GOD SHIP

OBSIDIAR FLEET BOOK 3

ANTHONY JAMES

© 2018 Anthony James
All rights reserved

The right of Anthony James to be identified as the author of this work has been asserted by him in accordance with the Copyright, Designs and Patents Act, 1988

The characters and events portrayed in this book are fictitious. Any similarity to real persons, living or dead, is coincidental and not intended by the author

This book is sold subject to the condition that it shall not, by way of trade or otherwise, be lent, resold, hired out, or otherwise circulated without the publisher's prior consent in any form of binding or cover other than that in which it is published and without a similar condition including this condition being imposed upon the subsequent purchaser

Illustration © Tom Edwards
TomEdwardsDesign.com

Follow Anthony James on Facebook at facebook.com/AnthonyJamesAuthor

THE WORMHOLE

The planet Vanistar was a place of no redeeming features. It was a huge, ancient rock on the edges of the Confederation's Hyptron sector, with thick clouds of ammonia and methane clinging to its surface like wet clothes on a drowning swimmer.

Were any explorer keen enough to pilot a spaceship through these toxic gasses, they would find only cratered plates of unending stone riven with ice-widened fissures. There was nothing of value here, at least not in quantities sufficient to be viable. Space Corps prospectors had visited Vanistar four times, each new vessel equipped with more advanced sensor arrays than the one before and on each occasion, these hopeful prospectors had left orbit without detecting anything new or useful.

On this day, twelve spaceships waited a few million kilometres away from Vanistar. These spaceships were unusual in design – they had large spheres of dark metal at the front and back, connected to a central frustum by comparatively slender beams. Energy forced its way through the armour of the vessels, appearing as random sparks of putrid greens and sickly blues.

It was not only the shape of these spaceships which was

unusual. Their relative positioning formed the twelve points of a dodecagon, with exactly five thousand kilometres between each point.

Without any outward warning, the flickering webs of power coruscating on the spheres of the Vraxar Neutralisers built up in their intensity, the green steadily pushing the blue aside, until there was no variation at all. Each nullification sphere on each vessel now shone with sufficient light to illuminate an entire moon.

In the centre of the dodecagon, an area of dark energy came into being – an amorphous shape of infinite depth a few hundred kilometres across its widest part. After a short while, a spaceship came through – a battleship from its size. The Vraxar battleship didn't simply *arrive*. It was hurled into local space at an immense velocity and it travelled for several million kilometres before its onboard navigational system brought it under control.

Another spaceship came through and then another. However, it wasn't these smaller craft which the Neutralisers had gathered for. The output from the twelve spaceships increased again, the magnitude sufficient to rival a month's power generation from the entire twenty-six worlds in the human Confederation. There was no air to carry a sound, but the entirety of space seemed to thrum as if in warning of what was to come.

Something else arrived, disgorged from the Vraxar's temporary wormhole like a vast parasite bursting free of its host body. This *something* utterly dwarfed any other crafted object to have flown through Confederation Space. The closest word to describe its shape was *ovoid,* though there was nothing pure or noble about what the Neutralisers had brought.

Having arrived, the vessel flew on with no deviation in its course, as if it knew its precise destination.

The Neutralisers weren't done. The nullification spheres blazed ever brighter and the thrumming became the distressed shriek of overstressed, modified Obsidiar. The area of dark energy wavered for a moment and then expanded, growing in size until it almost filled the imaginary dodecagon.

Whatever monstrous additional creation the Vraxar intended to drag through to this area of space didn't arrive. Maintaining a wormhole of this size required fifty or more Neutralisers. The strain was too much and one of the Neutralisers simply exploded, creating a wave of dark flame which washed across the two closest spaceships. This was sufficient to overload their nullification spheres and they, too, exploded.

A chain reaction followed, destroying the Neutralisers in pairs before they could break away. When it finished, only two remained from the starting twelve and these were badly damaged. The first was a smouldering mess of heat-scarred armour plating and it tumbled on an uncontrolled course which would eventually see it crash into Vanistar. The second Neutraliser made no attempt to rescue the crew from the stricken vessel. Instead, it limped away into a low lightspeed, apparently leaving the first ship to its fate.

The Vraxar fleet didn't have so many Neutralisers that it could dispose of them cheaply, but in this instance, the spaceships had done what was required. The gargantuan vessel was in Confederation Space and it was definitely not on a mission of peace.

CHAPTER ONE

FLEET ADMIRAL JOHN NATHAN DUGGAN was not happy. He laboured under this emotional state so frequently that his wife was beginning to worry for both his mental and physical health. She wasn't alone – even Duggan himself was aware that so much negative energy would eventually put him out of action and given his age, it could end up a permanent outcome. On the other hand, he was aware his family were planning a surprise celebration for his birthday in a few days and he was damn well going to be there for it with a party hat on his head and a smile on his face.

There were several reasons for his current irritation, but the overriding cause was the number of times his many teams had used the words *no luck* when he'd enquired about the degrees of success on their various projects.

The leader of one such team – a department head by the name of Shelby Timm - sat in a chair on the far side of Duggan's desk, trying to maintain an air of positivity having delivered his unwelcome news. Duggan was all for positivity, except when it was used as a make-do polish for particularly malodorous turds.

"A year's *additional* delay is unacceptable," Duggan said flatly. It was a tone which brooked no argument.

"We just can't get the efficiency up to where we need it," said Timm. "We're getting there."

"Slowly."

"We've had no luck with the prototypes."

There were the words again. *No luck.* Duggan's eyes bored into Timm. "It's been a year since we last saw a Vraxar warship. I had reassurances we'd have these new Obsidiar lightspeed propulsion systems fitted to the Shimmer missiles by now."

"You'll have them, sir. I give you my personal assurance."

"Don't treat me like a fool! The Vraxar could appear in New Earth orbit tomorrow morning! What then for your personal assurances?"

Timm shuffled in his chair, the cracks in his veneer of confidence unmissable. "All I'm trying to say is..."

Duggan raised a hand to interrupt. "I know what you're trying to say, DH Timm. I realise we've always been behind the curve when it comes to missile guidance and propulsion and I know how hard you've worked at catching up." He sighed. "Go back to your department and see what you can do to bring forward the release of a working prototype."

Timm nodded gratefully at this let-off, took the presented opportunity and exited the office in four long strides.

With his office empty, Duggan did his best to look on the bright side. After the near-total annihilation of the Vraxar fleet in the Cheops-A system a year ago, there'd been no sign of the aliens. The Obsidiar found in the crashed Estral Interstellar *Astrinium* had been fully salvaged and a reasonable percentage of the Confederation's share was now making its way into the fleet's warships, providing them with energy shields and giving them a chance to fight back against the power-draining Vraxar Neutralisers.

For the people of Atlantis, it had been a time of incredible upheaval. The evacuation of the planet was as close to completion as could be reasonably achieved. Much of the population was waiting impatiently out in deep space on the Space Corps' own fleet of vast Interstellars, whilst others had already been relocated to other Confederation worlds. It was a logistical nightmare, though one which had so far proceeded with few disasters.

Meanwhile, the Confederation Council had shown remarkable understanding towards the rebellious worlds Roban and Liventor. For their part, the councils of these worlds had agreed to extensive open-ended talks. Duggan was moderately surprised the offer of talks had been so readily accepted, especially in the circumstances of the entire Confederation being in a state of total war. Personal taxes were near enough a thing of the past but during periods of strife, there were numerous mechanisms in place to compel citizens with certain skillsets to work in research labs, shipyards, weapons factories and so on. The people of Roban and Liventor were just beginning to discover that it was possible for a working day to extend beyond four hours.

So, the political distractions were currently in hand and the Space Corps fleet was strengthening day by day, with new warships coming from the yards with uplifting regularity. It wouldn't be enough, of course, even with the Human-Ghast alliance working out as well as it was. The Vraxar couldn't produce offspring and they could only sustain their existence by killing and converting the other species they found. The aliens had no choice other than to keep coming and coming until one side was utterly defeated. The Vraxar didn't care about their losses – they could rebuild their numbers from the bodies of those they vanquished.

Duggan swore under his breath at the thought, his bad mood returning.

"I have been made aware of a high-priority internal memo

between two personnel on Monitoring Station Delta," said the disembodied voice of his personal assistant Cerys. The tone sounded more feminine than normal and Duggan wondered if the computer behind it was trying to put him at ease.

"What have you found?" he asked.

Cerys was able to monitor most communications within the Space Corps and it occasionally unearthed a gem before the personnel involved were able to escalate their findings up through the chain of command.

"A Lieutenant Lorene Fox has requested a second opinion on an anomaly she has detected on a planet far out in Hyptron."

"Does she mention what sort of anomaly?"

"She describes an object which is potentially metallic in origin. The planet in question – Vanistar – has an atmosphere of a type known to produce false readings."

"Has Lieutenant Fox obtained her second opinion?"

"Not yet, Admiral."

Cerys was designed to be as human as possible and would sometimes only drip-feed information in order to encourage a more natural conversation. It could be a mildly frustrating experience on the occasions when Duggan would have preferred to have all the details provided up front.

"Are there any Space Corps vessels due to fly through Vanistar's solar system?"

"There is nothing scheduled, though we have warships within striking distance. I have checked the Helius flight database we share with the Ghasts and they have no warships within four days' travel of the area."

Duggan rubbed his cheek in thought. It was unlikely to be anything which needed his immediate attention. On the other hand, he had a few minutes spare before he was required elsewhere.

"Who is in charge of Monitoring Station Delta?"

"Captain Sherry Brock is the most senior officer currently onboard."

"She's about to receive a surprise. Get me a channel."

"Connection established."

Captain Brock did indeed give every impression of being greatly surprised, if not completely shocked, when she realised it was Fleet Admiral Duggan who had forced open a direct channel to her console.

"Fleet Admiral," she stammered.

"Good morning, Captain Brock. My assistant tells me one of your officers has detected an anomaly on a planet called Vanistar."

"Yes, sir. She advised me verbally and I have a second experienced comms officer double-checking the initial findings."

"I would very much like to hear the outcome."

"Yes, sir, I will send over the results..."

"By which I mean I would like to hear the outcome *immediately*."

"Yes, of course. One moment, sir."

Through the comms link, Duggan heard a series of shouted orders on the monitoring station, followed by rapid footsteps and a noise which might have been that of a cup falling onto a metal floor. He waited.

Captain Brock returned. "It's definitely a metal object, sir. We can't provide you with an estimate of the size owing to the atmospheric interference."

"It's not likely to be small, is it?"

"No, sir. It won't be small."

"Is there any chance it could be a natural occurrence?"

"No chance whatsoever."

"Thank you, Captain Brock. Keep two of your sensor arrays trained directly on the object and see if you can find anything more about it. Send the information directly to my assistant."

"Yes, sir. The rotation of the planet will take the target object out of sight in the next hour."

"Do what you can. Over."

Duggan ended the connection. A coldness gripped his body – for a man who unsuccessfully tried not to believe in anything scientifically unprovable such as hunches, he was finding it hard to ignore the feeling that this sighting on Vanistar heralded the beginning of something terrible.

"The Vraxar," he said, spitting the words out.

"What action would you like me to take, Fleet Admiral?" said Cerys.

"Send out a fleet-wide notification - I want every warship on high alert. Send a message to each Admiral telling them about the findings."

Cerys was nothing if not efficient. "Done," it said, less than a second later and with a near-imperceptible note of satisfaction.

"Which is the closest warship we have to Vanistar?"

"The Galactic class *ES Abyss* is twelve hours away."

"Captain Blake's ship. He's getting into the habit of being in the right place at the right time. Can you reach him?"

"They are not travelling at lightspeed; therefore a direct comms channel is available," Cerys confirmed.

"Patch me through."

If Captain Charlie Blake was anything like as surprised as Captain Sherry Brock, he hid it well.

"Hello, sir," he said.

"I've got a job for you, Captain Blake."

"I'm all ears, sir. It's been a little slow out here on patrol."

"What makes you think there's going to be some action?"

"There always is. Whenever I speak to you, it means something has either happened or it's about to happen in the near future."

"I'll try to be less predictable in future," said Duggan. "I need you to do something for me. You should be receiving the coordinates of a new destination – it's a planet out in the back of beyond. The staff on Monitoring Station Delta have identified a metal object which shouldn't be there. It isn't ours and it isn't Ghast, so I'd like you to fill in the gaps."

"Am I to expect a hostile response?"

"I think you know the answer to that one."

"Yes, sir."

"The chances are, it's Vraxar. Take a look and report back. We need intel and I'd also prefer it if you kept the ES *Abyss* in one piece – it's one of our more powerful warships and I don't want it confined to a repair dock for the next six months."

"I'll do my best, sir."

"Good – now get on your way. You will be aware of the urgency on this one."

With Captain Blake gone, Duggan turned his attention to the other matters scheduled for his day. Since it appeared certain the Vraxar had returned, he was obliged to cancel numerous smaller claims on his time, including a few catch-up drinks with his old friend Frank Chainer. He felt guilty but Frank would understand.

Having freed up five hours of his day, Duggan set about creating a new schedule – one which would ensure his most senior staff were fully briefed about what he wanted from them. He recalled a few of the most outlying fleet warships, diverting them towards the populated worlds in Hyptron and then he spoke to the New Earth Tucson base commander to emphasise the criticality of the building and refitting work underway on the facility.

Before he knew it, Duggan was lost in the world of his endless duties.

CHAPTER TWO

THE HEAVY CRUISER ES *Abyss* was several hours into its journey to Vanistar. Captain Charlie Blake was feeling cooped up and he paced around, keeping an eye on his crew. Most of the officers were known to him, but there were two others who had been assigned during the last scheduled maintenance check on Pioneer a couple of weeks ago. These two officers – Ensigns Toby Park and Charlotte Bailey – so far appeared to be competent and eager.

"I wish this smell would go away," said Comms Lieutenant Caz Pointer for the dozenth time.

Blake sniffed – the entire bridge stank of smoked fish and had done since they'd left Pioneer. None of the crew owned up to ordering fish from the replicators and none had been witnessed eating it. A brief and distracting investigation suggested the smell was coming in through one of the air conditioning vents. While it was unpleasant, there were no warning alarms on any of the spaceship's life support systems, so the mystery remained unsolved.

Privately, Blake suspected it was a practical joke played by one or more of the technicians on Pioneer. He'd almost built up sufficient interest to begin an audit on the maintenance teams in order to cross-reference with similar incidents on other warships, but the call from Fleet Admiral Duggan had forestalled this time-wasting exercise. He put it out of his mind.

"I think we need to focus on where we're going," he said, addressing the crew. "We've been out of action for a year and we've lost our edge."

"Sorry, sir," said Pointer. "It's just hard to ignore."

"We're going to enter local space in a few hours. At that point, we may find ourselves under immediate attack and it's imperative we're prepared. I don't need to remind you what the Vraxar want and how important it is that we blow the crap out of them before they achieve their aims."

Blake sat down and studied his console, alert for anything untoward. He was just killing time – keeping himself occupied in order to prevent his brain turning over the endless possibilities of the future. Before the Vraxar, he'd never been bothered by thoughts of what lay ahead. Now, it was as if a plague of tiny, biting insects whirled inside his mind, refusing to go away no matter how many of them he swatted. He chuckled inwardly and without much humour. *I'm starting to get old and there's a part of me that's unwilling to let it happen.*

He accessed the *Abyss*'s data repositories and looked at the files on Vanistar again. There was nothing new waiting to be unearthed and while they travelled at lightspeed, there would be no updates from Monitoring Station Delta. He was tempted to exit lightspeed for a brief time to allow the warship's memory arrays to synchronise with the Space Corps network. He rejected the idea - the first report from the monitoring station suggested it would have lost sight of the object several hours ago, meaning there was unlikely to be any new information.

So, Blake waited and did his best to suppress his fidgeting. He was just starting to realise that his perception of how time passed was accelerating with every year he got older and as a consequence, the remaining three hours went by quicker than he was expecting.

"Entering the Kopel system in two minutes," said Lieutenant Jake Quinn. "Vanistar is the third planet and we're aiming for fifteen million klicks out. That's enough for our fission cloud to escape notice and gives us plenty of opportunity to approach with the stealth modules active."

"What I'd give for a fission suppression system," said Blake.

"We're scheduled to have one fitted in six months, sir," said Quinn. He saw Blake's face. "I see. Not much use to us at the moment."

"Activate stealth modules as soon as we're able. I'll require an in-depth scan of the locality and please keep the Tucson base advised."

The warship's fission engines emitted the faint whine which indicated they were about to shut off. There was a brief silence, a hint of dislocation and then the *ES Abyss* emerged into the Kopel solar system, between the third and fourth planets. There was a flurry of activity on the bridge.

Blake preferred to keep the *Abyss* moving instead of leaving it a motionless, easy target for any potential enemies. As soon as he got his bearings, he aimed the *Abyss* towards Vanistar and pushed the gravity engines to full output. The *Abyss* rocketed forward, hitting a speed in excess of two thousand kilometres per second.

"Stealth modules online," said Quinn.

"Get our energy shield up as well."

"Shield online. Our Obsidiar core is holding steady."

"Beginning area scan. First indication is there's nothing in the vicinity."

"I have informed the Tucson base as to our arrival. We are to proceed as planned," said 2nd Lieutenant Maria Cruz. She was operating at a reduced rank during her on-ship training period.

"I know we're to proceed as planned," muttered Blake. "I'm the captain of this damned ship and I'm giving the orders."

With the heavy cruiser at full speed, the stealth modules and energy shield active, Blake felt reassured they wouldn't be susceptible to instant destruction while Lieutenant Pointer finished her far scan. He drummed his fingers until it was done.

"We're the only thing out here, except for a few dozen asteroids which are half a million klicks to starboard."

"Good – focus on Vanistar and find what we're after."

"Already on it, sir," said Pointer. "There's a big old storm covering a third of the southern hemisphere."

"Is that where the target was detected?"

"I'm trying to tally it up. Yep, that's where it was – right under the storm. We have hydrogen, helium and then we get down to the toxic crap."

"Can our sensors pierce it?"

"Maybe. It'll be slow, but at least we've got a head start in that we know where to look."

"Not quite the head start I was hoping for, Lieutenant. Luckily, we have almost two hours travel time ahead of us before it becomes an issue. Please proceed."

It didn't take two hours before they made their first discovery and it wasn't what Blake was expecting.

"There's some type of crazy reading in an area of space away from the planet," said Lieutenant Cruz.

"I'll need a better definition than *crazy*."

"Yes, sir. My mouth talks to buy my brain time to think. I'm not quite sure what it is. This is more Lieutenant Quinn's speciality."

Quinn was already concentrating on the data harvested by

the *Abyss*'s sensor arrays. "There are decaying traces of energy – it's an arrangement I don't recognize," he said.

"Do we need to worry about it?" asked Blake.

"It's an unknown, so I would suggest we give it due consideration, sir."

"It covers a huge area," said Cruz.

"That's my worry, Lieutenant," Quinn replied. "I can't imagine what it would have taken to generate so much energy across such a wide area. I'm trying to calculate when it was formed by watching the rate of its decay."

"Will that work if you don't know its original state?" asked Blake.

"You're quite correct to ask, sir – we're missing a required variable. However, I'll be able to generate a chart which shows the levels of energy against time. All we need to do is pick a point on the chart which we believe most accurately reflects the time of generation."

"We guess, you mean?"

"Welcome to the world of reverse predictive modelling, sir."

"I think I'm more interested in why it's here, whatever it is or was," said Blake.

"Every piece of the jigsaw gives us a better idea of the whole."

"I won't give you an argument, Lieutenant. Carry on."

Minutes passed.

"The sensors are reading faint signs of positrons filtering through Vanistar's atmosphere," said Pointer.

"Show me."

Pointer brought up an image of the planet on the bulkhead screen. The image wasn't quite perfect, but it was more than good enough to see the roiling brown cyclone of dirty, windborne grit and gas which covered a huge area of Vanistar. A computer-generated red circle appeared, highlighting an area a few thousand kilometres south of the equator.

"Based on the atmospheric density and speed of the wind, this is where I predict the target object is located."

"Any signs of the storm clearing?"

"No, sir. The ship's AI predicts this particular storm won't blow out for another three years, by which point it will have certainly been replaced by another storm of equal or greater magnitude."

"Will you be able to see through the storm when we're at an altitude of a few thousand klicks?"

"I think so."

The Space Corps only put the best on its fleet warships and this short discussion provided Lieutenant Quinn sufficient time to work through some advanced modelling, with assistance from the *Abyss*'s eight blisteringly fast Obsidiar processing units. The outcome wasn't quite the clear-cut conclusion Blake was hoping for.

"I don't know when this anomaly was formed, sir. If we predictively reverse the decay, you can see how quickly the line on this chart climbs upwards."

"In other words, whatever this was originally, it required an inconceivably large power source to generate it?"

"Yes, sir."

"And you're none-the-wiser as to what it was?"

Quinn chewed his lip. "If I didn't know better, I'd say it's consistent with the movement of atoms around a wormhole."

"Except we're a long way from a wormhole."

"A very long way."

"I don't like it. Send the data to the Space Corps. They can set a team onto finding out if it's significant."

"I sent them it already, sir."

Blake found it pleasing when he didn't have to micromanage

everything. The only problem was his own inability to stop doing it. He trusted his officers more each day, so he was obliged to concede the weakness was his own and he set himself a personal goal to improve himself in this regard.

The ES *Abyss* flew on. The grainy image of Vanistar became gradually more detailed and the two comms officers were able to narrow down the site of the target object to within fifty kilometres. There was no sign of hostile activity, though it was looking increasingly likely they'd need to descend into the atmosphere to gather the necessary intel.

"Is there anything other than unshielded Gallenium which can produce this quantity of positrons?" Blake asked when they were a hundred thousand kilometres away.

"Not that I'm aware of," said Quinn.

"What we're seeing is consistent with wreckage," said Cruz. "If it's Vraxar, I have no idea why they'd simply crash into a planet."

"Is there any seismic activity?"

"Bits and pieces – nothing out of the ordinary."

"Is there any sign of *recent* seismic activity?"

"Yes, sir. There usually is if you look hard enough," said Pointer.

"What about an impact crater? I'm trying to decide if there's an active enemy installation on the surface or if a Vraxar ship crash landed."

"I guess we'll need to poke our noses into those clouds before we find out," said Hawkins. "It can't smell worse than the air on this bridge."

"I think there might be a crater," said Cruz. "There's no clear picture, but there are what I first took to be naturally-forming ridges over here." She highlighted an area of the display which was thickly shrouded by the storm. "There's something similar a few hundred klicks to the south as well." She highlighted another area.

"That comes to about nine hundred klicks from north to south," said Ensign Park.

"If you ram an incredibly heavy object into a lump of rock at an enormous speed, you get a big hole," said Hawkins.

Blake piloted the *ES Abyss* on manual and brought it to an altitude of twenty thousand kilometres. Then, he handed off control to the autopilot which set the heavy cruiser flying in a tight circle directly over the target area. The evidence suggested this was a crash site, rather than a military installation. Nevertheless, he didn't like heading into a situation without a having a bit more than simple guesswork as backup. Whatever was down there, it was likely as blind as they were and Blake didn't want to make the first move. Before he could be forced into making a decision, his comms team came through for him.

"I got a sighting of it!" said Pointer.

"Oh crap," said Cruz. "Is that what I think it is?"

"What is it?"

"On the main screen, sir."

A static image appeared, enhanced by the ship's sensors and with the shrouds of choking grit filtered out by a series of complex algorithms. The resulting picture managed to be both indistinct, yet also far too clear.

"A Neutraliser," said Blake. "A damned Neutraliser." He turned to Lieutenant Hawkins. "Keep it targeted with every missile we've got. If it tries to lift off, we're going to blow it out of the sky."

"I don't think it's going anywhere, sir," said Quinn. "There's output from its aft nullification sphere, but everything up front from that is dead."

"Offline and recoverable or offline and completely out of action?"

Quinn shrugged. "I wouldn't like to guess. At this precise moment, they're going nowhere."

"What now?" said Blake to himself.

He stood and walked closer towards the image of the spaceship, as if proximity would bring him answers. It was an unexpected situation – for the Neutraliser to have crashed, it must have sustained catastrophic damage. The Space Corps hadn't inflicted the damage and there was no record of an engagement between the Ghasts and the Vraxar. Warships absolutely did not fail this badly without external influence.

"We were sent to check out what the hell is going on, so we'd better get on with it," he said at last. "I'm going to bring us through this storm and we're going to find out what happened."

"What if there's a fourth race of aliens and they attacked this Neutraliser?" said Lieutenant Hawkins. "That would stir things up, wouldn't it?"

"Don't. Just don't."

Feeling as if he needed to take hands-on control, Blake grabbed the control bars. The autopilot dutifully switched itself off, whilst providing an advisory notice to warn him how much better a computer was than a human at piloting a twelve billion tonne warship. Blake ignored it.

"This storm won't interfere with the stealth modules, will it?" he asked.

"It shouldn't do. It's generally radiation that causes the problems," said Quinn.

The storm was dense and violent. It raged with the force of a million atomic bombs from the surface of the planet, up to an altitude of two hundred kilometres. On the bridge of the ES *Abyss*, the crew felt nothing as the spaceship descended. Wind and grit pounded against the energy shield in wasted fury. There wasn't a planet in existence which could host a storm with the power to trouble a warship the size of this one.

At a height of eighty kilometres, the warship's sensors were able to penetrate the atmospheric conditions all the way to the ground and they provided a near-perfect reproduction of the Neutraliser. It lay at the bottom of an immense crater. At the place of impact, the crater was many kilometres deep and it sloped upwards, forming a shallow basin with a diameter of several hundred kilometres. It looked bad, but Blake was sure Vanistar had got off lightly – the Neutraliser had come in at a comparatively low speed.

The vessel itself was a mess – half of the front nullification sphere was missing and the remainder was partially flattened. Lieutenant Quinn confirmed it was generating no power whatsoever. The rest of the Neutraliser's hull was blistered, swollen and misshapen. The rear connecting beam was noticeably bent as if it had been subjected to extreme heat or force. It was a troubling sight.

"That's dispersed heat damage with no explosion crater," said Hawkins. "Whatever did this it wasn't a beam weapon and it wasn't a missile strike."

"Could it have been caught on the edge of the Inferno Sphere and somehow escaped this far before they suffered complete system failure?" said Quinn.

"I don't think so. When the Obsidiar bomb went off the Neutralisers were close to the centre of the blast and they didn't stand a chance. The analysts spent weeks checking the Blackbird's sensor recordings and they didn't find anything to suggest there was another Neutraliser in the vicinity."

"There's plenty of juice running through that aft sphere," said Quinn. "About a thousand times more than our maximum power output, including from our Obsidiar core."

Blake watched the uneven play of green and blue lights as they jumped erratically across the surface of the nullification sphere. There was something wrong, he was sure.

"Is it stable?" he asked.

"I don't know, sir," said Quinn. "It's an excellent question and I'm not sure if I'll be able to provide you an answer. I'll get on with it at once."

"I wouldn't like to think what might happen if it were to go critical."

"Nope."

"What are you planning to do, sir?" asked Pointer.

"Fleet Admiral Duggan sent us out here to gather intel, Lieutenant. There's only so much intel you can find from looking at the outside of a ship."

"Should I launch the drones?" asked Pointer.

"Yes – I'm exceptionally interested to see what lies inside that Neutraliser."

The recon drones were designed to be launched at a moment's notice. Lieutenant Pointer sent a dozen racing towards the Vraxar spaceship beneath. The drones were robust and designed to withstand the elements, so they sped easily to their destination. Blake watched, fascinated, as they flew over and around the Neutraliser, scanning and searching.

"Are we learning anything new from this?" he asked.

"No, sir," said Pointer. "Our sensor arrays can see from this distance what theirs can only see from close-up."

"Wait on – what's this?" said Blake.

"Looks like Drone #9 has found a breach," said Quinn.

"Where is it in relation to the rest of the ship?"

"That drone is near to the place where the front nullification sphere joins the connecting beam."

"Look at that damage!" said Blake. "Any idea what caused it?"

"A combination of heat and impact," said Hawkins. "It's dark in there."

The hull breach was a jagged tear through the Neutraliser's

armour plating and was only half visible, with the remainder vanishing out of sight underneath the spaceship. The drone was equipped with high-intensity lights and it made directly for the widest part of the breach, with its light beams skittering over the black metal. The image feed from Drone #9 ended abruptly.

"What the...?" said Pointer.

"Has it failed?"

"I don't know, sir. Drone #10 has located the hole now."

The second drone followed the first, relaying a brief, confused image of the Neutraliser's interior. It, too, shut down almost immediately. Blake guessed what was happening.

"Their Gallenium engines are going offline."

"I still can't detect anything from that front sphere," said Quinn in puzzlement. "Nothing at all."

"It doesn't appear as if the enemy vessel has entirely lost its potency," said Blake. "With or without the power flowing."

"Should I recall the remaining drones?" asked Pointer.

"There's no point in throwing good after bad. Bring them back."

"I've sent the command and they should be back with us in the next few minutes."

"We're not going to see much of the interior without the drones," said Hawkins.

"There's a way for us to get the information we've been sent to find, Lieutenant. It just means taking a bigger risk."

Blake wasn't pleased with what he needed to do. Unfortunately, there was no choice and he opened up a comms channel in order to pass on the news.

CHAPTER THREE

LIEUTENANT ERIC MCKINNEY sat in the mess room of the *ES Abyss*, watching the sensor feed on one of the wall-mounted screens provided to give ship-bound troops an eye onto the outside world. A few of the other soldiers were in the room with him, eyes glued to the display and their mouths half-open.

"What's a Neutraliser doing here?" asked Rank One Trooper Dexter Webb, his plate of replicated fried meat forgotten in front of him.

"That's what we're here to find out," said McKinney.

"Did the Space Corps know about it?"

"I don't know."

Webb was a natural with a plasma tube but he had a habit of asking too many questions. "What do you think Captain Blake will do?" he pressed.

Sergeant Johnny Li took it upon himself to answer. "The way I see it, there are only two possible choices. One: we hover here for a while and stare at the Neutraliser and then fly somewhere else. Two: Captain Blake decides he needs someone to go check it out. I reckon this is the most likely outcome."

Ricky Vega had been silent so far, staring at his new hand. He'd lost the original in the same engagement with the Vraxar that had seen Webb badly hurt, and the Space Corps had given him a new flesh-and-bone copy which was a slightly different hue to the rest of his skin. "Don't they have drones for this sort of mission?"

"You losing your nerve, Vega?" asked Huey Roldan.

"Nah, course not. They can't replace guys like us with drones."

"You can't beat feet on the ground," added Martin Garcia.

McKinney felt something buzzing in his pocket and he pulled out a short blue cylinder made from some kind of polymer the name of which contained in excess of fifty letters. There was a tiny screen on the cylinder, informing him of an inbound communication from the bridge.

"Here we go," he said.

With a twist, he detached the end of the pocket communicator and a tiny combined earpiece/microphone fell from the hollow centre into the palm of his hand. He pushed it into his ear.

"This is McKinney."

The group of soldiers kept their eyes fixed on McKinney and tried to figure out the direction of the conversation from his one-word responses to Captain Blake. After a couple of minutes, McKinney removed the earpiece and replaced it in the communicator.

"They did send drones and the drones didn't work," he said, getting up from his seat. "Let's go."

The others climbed to their feet, questions spilling out.

Without further explanation, McKinney strode off towards the main exit from the mess room. There was a mini-console mounted on the wall at the entrance to the passage. He paused to issue a command to muster and selected the location. Immediately, the usual subtle white-blue lighting changed to a deeper, rich blue and the androgynous tones of the *Abyss*'s computer spoke instructions.

"All troops to the rear shuttle bay armoury. All troops to the rear shuttle bay armoury. This is not an exercise."

"They're really sending us," said Roldan, falling in behind McKinney.

"It's a Neutraliser," McKinney replied. "I'm not surprised they want to get some human eyes on it."

"That thing's massive. We've only got a hundred and twenty men on the *Abyss*."

"There's a breach into its hull and our scans suggest the life support systems failed. Captain Blake is confident there's nothing left alive."

"I've heard that one before."

"Look on the bright side – you might get to do some shooting."

"I'm going to take me a crap on a Vraxar toilet," said Jeb Whitlock happily.

McKinney shook his head in wonder at the priorities of some in his squad.

"Do the Vraxar even have toilets?" asked Webb. "Someone told me they got sewn up *down there*."

"Enough," said McKinney.

"But Lieutenant..."

"That means *shut up,* soldier."

The *ES Abyss* was a shade under four thousand metres long, yet the liveable space inside took up only a fraction of that. It was less than a thousand metres from the mess room to the rear shuttle bay. The corridors were wide enough for three to pass and a cool breeze blew in McKinney's face as he walked. He'd spent most of his service years on the ground and he was still getting used to the feeling of being permanently stationed onboard a fleet warship. He understood what the old timers meant when they described becoming attuned to the engines and what the different tones and vibrations signified. It was a new world and one he embraced.

Other soldiers joined in the procession and McKinney's practised eye estimated that more than a hundred were following him when he reached the bay armoury. The armoury was a square room with a claustrophobically low ceiling and lit permanently in red, as if the colour would somehow impress a sense of urgency upon the soldiers kitting up. There were racks of suits dangling from a rail in a long alcove along one wall. Elsewhere there were a couple of metal boxes filled with the associated visors, these expensive technological marvels thrown inside without apparent care. Elsewhere, racks and cabinets carried a variety of weapons designed to efficiently convert the living into dead.

"Command code: McKinney. Unlock all."

Around the room, dozens of tiny red lights which indicated the weaponry was locked down, turned to green. McKinney climbed onto one of the metal benches, his short hair brushing against the dull alloy of the low ceiling.

"Listen up!" he bellowed once he judged everyone was present. "You're taking a suit, a repeater, rifle and grenades. Comms packs and plasma tubes for those trained to carry them."

"What's the job, sir?" asked Joy Guzman.

On a warship, news travelled faster than a gauss slug in a vacuum and McKinney had no doubt everyone had a good idea where they were going.

"There's a disabled Vraxar Neutraliser on Vanistar. It's badly damaged and we've been asked to poke our noses inside and check out what our favourite alien scumbags have been up to."

"That's it?"

"I expect the mission goal to change once we land and learn more about the situation."

"Are we taking any heavy armour, Lieutenant?" shouted Elias Mack from the back of the gathered soldiers.

"Negative - we're going in the two biggest shuttles and the tanks are staying behind. The ES *Abyss* will provide cover for our approach. There's a breach in the enemy hull at ground level and that's our way in. It's not tall enough to fit a tank through and even if it was, and as big as the Neutraliser is, I very much doubt there's space to drive a Gunther around the interior."

"That's the polite way of telling you not to ask stupid questions, Mack!" shouted Ronnie Horton.

There were a few jeers and whistles, which died off quickly when McKinney called for silence.

"Most of you haven't fought the Vraxar before. You've been in the simulators and read the files, but you haven't faced them for real. They're fast and I still don't know if they care for their own miserable lives or not. It makes them unpredictable."

"And they stink worse than Whitlock's breath," said Garcia.

There was further jeering and this time McKinney was more forceful when he demanded silence.

"The next man I catch pissing around travels to the surface tied to the shuttle's nose cannon. That means you, Garcia."

"Sorry, Lieutenant."

Rudy Munoz raised a hand. "I know you said all the Vraxar down there are dead and everything, sir, but I prefer to look on the pessimistic side if I think it's going to increase my chances of getting out alive."

"Get to the point."

"If we see any Vraxar, are we shooting the bastards first or should we try and parlay?"

"Shoot the bastards first. Any more questions?"

When nothing was forthcoming, McKinney repeated his order for the soldiers to get kitted up in preparation for the mission. Soon, he was listening to the coarse chatter as his troops struggled into their spacesuits. While he dressed, McKinney tried to get a sense of the mood. Those he classed as his experienced men laughed and joked without a care. The others made forced jokes and wisecracks that suggested they weren't quite so unconcerned. *Everyone has to start somewhere,* he thought.

Getting into a spacesuit was a standard drill exercise and it wasn't long before the entire warship's complement of soldiers was suitably dressed for a deployment into a low-temperature atmosphere filled with toxic gas. Most had their visors resting on top of their heads whilst others lowered them into place, hiding their expressions.

Afterwards came the superstitious checking of the gauss rifles. The soldiers picked them up and replaced them, checked the heft and looked along the barrel. Occasionally a man or woman would test four or five rifles before settling on a satisfactory example. McKinney had never understood the need for this particular routine and he shook his head inwardly. The weapons were produced with a variance percentage that was many decimal places long and made up entirely of zeroes apart from the last digit, which was rounded up to a one. Even the most expert sniper in the entire Space Corps wouldn't know the difference if you swapped his favourite gun for another.

For whatever reason, repeaters and plasma tubes were exempt from this careful examination and soon, McKinney was facing six rows of fully-armed soldiers. A few shuffled nervously or transferred weight from foot to foot. Mostly, they looked ready for anything.

He climbed back onto his bench. "Move out to your designated shuttle," he said. "Once I've been given the go-ahead, we'll leave. Vanistar isn't the sort of place you'd go on a first date, so don't be stupid enough to lift your visors."

McKinney jumped down with a thud onto the floor, gathered up his rifle and clipped it onto his plasma repeater's ammo pack.

There were two wide corridors leading from the armoury, both going to the same place. He picked one and headed along for fifty metres. It opened out into a room that was seventy or eighty metres wide and only ten across. There were airlock doors to the left and right, whilst a set of steps climbed upwards from the middle of the opposite wall. A sign hung from the ceiling above the entrance to the steps. *Docking Bay - Shuttles Three and Four.*

McKinney ignored the steps and went to the left-hand airlock door. It spun open automatically at his approach, allowing him access to a tunnel with a grated floor and a console at each end. The red light from the armoury was replicated inside. There was plenty of room for sixty of the *Abyss*'s troops in the airlock. Once everyone was within, McKinney used one of the consoles to activate the end door. There was a short pause during which the warship's life support systems ran through a series of checks. Then, the first door closed and the second door opened. Stark hospital-white light from the shuttle's passenger bay flooded out and mixed with the red inside the airlock, making a pink hue.

He stepped across the threshold and immediately noticed the lack of solidity underfoot. The shuttle was heavily armoured, but its hull wasn't anything like as dense as the *ES Abyss* and his footsteps had the faintest of hollow notes.

The Space Corps didn't spend its money on the sort of frivolous luxuries that would cause uproar amongst the Confederation's citizens. Therefore, the shuttle's seats were meagrely padded, the passenger bay viewscreen was an older model and there was no chandelier hanging from the ceiling. The craft was little more than an over-chilled grey box with an engine and a top-of-the-line twelve-barrel Gallenium-driven rotating gauss repeater that, given the opportunity and a murderous intent, could mow down a thousand penny-pinching bean counters in under five seconds.

McKinney crossed directly to a door in the front wall of the bay. It hissed opened with the press of a button and allowed him into the cockpit. There were three seats in front of the main console, their black cloth coverings showing signs of wear and tear. He dropped into the middle one and began the process of bringing the shuttle into a state of flight readiness. The engines of all four of the *Abyss*'s shuttles were kept warm, so it didn't take longer than a few seconds until the *Ready* icon appeared on the pilot's central screen.

The cockpit door opened and a figure leaned inside.

"Need a hand?" asked Corporal Nitro Bannerman.

"Sure. Jump on the comms."

"Want me to get someone up front who can use the nose cannon?"

"Don't worry about it, Corporal. We'll have the *Abyss* watching over us and I know which I'd feel safer with. Besides, I can control the chaingun from here if I need to."

He activated a secondary screen to his left. It showed the view from a sensor positioned dead in the centre of the nose cannon's barrels, along with a targeting circle and various other details such as distance and the number of hostiles it was tracking.

"It hasn't detected anything it doesn't like, huh?" said Bannerman, looking over.

"Just hope it stays nailed on zero. Even with the *Abyss* providing cover, I don't want any surprises on this mission."

"A quick in and out. Easy."

"I'm not going to tempt fate, Corporal."

"It keeps life interesting."

The shuttle was ready to fly. "Speak to the bridge and tell them we're ready to go."

It only took a moment for Bannerman to send the message and get a response. "Captain Blake asks what we're waiting for. He's even opening the outer bay door for us."

The thick door protecting the ES *Abyss*'s shuttle bay dropped into its recess with a serenity belying its incredible weight. The shuttle was facing outwards and its front array showed the swirling patterns of dust hurtling past as they were dragged along by the furious winds.

"We've got the coordinates in our nav system. I'm activating the autopilot. Corporal Bannerman, make Shuttle Two aware."

"Roger."

McKinney touched an area on his screen and a number of electronic gauges climbed. The shuttle's engines rumbled, causing the third seat in the cockpit to buzz gratingly. The gravity clamps holding the vessel in place shut off and the shuttle decoupled from the bay wall. There was a sensation of acceleration and the outer bay doorway grew rapidly larger on the sensor feed.

"Shuttle Two will undock once we're through the energy shield," said McKinney.

Shuttle One flew out of the ES *Abyss*'s bay, still within the protective sphere of the energy shield. The effect was strange to witness – within the shield, it was calm and still. Outside, the potent anger of Vanistar railed fruitlessly against the power of Obsidiar.

"We haven't even landed and already I hate the place," said Bannerman.

Something in the man's words made McKinney shiver. He didn't count himself superstitious, but he couldn't shake the sudden feeling something bad was going to happen. He did his best to ignore it and sat back while the autopilot took the shuttle through a gap in the energy shield opened for them by the ES *Abyss*'s battle computer.

As soon as they were outside the shield's perimeter, the howling winds gripped the shuttle and did their best to carry the craft along in the madness.

CHAPTER FOUR

IT WAS a bumpy ride to the surface. The shuttle's sensors were considerably less advanced than those on the *ES Abyss* and they struggled to pierce the storm. Then, at an altitude of ten kilometres, there was a brief lull which allowed McKinney to see the extent of the challenge ahead.

Bannerman realised it too. "Assuming all the Vraxar onboard *are* dead, and I sincerely hope they died in agony, that's a lot of ship to search," he said.

"Have you left the oven on or something?"

"Reprimand accepted, Lieutenant, but you can see the problems."

"It's not ideal," said McKinney. "Maybe we'll only be required to do some advance recon before the Space Corps sends in a dedicated team and a recovery vessel."

"The *MHL Titan* is the biggest lifter in the fleet and even that's only twelve klicks long. Assuming it was big enough to carry off an eighteen klick Neutraliser, do you really think they'll send such a valuable asset into a place where the enemy have been detected?"

"That Neutraliser could be full of Obsidiar," said McKinney. "If it is, they'll do whatever it takes. Hell, they'd build a whole new lifter if they needed to."

"Yeah they might. In the future. We're the only ones who are here now and capable of completing a full search of a spaceship type that's causing the biggest worry in the high command."

McKinney couldn't deny the logic. "If it's to be a full search, then that's what it's to be."

"It's not the searching that worries me, Lieutenant." Bannerman gave a short laugh. "The searching part will be interesting – something to tell the grandkids when we've forced the Vraxar into long-overdue extinction. My worry is the enemy might want their Neutraliser back."

"You think they could turn up?"

"At any moment, sir."

"We'd better not stop to admire their women, then."

"I'd rather not think about Vraxar women if you don't mind."

McKinney laughed. "Me neither. Not that we've seen any yet."

"Not that we know of. It's not as if they get nicely dressed and wear makeup, is it? Who knows what the Vraxar do to the bodies of the dead – we could have been shooting women and thinking they were men."

"Nah – most of the Vraxar are dead Estral. You've seen Ghost women before – they're much smaller than the males."

"Almost attractive some of them. In a grey-skinned, alien kind of way."

"They're not my type, Corporal."

"Nor mine. Doesn't stop the talk though."

The conversation tailed off, with neither man desperate to pursue it. A new thought came to McKinney.

"If I die, do me a favour and make sure there isn't enough of me left to make into a new Vraxar."

"If you'll make me the same promise."

For some reason it seemed important and McKinney stuck out his hand. Bannerman grasped it and the two men shook on their agreement.

"Better to go home in pieces than spend a thousand years rotting with nothing more than a few metal struts keeping me upright."

"Amen to that, Lieutenant."

The moment passed and McKinney saw they'd descended to an altitude of three kilometres, which meant the shuttle's autopilot was slowing them in preparation to land. Shuttle Two was many kilometres above and coming in steadily.

"They sent drones first, but their engines shut off," said McKinney.

"This shuttle runs on Gallenium, doesn't it?" asked Bannerman.

"It does. Captain Blake reckons we'll be fine as long as we don't come in too close. The drones weren't affected until they got inside."

"How close is close?"

"We're programmed to land five hundred metres away – wherever the autopilot can find that's suitable."

"There's no way we'll be able to set down properly. There's far too much slope from this crater."

"You're right – it's going to be a rough landing. I'll need to leave the shuttle on autopilot to keep it from sliding down the slope."

"I can't say I'm excited about a five hundred metre scramble down the side of an impact crater in this storm, sir."

"The crew on the *Abyss* have already done the looking – there's a dramatic fall-off in the wind speed once you get right near to the bottom. Believe it or not, that Neutraliser's going to act like a big wind-break."

"Great. Just like being on a beach holiday again."

McKinney smiled and shook his head in mock-despair at the cynicism of his fellow man. He accessed the shuttle's internal comms and told the soldiers in the passenger bay to get ready.

"This is your one-minute warning. Get your visors in place."

In spite of the reassurances, the shuttle reached an altitude of a thousand metres without any let up in the storm. Some of the gusts were in excess of two hundred kilometres per hour and McKinney was seriously worried he'd lose half his men before they even reached the Neutraliser. Then, with only a few seconds until touch-down, the winds lessened significantly. The external monitoring tools on the shuttle showed the average windspeed at nearly sixty kilometres per hour, with frequent gusts reaching past one hundred kilometres per hour.

"That's not so bad," muttered Bannerman. "Just like exercises on Tourmaline."

McKinney smiled at the memory. "The Space Corps' favourite torture chamber."

In spite of the lightness in his tones, McKinney was nervous about the landing. The shuttle was designed to handle pretty much anything, but it only needed a small miscalculation from the autopilot, or a misread from one of the sensors and the whole mission could become a disaster before it started. He watched the approach intently.

"The autopilot's going to set down the four portside landing legs and use the engines to keep the starboard side level. We'll jump out through the portside exit and come around the nose. After that, it's all downhill. Shuttle Two is ninety seconds behind up and they're aiming to set down three hundred metres to our north."

Bannerman didn't respond and the set of the man's jaw indicated he didn't relish what was coming.

The sound from the shuttle's engines increased in volume

and they grumbled under the strains of the autopilot's fine tuning. If this had been a normal landing, McKinney would have already been in the passenger bay with the others waiting to disembark. In the circumstances, he thought it better to stay in the pilot's chair and keep an eye on things.

The altimeter counted down the last few metres until a thump in the cockpit indicated the port legs had made heavy contact with the ground. The gravity engine developed a lumpy note which suggested to McKinney the autopilot was having to vary the power constantly in order to keep the craft level.

"Is that it?" asked Bannerman.

"As good as we're going to get."

McKinney spoke briefly to the pilot on Shuttle Two – a sergeant called Chester Goodman – to ensure he knew what to do. When he was satisfied, McKinney pulled down his spacesuit visor and left the cockpit. The rest of the soldiers were on their feet, their faces pointed towards the port exit door. There was plenty of nervous chatter in the comms open channel and McKinney asked for silence so that nothing important would get lost in the noise.

"Everyone get your visors down or you'll die an agonising death within ten seconds of departure. This is the real thing folks – your chance to put all that training into practise. Maybe even shoot yourself a genuine alien instead of one created in a simulator."

There was no indication the troops were anything other than fully prepared, so McKinney activated the portside exit door. The shuttle's life support knew this was a hostile environment and it demanded confirmation, which he provided. Without further delay the rectangular door fell open, becoming an exit ramp for the soldiers to disembark.

Details flooded into McKinney's brain, fed through the visor sensor. It was much gloomier outside than he'd expected and it was easy to forget the shuttle's sensors were programmed to boost the natural light. A rocky slope stretched upwards until it was lost in the swirling clouds of windborne dust. Grit covered the uneven ground, moving constantly as it was whipped up by the larger gusts. Warnings on McKinney's HUD advised him it was well below zero – easily cold enough to kill a human in minutes. As well as that, the gravity was higher than usual, meaning the squad was going to feel like crap if they needed to exert themselves too much.

"Welcome to the Space Corps, lads and lasses," said Sergeant Li.

"Shuttle Two is due in less than ninety seconds. I'm going to take a look outside while you wait here," said McKinney. "Once the second shuttle is down, we'll move."

McKinney went down the ramp. He was immediately caught by a strong gust and he staggered to the side before recovering his balance. The gust faded, to be replaced by a persistent wind which changed direction at irregular intervals. It took most of his concentration to keep from being swept off his feet. He looked towards the shuttle's nose a few metres away and staggered towards it, keeping one hand pressed to the side wall of its hull. The sporadic beat of its engines was easily felt.

While the other soldiers waited anxiously in the passenger bay, McKinney advanced along the shuttle's flank. The angle of the craft kept the Neutraliser hidden until he reached the wedge-shaped nose and was able to see around. It was an awe-inspiring sight. The Vraxar ship rose from the gloom, towering hundreds of metres above the tiny Space Corps vessel. Much of it was lost from sight in the dust and the darkness, but it was the hints and suggestions of size which make McKinney shudder. Seen through a warship's sensors from half a million kilometres, the Neutraliser appeared spindly. Here, viewed from five hundred metres away, it was nothing of the sort.

A figure joined him, hunched against the wind and with its visored face aimed towards the Vraxar spaceship.

"Holy cow," said Sergeant Li. "You wouldn't want that thing landing in your back garden."

McKinney was accustomed to Li's approach to the universe and didn't respond to the comment. "Can you get a visual on Shuttle Two?" he asked, his neck craned to the skies. "They should be on the final approach." The visor sensor showed nothing.

"Can't see a damn thing," said Li.

McKinney opened a channel. "Shuttle Two, please report."

The spacesuit comms spat and squealed.

"Shuttle Two, please report."

"No answer?" asked Li, his voice filled with concern.

"I'm going to try the *Abyss*." McKinney requested a channel and got one immediately, though the static remained. "We've lost contact with Shuttle Two."

It was Lieutenant Cruz who answered. "Same here. Lieutenant Pointer is trying."

The background sounds of activity on the warship's bridge came through the channel, though McKinney wasn't able to determine exactly what was going on. Cruz spoke again.

"They've lost power, they've just gone into freefall."

"Oh shit."

Cruz spoke quickly and with a tautness to her voice. "Lieutenant Quinn is attempting a remote restart on their engines."

The movement sensor in McKinney's suit picked up an object a few hundred metres overhead and highlighted it in a smear of orange. Shuttle Two was coming down. Its descent appeared gradual and his heart jumped at the thought they might have got the gravity drive online again.

"You got them working?"

"Negative, they're still offline."

Then McKinney realised it was his viewpoint which made the approach appear to be a controlled one. As it neared the ground, the shuttle seemed to accelerate until it was hurtling at an unstoppable speed.

"Get their engines started!" he shouted.

It was too late. Shuttle Two smashed into the ruined front nullification sphere of the Vraxar Neutraliser. The shuttle's armoured hull was built to withstand high-speed impact and it only buckled, rather than breaking apart. The vessel bounced once, hit the sphere a second time and then fell several hundred metres until it landed nose-first on the stone ground at the base of the Vraxar spaceship. Slowly, it toppled to one side before coming to a rest.

McKinney swore and began running down the slope, heedless of the danger.

"Lieutenant, wait up!" Li called after him.

"Help me! Get Grover and Sandoval. Tell them to bring their kit."

This part of the Neutraliser's impact crater was steep and treacherous with grit. McKinney lost his footing and slid for a few metres, his body fighting for balance and against the wind's determination to knock him into a headlong fall.

"Lieutenant, stop!" said Lieutenant Cruz.

It took McKinney a moment to realise the crew of the *Abyss* must be tracking his movements from above. "I can't. They might be alive."

"They're gone. The life support unit went offline along with the engines."

"I've got to see."

"Eric, stop! You'll break your neck."

Cruz had that touch and the use of McKinney's first name brought him to a slithering halt.

"Gather your men. You need a controlled approach," she said.

McKinney took a deep breath, numbness seeping into his brain. He shook it off angrily. "Yes."

For the next few seconds, he barked out orders. He instructed the two onboard medics to leave the shuttle, along with a handful of the other soldiers. His sprint towards the crash site hadn't lasted long and he was surprised at how much distance he'd put between himself and the shuttle. It was two hundred metres away, its edges made indistinct by the storm.

A group of soldiers came towards him, their tentative footsteps clearly at odds with their desire to make haste. They had their rifles ready, which made the approach even harder. By the time they reached him, McKinney had accepted everyone on the second shuttle was dead. The network he'd set up between the spacesuits allowed him to access the vital signs of his soldiers and there was no reported life from the squads on Shuttle Two.

Medic Amy Sandoval put her arm around him for the briefest moment to show she understood. Then, she walked by, her heavy med-box dangling by its strap from one hand and bouncing against her leg with each tortured stride.

Confirmation of the sixty deaths, when it came, made McKinney feel no better and no worse. The doors to Shuttle Two could be opened by mechanical means when there was an emergency and the interior was a jumble of broken, lifeless bodies. The vessel had ended up more or less on its base and the two medics were able to move from body to body, until they were absolutely sure there was no one who could be saved.

Captain Blake spoke to McKinney privately. "I'm sorry, Lieutenant," he said simply.

"What happened, sir? Shuttles don't fail like that."

"We think their autopilot took them through a randomly-generated negation zone."

"I thought the Neutraliser was no longer functioning."

"So did we. It seems likely there's sporadic activity in there somewhere."

"Are we aborting, sir?" asked McKinney.

"We can't. This is a mission to gather intel and we can't allow tragedy to put an end to it."

"What about our return flight? Will we hit another negation zone?"

"I don't know, is the honest answer. I've got my crew working on finding you a definite answer."

It wasn't what McKinney had wanted to hear, though he had no choice other than to accept the situation.

"Do you have any more specifics on what we're looking for, sir?"

"Anything you can find, Lieutenant. Examples of their technology, weapons. Whatever your eyes see, chances are it'll be new to the Space Corps."

"I'll gather my men, sir."

"Thank you."

The comms link went dead and McKinney set himself to the task of organising the remaining sixty soldiers for the coming job. It didn't take long and within twenty minutes, they were standing at the base of the Vraxar Neutraliser. The hull breach was vast and it vanished through two hundred metres of black armour plating as well as another metallic substance which neither McKinney nor his visor computer recognized.

"Plant the comms beacon right here," he said, pointing at the ground nearby.

Two of the soldiers were carrying the booster device, which was a cloth-wrapped metal cube with a screen, an input pad and an extendible aerial. They placed it carefully at the place indicated and pulled out the aerial. As soon as it was switched on,

McKinney noticed the signal strength on his suit comms became much better.

"You're aware that booster won't do shit once we're inside, aren't you Lieutenant?" said Bannerman. "The walls of the Neutraliser are far too thick for the suit comms to penetrate."

McKinney was lost for words. "What the hell did we bring the booster for? Are you saying we'll be comms blind once we get inside?"

"I thought you knew, sir."

"I wasn't expecting perfect clarity on the comms, but I thought the booster was enough to get around that."

McKinney felt sick. Out of the entire Space Corps, he was amongst the small group which had real combat experience, yet it wasn't enough to prevent him making mistakes like this.

"Look on the bright side, Lieutenant – we'd be going into that ship regardless of whether the comms were working or not."

"Yeah. We'll have to make do."

He connected to the *ES Abyss* and advised the crew what to expect. Either they'd also overlooked the facts about the comms or assumed the soldiers would know what they were doing. There was no finger pointing and McKinney finished his conversation quickly.

"If it's a maze inside, we're splitting into groups," he said to Bannerman. "I assume we'll not be able to speak to each other once we go our separate ways?"

"That would be correct, sir."

"It just doesn't get better."

With no other way, McKinney set a six-hour time limit for the different squads and made sure the group leaders fully understood they were to get out right on schedule. It wasn't going to be easy, especially when they had no idea what lay ahead.

With preparations as much in place as he could make them, McKinney turned his attention to the gathered troops. The delay hadn't been long but they were getting restless and a jumpy soldier was far more prone to error.

"We're set," said McKinney.

"I think there's light through there," said Sergeant Woods.

"Someone's home," said Mills.

"The Vraxar are dead," said McKinney. He didn't even try to make it sound convincing. The bad feeling he'd experienced on the shuttle flight earlier hadn't left him, even after the deaths of everyone on Shuttle Two. In fact, his entire body was tingling with a feeling that something was wrong. He ignored it and walked towards the opening in the vast spaceship's hull.

CHAPTER FIVE

TO ERIC MCKINNEY, walking into the Vraxar Neutraliser felt like stepping into his own version of hell. The storm winds howled along the length of the ragged breach in its hull, and the grit rattled off his spacesuit. Overhead, the black metal armour loomed like an overhanging cliff, ready to collapse upon him at any moment. Beneath his feet, the surface was rough and deeply grooved, presumably from its contact with the surface of Vanistar. It was also warm enough for him to feel the heat through the material of the spacesuit and the soles of his boots.

The breach tapered drastically as he advanced, until it was only a few metres high. The light which Sergeant Woods had mentioned became stronger, whilst the winds of Vanistar weakened reluctantly, unwilling to give up their claim on this monstrous construction of metal.

During his cautious approach, McKinney's brain turned over the same words again and again. *Everything's dead, except us.* He wanted to believe it more than anything.

"If I didn't have balls of steel, this place would give me the creeps," said Garcia in a hoarse whisper.

"We're not even inside it yet," answered Roldan.

"There's more light a couple of hundred metres to the left," said Sergeant Li. "I reckon this ship got unzipped for half its length and the crew on the *Abyss* can't see it from up there."

"A little hole probably wouldn't have killed everything onboard something like this," said Vega.

"Their life support failed," said McKinney. "That's what killed them – they came in fast and got turned to pools of mush by the impact."

"These Vraxar deserve plenty of additional freezing air and ammonia to make absolutely sure they're properly dead."

"Amen to that."

McKinney was tempted to send three of the six ten-man squads to investigate the area Sergeant Li had noticed. It didn't seem wise to split up quite yet and he waved his arm forward. After a few more paces, he squinted ahead. The greenish light was coming from somewhere deeper within the Neutraliser and it wasn't nearly strong enough for him to get a clear picture of what lay inside. He adjusted the visor sensor to try and reach a comfortable medium, but the only impression he got was of a roughly-square opening at the deepest part of the furrow in the hull.

"It gets narrow here," he said. "Spread out to the sides and I'll go in with Squad A."

"Want me to put a rocket through, Lieutenant?" asked Webb.

"Save it for later."

The ceiling came lower and lower, though not so much that McKinney needed to duck. He reached the opening and stepped through it. The floor became perfectly flat and the ceiling rose above him. His visor sensor finally began to provide him with reliable details and it showed him the opposite wall of a long, wide room. There was no available cover, so he stepped to one side of the opening and crouched with his back to the wall and held tightly to the barrel of his plasma repeater. His visor detected no movement, no heat and no life. In fact, it was utterly deserted. Even the wind was totally gone, its absence making him realise how much he'd grown to hate it in such a short time.

The purpose of the room wasn't easy to guess. The walls were as dark as the exterior of the spaceship, except these ones were clad in what he initially thought were huge, rectangular tiles, without visible indication of how they'd been fixed in place. McKinney ran his fingers along one of the grooves and was left asking himself if these were indeed tiles or simply marks etched into the walls. The ceiling was five metres above and covered with the same tile pattern.

The two drones from the *ES Abyss* were on the floor a few metres away, resting on their sides. McKinney didn't need to come closer to see they were completely dead. They hadn't lasted long.

"Lieutenant?" whispered Rudy Munoz.

McKinney's distraction had caused him to delay too long. "Clear," he said.

The rest of Squad A entered one-by-one and spread themselves around the vicinity of the opening.

"Impressive," said Jeb Whitlock.

"It's two hundred metres to the far exit, with three exits in the wall opposite and another over there to our left," said McKinney. "The light is coming from the middle one of the three."

"The atmosphere in here isn't breathable," said Grover. "So unless these Vraxar are immune to practically everything, they're all dead and that light is coming from some sort of leftover power source."

"We can't be complacent," said McKinney.

"Not even a cockroach could survive in this, Lieutenant. And if you fire one of them towards a wall at a speed in excess of four hundred klicks per second, there'll be nothing left to wipe up afterwards."

"I understand the theory, Medic. I still don't like it."

Although there was no sign of enemy activity, McKinney wasn't willing to call in the other squads yet. With a series of brief commands, he sent the men of Squad A to investigate the exit passages. None of them was keen to find anything alive and they crept off without a sound.

McKinney joined in with the scouting and made for the furthest exit, accompanied by the squad's explosives man Clifton. They kept close to the wall for the illusory comfort it provided. After a short distance, they passed a screen flush to the wall, with a panel beneath it.

"There are symbols on it," said Clifton. "Alien mumbo jumbo crap."

The alien characters were exceptionally faint and difficult to see even in the near-darkness. McKinney watched them for a moment and grimaced when he saw them change to a new arrangement.

"This isn't good," he said. "There's something still working on this ship and I don't like it."

"As long as the Vraxar are dead, their ship can do what it likes as far as I'm concerned, sir."

"That's not how I look at it."

Clifton reached out a finger towards the control panel under the screen.

"Don't touch!"

The finger retreated.

"Probably not wise, huh?"

"Not wise," McKinney agreed.

They reached the end of the room. The exit passage was a few metres wide and high, which suggested it was expected to carry traffic larger than a standard Vraxar soldier. It went off into the depths of the spaceship, with no visible end.

"Do you think this goes towards the central section?"

"It seems likely."

"Strikes me that's where the Vraxar captain would keep himself."

"You're assuming they act the same way we do."

"What's the point in living if you can't make a few assumptions, Lieutenant?"

Clifton was a strange one, though in an eccentric way rather than in a manner that might cause concern. McKinney clapped him on the back.

"I've seen enough."

He spun and made his way along to the entry point. The others of Squad A had little to report – there were passages leading off to unknown areas of the Neutraliser, all of which would need to be explored.

"Everyone get inside," said McKinney to the other squads.

The rest of the soldiers were keen to escape the wind and it was enough to overcome their reluctance to set foot on a vast enemy spaceship. They practically dashed inside and it took only a couple of minutes until they were assembled by squad.

Without having sufficient knowledge of the vessel's interior to formulate a plan, McKinney made a series of snap decisions.

"Squad B – you're going to the left. That passage looks as if it leads to the forward nullification sphere. I have no idea what you'll find, but I'm damned sure the Space Corps will be very interested. If you can obtain any samples, please do so."

"Does that mean we can steal stuff, Lieutenant?" asked Joy Guzman.

"If it looks interesting and it's not nailed down, I want it back on the shuttle."

"It's just like being a pirate."

"This is Confederation-approved, soldier. That makes it legit."

McKinney turned his attention to the remaining soldiers. "Squad C, take the first of the three passages, Squad D take the second. Squad E, I'm sure you can work out where you're going. The first person who gives me a wisecrack answer gets to guard the comms beacon outside in the wind."

Nobody wanted that particular duty and the four squads waited to be dismissed without any jokers making themselves heard.

"Squad F, you get the easy work. You're going to wait here in case you're needed. Corporal Evans, I'm trusting you to make the right call if there are any signs of trouble."

Evans had matured considerably since the first time McKinney had met him in the Tillos bunker on Atlantis. He'd changed from a man accustomed to lax discipline to someone of level-headed reliability.

"We'll keep an eye out, sir."

"That leaves one squad and one last corridor to explore," said McKinney. "We've got some running to do from the looks of it."

"A high-gravity slog to the Vraxar captain's office," said Clifton.

"With no guarantee of a medal at the end of it," grumbled Vega.

"You got a new hand out of the Space Corps already, didn't you?" asked Garcia. "I thought you'd be grateful."

"Yeah, the trouble is only this middle finger works properly," said Vega, flipping Garcia the bird.

"Nice one, man," laughed Roldan.

McKinney's own grin was hidden by his visor, though it was harder to keep it from his voice. "Everyone set your timers – we need to be back here in six hours. Two would be better. Move out, everyone and be aware you're going to lose comms. Stick with your party and don't get separated."

Sixty of the *ES Abyss*'s troops went off with their teams. McKinney took note of the purposeful strides and the readiness of their weapons. He'd assigned a known officer to each squad where he could and hoped it would be enough.

With Squad A spread out around him, McKinney led the way to the far exit. He used the opportunity to connect to the *ES Abyss* and was pleased when Lieutenant Cruz answered.

"We're heading into the Vraxar spaceship now," he advised. "I'm streaming the data from my visor sensor through the beacon we've got outside. I don't know how long it'll be until we're cut off."

"There's already significant attenuation in the signal, Lieutenant. You'll be comms blind in a few minutes."

"Understood."

"Come back safe, please."

"Yes, ma'am."

The comms went dead, leaving McKinney in what was becoming a familiar position for him – alone except for his squad and facing the unknown.

A voice caused McKinney to turn.

"Hey, what's this?" asked Casey McCoy.

The soldier was standing in front of the barely-lit screen McKinney had walked past earlier.

"Leave it!"

The warning came too late and McCoy ran his fingertips across the panel beneath the screen. At once, the panel sprang into life and the Vraxar symbols illuminated brightly. They started changing rapidly and something inconceivably heavy clunked through the ceiling.

McCoy jumped back. "Sorry, Lieutenant."

"I could happily beat the crap out of you right now, Soldier," said McKinney.

"Sorry," stammered McCoy again.

"Think yourself lucky I'm not the violent type."

"Except when it comes to the Vraxar," said Roldan.

McKinney was furious but wise enough to accept he couldn't change what was done. He waited for a few moments, listening intently. The clunking wasn't repeated and although the display screen continued to change, there was no sign McCoy's actions had caused any direct harm.

"This ship ain't dead. Not by a long stretch," said Whitlock. "I don't care what the sensors on the *Abyss* say."

"This thing can shut down a whole planet," added Roldan. "It makes sense for it to have lots of its own backup power systems."

The logic didn't necessarily follow, but McKinney found himself in agreement with Roldan's assessment. "Just as long as the Vraxar are dead, we've got nothing to worry about."

"Maybe you should tell McCoy not to stick his fingers in anything that looks like a power socket. That would be my major worry," said Garcia.

McCoy's response was short and blunt.

"Enough," warned McKinney. "We're in hostile surroundings – I don't want anyone getting distracted because you two are pissing on each other."

The bitching stopped as quickly as it started. McKinney didn't usually mind the banter – it served a useful purpose when the men were cooped up in their quarters on the *ES Abyss*. Here in a situation that was potentially dangerous, he didn't want the hassle of dealing with the fallout.

They reached the exit corridor and set off warily along it in a column two abreast. The lead men had their repeaters trained forwards, whilst those behind kept their rifles ready. If there was any movement, the front two would drop to their knees and those to the rear would spread out to the sides in order to get a clear line of sight.

McKinney was accustomed to enclosed spaces, yet there was something about this Vraxar ship which beat against his resolve. He could imagine the vast weight of metal pressing in on him and the feeling grew with every step. The others were uneasy too and they muttered the type of throwaway comments which people made when they were trying to distract themselves from something unpleasant.

They walked at a rapid pace for fifteen minutes without seeing any side passages or variation. There was no light and the visor sensors weren't capable of generating a good image. Every time McKinney thought he saw a side passage in the distance, it turned out to be a false alarm. He wanted to use the conventional torches built into the suit visors, but the light would give them away from a good distance. So, they walked in sensor-enhanced darkness. The extra gravity was enough to make them sweat and it was fortunate the Space Corps insisted on a high degree of fitness.

"How long do you reckon this tunnel is, Lieutenant?" asked Webb.

McKinney had been asking himself that exact question. "The two nullification spheres are more than three thousand metres in diameter and the central section is four thousand metres at its longest point. That means each of these connecting beams is four klicks from sphere to central section. We came in a little way along from the front, so I'd guess this corridor is nearly four klicks long, assuming it terminates at the central section."

"What if it goes all the way to the end of the ship?"

"Then we turn around and we come back."

It was Ricky Vega who saw it. The others walked by without noticing a series of shallow indentations in the wall.

"Lieutenant, look at this."

McKinney drew to a halt and the others stopped with him. "What is it?"

"It looks like a ladder to me," said Vega. "There's something on the ceiling."

"Let me have a look."

McKinney clipped his rifle onto his repeater pack and sized up the ladder. It was more like a series of wide, deep slots in the wall, spaced half a metre apart and climbing as high as the ceiling four metres above.

"Looks like a hatch or something up there," said McCoy.

"We're here to explore, so let's see if it'll open."

McKinney pushed his hand into the highest slot he could reach and jammed the toe of his boot into one of the lower openings. With a grunt, he hauled himself upwards. It was awkward and his hand almost slipped when he was halfway up. His fingertips stung from the effort of holding himself in place.

The hatch was a square section of the ceiling, about one metre to each side. It was the same colour as the other metal and only a thin seam betrayed its presence.

"Good eyes, Vega, McCoy," he said. "It's hard to make it out even with my face pressed against it."

"Does it open?" asked Roldan.

Keeping a tight grip with one hand, McKinney reached up with the other and thumped his palm against the hatch. There was no indication it was any less solid than the metal around it. He struck it again.

"If it does, I can't figure it out."

McKinney was about to give up and climb down, when he noticed something in the wall next to the topmost ladder slot. There was a square groove about three fingers wide. There was no reason for it to be there, so he shuffled carefully towards it.

The men below craned their necks to see, curious to find out what McKinney was up to.

When he was close enough, McKinney stuck out his hand and tentatively put his middle and forefinger into the hole. The opening went inwards and then down and he was able to hook his fingers over the lip. Without allowing himself time to wonder if this was the best course of action, McKinney pulled hard. A long, narrow section of the wall came away easily and smoothly – the groove was the top of a lever made to be flush with the wall. The hatch opened silently – it rose a few inches into the ceiling and then slid to one side. McKinney's suit detected a faint breeze coming out, suggesting the area above was pressurized.

The ladder continued upwards and, having come this far, McKinney continued his ascent.

CHAPTER SIX

CAPTAIN CHARLIE BLAKE couldn't settle. The climate-controlled air on the bridge felt alternately too hot and too cold. His chair had developed bumps and lumps where there had previously been none and the bridge replicator was emitting a high-pitched whine he was certain hadn't been there before.

The surviving troops had been out of comms sight for fifteen minutes, except for Corporal Evans and his men. Corporal Evans hadn't heard from the others since they'd left the entry point room and therefore wasn't able to give any more detailed responses than *I don't know, sir* or *I'll let you know as soon as they return, sir*.

"When I find the technicians responsible for this damned smell I'm going to wring their filthy, rotten necks!" Blake snarled.

He sat down once more, cursing the factory which had covered his seat. A minor alert on the tactical screen required his input and he touched it with a fingertip. The warning didn't clear immediately and he banged at it with his knuckles, swearing loudly.

He heard quiet footsteps and a figure appeared at his side.

"They're gone, sir," said Pointer. "We can't bring them back and we can't mourn them yet, but we need to put everything to one side until the living are safe."

"I hate these Vraxar," he said. "I always prided myself in being above hatred, but I can't help myself."

"We all want the same thing, sir."

"The extermination of another species."

"That's what it's going to take. We can't allow our humanity to weaken us. If we don't win, we'll become Vraxar and we'll be the ones carrying their guns when they reach the next civilisation on their route."

He twisted in his seat and studied Pointer's face. There was a strength there he'd never seen in her before – a determination that was non-existent in the Caz Pointer he'd once known. *Or thought I knew.*

"We'll finish this mission and we won't be diverted," he said. "This is too important for us to mess up."

She smiled in understanding and returned to her seat. Lieutenant Quinn interrupted the following silence and the news he brought wasn't in any way welcome.

"Look at this, sir," said Quinn.

Blake leapt from his chair and crossed the bridge until he was standing next to the man. There was a stack of empty cups about thirty high on the edge of the engine monitoring console which Quinn had evidently been cultivating and Blake struggled against the urge to knock the tower over.

"I can see from your face I'm not going to like this."

"No, you aren't going to like it, sir. You *really* aren't going to like it."

Blake's eyes darted over the numerous gauges and charts on the console. "Which one am I looking at?"

"This one here. I've been monitoring the fluctuations from

the rear nullification sphere. It's been spiking since we arrived and if you look at this chart here..."

"Going up."

"Yes, sir, it's going up and at an increasing rate. I can't tell you what that thing is made of or how it works, but I'm absolutely certain it's failing."

"Not a gentle failure from the looks of this chart."

"It's going critical."

"What happens then?"

"There's a chance it'll simply shut down like the front sphere."

"You don't think so?"

"I wouldn't like to be here to witness what happens. If even a fraction of its known power generation capabilities are converted into a more destructive form of energy, we could end up with a crater the size of a moon."

"Or worse."

"Much worse."

"How long?"

"This is guesswork – somewhere between one hour and four. I can run it through a standard simulator if you want something more exact."

Blake wasn't sure if he was more shocked at the imminent failure of the Neutraliser or that there was a premade simulator to predict it. "Run the sim. And can you provide an estimate of how long our energy shield will hold out if we remain at an altitude of eighty klicks and that Neutraliser blows up?"

"Assuming it doesn't simply shut down and reaches critical mass..." Quinn furrowed his brow. "Do you remember when we left that bomb in the middle of the Vraxar mothership and what happened to those battleships they had parked nearby?"

"Our shield won't help us?"

"If I was a betting man, I'd say it won't last longer than half a second."

"One day you'll give me a happy surprise, Lieutenant. How long until the sim is finished?"

"It's finished, sir. You might have misunderstood when I described it as a *standard* sim. We know so little about the Neutralisers that it's entirely guesswork."

"There's a simulator that tries to derive a probability from guesswork?"

"There are a lot of clever men and women in the research labs, sir. This isn't so much a guesswork simulator as such. More of a chaos distiller."

Blake shook his head in wonder. "Just tell me how long."

"Two hours and ten minutes, sir."

"What's the expected degree of accuracy?"

"Thirty percent."

"Not at all accurate, then."

"Nope."

The results of the *ES Abyss*'s simulator software were so inaccurate it was impossible to have any confidence in them. Blake mulled things over briefly; when it came down to it, there was no choice in how to proceed.

"Lieutenant Pointer, speak to Corporal Evans. Tell him to locate the other squads in preparation for a fastest-speed withdrawal. Stress the urgency so there is no scope for misunderstanding."

"Yes, sir."

"Ensign Bailey – send our remaining two shuttles out on autopilot and programme them to hover at an altitude of one hundred metres, without coming close to the Neutraliser. This may be a staged withdrawal."

"I'm on it, sir."

Pointer finished speaking with Corporal Evans. "He's going to look for the other squads and will order them to the shuttles."

It was frustrating and Blake wanted to do something that would give him a semblance of control. Apart from sending his crew out to the Neutraliser, there was nothing he could do and he clenched his fists. It was about to get worse.

"When the shuttles have launched, we should climb to an altitude of not less than forty thousand klicks and keep two of our cores wound up for short range transits," said Lieutenant Hawkins.

Hawkins was absolutely correct, though it felt to Blake like a failure when he gave the order. The ES *Abyss*'s two shuttles left the hangar bay and the heavy cruiser climbed higher until it was at an altitude of exactly forty thousand kilometres. If anything went catastrophically wrong it wasn't going to be far enough, but Blake couldn't bring himself to sit half a million kilometres off world and watch events unfold like a coward hiding behind the curtains.

"The comms beacon is going to struggle to push a signal through the storm," said Cruz. "The beam strength is less than ten percent and it fluctuates with the weather conditions."

"This is the hand we've been dealt, Lieutenant."

"I thought you didn't believe in fate, sir?"

"I don't, but I'm beginning to learn I'm not right about everything."

"The knowing makes you stronger, not weaker," said Hawkins.

Blake smiled though he didn't feel it inside. With the lives of sixty men and women no longer in his control, he resumed pacing.

AT THE TOP of the ladder, there was a space. It was too small to call it a room – the ceiling wasn't high enough for McKinney to stand and if he'd been interested enough to try it, he could have touched the opposite walls by reaching out with both arms. There was a narrow tunnel, which his sense of direction told him led towards the centre of the Neutraliser's connecting beam. There was no light and he couldn't see how far the passage went.

"Anything up there?" asked Roldan.

"Another tunnel. I'm going to have a look."

"If you find any Vraxar valuables, remember we're a team, sir."

"I'll keep it in mind."

The tunnel was just wide enough for him to walk front-on, though he was forced to stoop to avoid knocking his head on the metal ceiling. His visor's image intensifiers were running at 100% and the best they could manage to show were a few areas of green and lines where the walls met with floor and ceiling. He turned on his visor torch and continued.

"Doesn't look like there's much here," he said.

There was no response from the comms – not even a background hum. Whatever material he was passing through it was dense enough to block a comms signal after only a few metres. He pressed on and gradually he became aware of a buzzing sound, coming from an unknown source. The walls carried no vibration, leaving him mystified as to what it might be.

McKinney guessed he'd walked for two hundred metres when he reached the end of the tunnel – it simply terminated at a blank wall. By this stage, the buzzing sound was so persistent he needed to reduce the feed level from his visor microphone. It wasn't enough and the buzzing seated itself in his joints and bones, making his entire body ache.

At the discovery of this apparent dead-end, McKinney's brain was stumped. His hand knew what to do and it reached out to the side wall, finding another of the lever grooves. He poked his fingers inside and pulled. A large section of the smooth wall slid sideways into a recess. Green light flooded in and McKinney closed his eyes until he felt everything adjust.

He walked another few paces and stepped into an area like nothing he'd seen before. He found himself standing on a narrow walkway close to the bottom of an immense, cylindrical space. This space continued for a thousand or more metres to the left, while to the right it went so far it confounded the efforts of his sensor to locate the end.

The highest point of the ceiling may have been a thousand or more metres above. It was impossible to tell, since there was a thick bundle of black-metal cords along the entire length of the Neutraliser's interior. These cords were held in place by huge crossbeams and were of many different sizes, intertwined in such a way as to defy the eye. They twisted this way and that, like the entrails of a gigantic world-destroying beast.

The green light came from sparks running through this metal vine. The sparks jumped and flashed, racing from one end of the spaceship to another. The buzzing, which had been loud before, was almost too much to bear and McKinney ground his teeth together and placed a hand over the visor earpiece.

He stumbled, only dimly aware of a red alert inside his visor advising him that his heart had stopped. A sharp, terrible pain squeezed his chest until he thought his ribs would crack from the agony. He fell to one knee and his sight dimmed. He fought to stay awake in a battle his mind couldn't win.

The spacesuit's defibrillator thumped off his chest, once, twice, three times. Its medical computer made the decision to inject him with a fatal dose of battlefield adrenaline. The combination brought McKinney back to consciousness, gasping, retching and feeling as if he'd been dumped into a vat of icy water. His heart rate began to fluctuate wildly as the excess of adrenaline caused it to fail again. At just the right moment, the suit computer injected him in four places with a second substance, this one designed to bring a soldier down from the highs of running too long on boosters.

Got to get out of this room!

His heart went into spasm again and recovered. The battlefield adrenaline cleared his mind and gave strength to his limbs. McKinney threw himself into the passage and his fingers fumbled for the lever. He pulled it hard and kept running. The door closed, cutting off the light in the passage and leaving him once more in the darkness.

McKinney didn't allow himself a second to rest and he ran back towards the hatch in a half-crouch, his shoulders scraping against the side walls. He reached the top and saw his squad milling around uncertainly. His suit re-established a connection with the Squad A channel and he caught a few snippets of the conversation.

"We should go up there."

"Nah, the Lieutenant will be fine."

"It's been too long."

"Look, here he is," said Vega. "Welcome back, sir."

McKinney came down the ladder at speed, closing the upper hatch as he did so.

"Grover, plug me into that machine," he said, pointing at the med-box on the floor.

Grover was a man who acted and talked at once, rather than queuing the two up. "What's up?" he asked, plugging a wire into the interface on McKinney's suit.

"I found the Neutraliser's central power conduit. It stopped my heart."

"You got lucky, then. You've got a significantly elevated heart rate and enough battlefield adrenaline in your veins to kill fifty percent of the entire Confederation's population. Other than that? No lasting damage that I can see. You should get back to the entry point."

"Negative. We press on and I'm leading."

"Fine, ignore the advice of your trained medical staff and piss off deeper into the bowels of an alien spaceship. See if I care."

McKinney clapped Grover on the back in response and set off once more. He wasn't sure what conclusions he could draw from the Neutraliser's central conduit – doubtless there were people in the Space Corps who would be very interested and could make a few educated guesses. The one overriding feeling he had was that the Vraxar followed a technology path which was very different to that of either humans or Ghasts.

What do I know? he thought. *I'm only a soldier.*

Squad A continued along the wide corridor, this time at an increased pace.

CHAPTER SEVEN

"ACCORDING TO MY VISOR READING, we've walked four thousand metres, and for nearly an hour," said Huey Roldan.

"We should be in the central section," McKinney replied. "There's got to be a way up soon."

"Do you reckon this is only a maintenance corridor?" asked Garcia. "I've counted ten ceiling hatches."

"It seems like wasted space if you ask me," said Vega.

"I doubt they added this corridor without a reason," said McKinney. He stopped suddenly, bringing the others to a halt with him. "It looks like the corridor ends ahead. What's that I can see to the side?"

"On the left wall?" asked Webb.

"Yes."

"An opening."

The opening turned out to be a long flight of steps with high risers and a deep tread. The men gathered at the stairwell entrance and tried to determine what might be at the top. It was no good – there were too many steps and the distance was too great.

"No sign of a lift," said Clifton.

"These Vraxar must like climbing," said Webb.

"I don't think they feel pain, soldier. Seems to me that they'll keep doing what they're told, even if it kills them."

"What's the point?" said Munoz.

"Eh?"

"Who'd want an existence like that? Why bother with living if you've had everything taken away from you?"

"None of them had a choice," said McKinney. "The Vraxar killed them and used their bodies."

"There's got to be some original Vraxar out there, hasn't there?" said Whitlock. "The ones we've seen are treated like slaves. I'll be there're some head honchos hiding in the shadows and ordering these other ones about, while they sit back with a glass of cold beer."

It was an idea which had enough appeal to take hold and soon the soldiers were nodding sagely as if they'd figured out a significant part of the Vraxar's motivations. McKinney was fairly sure there was no fairness or equality within the Vraxar ranks but it didn't take a genius to figure that out. Martial races weren't known for their adherence to democratic rights.

"We're going up," McKinney said, letting the men know what they'd already guessed.

To the squad's credit, they got on with it. The effects of extra gravity, along with the weight of their equipment and the height of the steps soon cut off any inconsequential conversation and the squad toiled its way upwards.

McKinney was still burning with battlefield adrenaline and he found the climb easy, though he was aware there'd be a price to pay in the future. His brain idly rotated the jigsaw pieces of what they'd discovered so far on the Neutraliser. It wasn't difficult to assume the entire ship was designed around the single task of shutting off other power sources, but as far as McKinney knew, most in the Space Corps believed it was the forward and aft spheres which did all the work while the central section was thought to be packed with their troops.

What McKinney saw made him think there was something in the central section which was doing the nullification, whilst the spheres were more likely to be amplifiers. He found the idea interesting, though admitted to himself there was little chance of gaining a tactical advantage if there was any proof to his theory.

The steps ended after an interminable time and McKinney was sure everyone in his squad had taken some kind of booster. He didn't blame them.

After checking for signs of life, they entered the top room. It was a big space, eighty metres or more to each side. At floor level, there were rows of metal workbenches arrayed in neat rows and there was a jumble of objects piled untidily against one wall. Higher up, there were ladders and gantries, with connecting walkways of grated metal, and the ceiling itself was lost in the gloom far above. McKinney got a ping off the highest visible point – it was three hundred metres away.

He paused to listen - it was silent.

"This place looks like its centuries old," said Roldan, putting words to what they were all feeling.

"I've seen pictures of factories on Old Earth that looked newer than this," said Garcia.

"This reminds me of a mineshaft."

"I don't like it," said McKinney. "We'll be easy to pick off from those gantries."

"There's another exit," said Clifton. "Unless you want to go up?"

"I don't want to stay in here. We'll head towards that far exit. Keep on your guard."

They spread out across the room, the soft hum of their plasma repeaters rising to prominence above their footsteps.

McKinney had positioned himself so he would be closest to the pile of objects. He stooped to examine one or two – whatever they had originally been intended for, they'd been smashed off the wall of this room when the Neutraliser crashed down and they were flattened or broken.

"Nothing worth having, Lieutenant?" asked Vega.

"Only for scrap."

"There could be dead bits of Vraxar in there."

McKinney dropped the alloy bar he was examining and suppressed the urge to wipe his hands on something.

They left the room without incident and headed deeper into the Neutraliser's central section. McKinney was aware of the passing time, so he kept the squad moving. He didn't want to be here any longer than necessary, but more importantly he didn't want to return empty handed.

After following three long corridors, each of which connected to a small, empty room, they reached a second set of upward steps. The passage continued on by, so there was no need to climb if McKinney chose not to.

"You know what they say about shit?" said Garcia. "The higher you go, the more of it there is."

"I thought it was *shit falls on those underneath?*" said Webb.

"Whatever it is, down here is where all the Neutraliser's maintenance stuff happens. These rooms were probably stuffed with whichever poor bums the Vraxar conquered before they reached the Estral. Ruined husks with lumps of skin falling off."

Garcia was likely trying to be sympathetic towards the dead in the only way he knew how. There were occasions McKinney wished the man wouldn't bother trying and kept his mouth closed instead.

"The Vraxar represent thousands of years of tragedy and extinction, soldier. I think we should try and show some respect for their victims."

"I'm no good with words, sir. I hate this place."

The words were sincere and McKinney let it drop. He was feeling on edge and it wasn't because he'd almost died a short while ago. The battlefield adrenaline contained all sorts of other substances to make a soldier forget about his own mortality. It couldn't suppress every emotion and McKinney was fighting with the pressure of standing inside what felt like a coffin of endless death and misery. In a way, it would have been easier if the Neutraliser was filled with Vraxar – shooting the bastards was far easier than thinking about their past deeds.

"We're going up," he said. "If there's no Vraxar gold, we're returning to the shuttle."

This staircase wasn't as long as the previous one. Even so, it took the squad a few minutes to reach the top. To McKinney's dismay, there were more corridors, rather than a room filled with portable Vraxar technology, waiting to be carted back to the shuttle. There was also light – a dingy grey illumination which appeared to emanate from the metal.

"We've got power," said Grover.

"Is that a good thing or a bad thing?" said Webb.

McKinney looked each way along the corridor – he thought there might be doors and side passages in both directions. "I don't like it."

"We could leave?" said Roldan hopefully.

"Fifteen minutes and then we head back," said McKinney.

"Which way?" said Roldan, unable to hide his disappointment.

McKinney chose to go right. He was starting to feel like a gambler who, having called heads ten times in a row and lost each one, had convinced himself that the next flip of the coin was more likely to be a head. *And I'm doubling the bet each time,* he thought.

He ignored the whispers of self-doubt and strode off, letting the others catch up to him. They reached the first door and Clifton idly thumped the featureless surface with his fist.

"Half a metre thick," he said.

There was an access panel to one side – it was a square, polished area flush to the wall. The panel looked as if it was made from glass but probably wasn't. Unfamiliar Vraxar symbols cycled through a pattern with no sign of repetition. McKinney was tempted to try and activate the panel, to the point where he reached out a tentative hand towards it.

"Best not," he said, pulling the hand away.

They passed two more sealed doors and then the corridor ended at a T-junction. The right turning continued until the end was lost in the distance, while the left branch ended at a closed door thirty metres away. They were running out of time in which to accomplish anything.

"Let's give that door a try," said McKinney.

With his mind made up, he strode to the end of the corridor and the rest of the squad moved to follow.

"Are you sure this is wise, Lieutenant?" asked Whitlock.

"No."

"Maybe we should..."

"No."

McKinney reached the door. From his periphery, he could see the access panel in the adjacent wall, perfectly positioned for him to brush his fingers across its smooth surface. In two quick gestures, he pressed his palm to the panel and followed up with a swipe of his fingertips.

The door opened.

"Oh crap," said Garcia, peering inside.

The room was a huge, rectangular, open space. Its longer walls were a hundred metres or more and the shorter walls closer to sixty. There was a viewing window set into the far wall, the contents of the room beyond hidden by a tint on the clear surface.

The dirty lighting was stronger here and somehow reminded McKinney of a deserted hospital viewed through the eyes of a nightmare. There were hundreds of raised platforms on the floor – most of them a metre wide and three in length. Others were much larger. *Biers,* thought McKinney as soon as he saw them.

The high ceiling was covered in a criss-cross of deep runners, to allow free movement for the many-jointed robotic arms which reached down from above. These arms were made from some type of grey polymer and they were fitted with several different types of implements. There were scalpels, tubes, syringes and more. Elsewhere, there were mobile medical units, floating quietly above the floor. The walls were covered in panels and screens, their alien texts constantly updating and changing.

Worst of all was the blood. It covered every single bier, in thick, glistening smears. In places, McKinney could see it oozing onto the floor. *It should have dried or been stripped away by the force of the impact with Vanistar,* he thought. Then he was struck with the realisation.

"The life support is still functioning in this area of the ship," he said. "The failure mustn't have been complete."

"That's what's keeping all this blood wet?"

"I guess."

"Does that mean...?" said Roldan.

"There might still be Vraxar alive," McKinney confirmed.

The squad were instantly more alert and the worry – bordering on fear – was apparent in their voices.

"Why haven't we seen any?" asked McCoy.

"I think we might have breached the central area of the Neutraliser when we came through that door," said McKinney.

"Time to get out of here?" asked Vega.

McKinney didn't answer at once. His feet were on the move and it felt as if his brain had no say in the matter. The floor was sticky with more than just blood – there were other fluids mingled in congealing lumps. He walked between two of the biers and tried hard to pretend he hadn't seen the gobbets of flesh on the surface. A medical robot hummed nearby, from its shape appearing more like a mobile repeater than a device to save lives.

Of course - its purpose really isn't to save lives.

"Where are you going, Lieutenant?" asked Whitlock.

"I need to see what's on the other side of this window."

"What is this place?"

"A conversion room. Where the living and dead become Vraxar."

It was like a slaughterhouse and McKinney was incredibly glad his visor blocked out the smells. Just when he'd become accustomed to his level of hatred for the Vraxar, he found there were new depths waiting to be plumbed and he blinked back tears of fury.

It's going to make me stronger.

He reached the window and stepped close enough to see through. What had appeared to be a tint was, in fact, a coating of some kind of dirt. He didn't want to touch it, but he nevertheless swabbed an area away with the side of one hand. The dirt was moist and the best he could manage without having a cloth in his possession was to leave a thickly blurred section through which to peer.

"Look at this," he said.

The rest of the squad came over. They didn't want to be here and they cursed amongst themselves as a distraction from the filthy squalor of the conversion room.

Garcia was a moaner, but he could be relied on when the going got tough. He crossed the room quickest and waited next to McKinney, unwilling to take the next step.

"I'm not sure I want to look through there, Lieutenant."

"Look."

Garcia did as he was asked. He stepped back from the window without saying anything.

Ricky Vega was next. He spent a long moment staring into the next room, unleashing a string of quiet expletives as he did so.

The others took their turns. Armand Grover was the slowest to cross the room, since he took a few moments to study one of the medical robots.

"I reckon we could probably push one of these back to the shuttle," he said. "That would make a good prize, wouldn't it? We could learn what sort of medical tech the Vraxar use."

"We aren't taking a medical bot," said McKinney.

"What, then?"

McKinney thumbed at the smeared patch on the window and Grover put his visor up close.

"I don't think opening that room is a good idea, sir."

"You reckon?" McKinney took another look to remind himself of a sight his brain would never forget.

The room within was filled with Vraxar. It wasn't possible to see how many – certainly there were tens, possibly hundreds of thousands - since the far walls were hidden in the distance. The aliens stood in staggered rows, their bodies held upright against ten-feet metal posts, to which they were bound by metal straps across their necks. Their arms were pulled back and twisted around the posts, though it was impossible to see if they were tied in some way. The fixing method would have killed a human in a few hours and it made McKinney wonder if the Vraxar were determined to make their existence as vile as possible, even as they pursued its extension at any cost.

"The Space Corps has never been given the opportunity to question a live Vraxar," said McKinney.

"How do you know they're alive?" said Clifton.

"Their eyes are open. They're alive and we all know it."

"Yeah."

"What if we open that room up and it somehow releases them?" asked Munoz. "I didn't see any weapons in there with them, but there are only so many rounds in these repeaters."

"It's a chance we'll have to take. Our prize is in that room, gentlemen – it's the Vraxar gold we've been looking for."

If any of the squad disagreed with McKinney's decision, they kept it to themselves. The door to the room filled with Vraxar was set in the middle of the conversion room wall. McKinney approached it with the trepidation of a barefoot man stepping into a darkened room filled with poisonous snakes. This door was three times the width of the others and with a slightly larger access panel to one side.

"Here we go," he said.

McKinney pressed his hand to the panel.

CHAPTER EIGHT

THE DOOR ROSE into the ceiling, permitting access to the room beyond. The air from within came soundlessly through the opening, bringing a variety of compounds which McKinney's visor didn't recognize and which it warned him strongly against inhaling. He had no intention of removing his visor; instead he waited on the threshold with his plasma repeater ready to fire if there was any sign of movement. Thousands of Vraxar eyes stared at the squad. They didn't speak, but there was a sound, which McKinney recognized as air rattling through countless pairs of rotting lungs.

Now that he wasn't viewing this *storage facility* through the semi-opacity of the soiled window, McKinney was able to see more details. The majority of these Vraxar had once been Estral, though here and there he saw other types, most of them physically smaller specimens. They were in various stages of decay and the floor was littered with pieces of their flesh. Motes of skin floated in the air, contrasting with the diffuse grey light.

Each Vraxar had different shapes and sizes of metal implants, without rhyme or reason for why that might be. Some were missing eyes, limbs, jaws, feet and it was only in most cases that metal was used to fill the gaps.

None of the squad knew what to say and they shrank away from the door, not wishing to be the focus of so much attention. McKinney didn't like it either, but he stepped over the threshold. He was finally able to see the extent of the room – it was roughly square and approximately eight hundred metres along each wall. There was about a metre between each Vraxar - he tried to work out the numbers and gave up quickly.

Without warning, the diffuse grey light faded out and was replaced a moment later by a steady green light.

"Oh shit," said Webb.

The other men pointed their repeaters this way and that, as if they expected the Vraxar to detach their collars and coming sprinting towards them. McKinney was within a hair's breadth of ordering an immediate withdrawal, when he gave himself a shake. Only the light had changed and the Vraxar remained where they were.

"Hold!" he ordered.

"What the hell is going on?" muttered Garcia.

"Nothing is going on. The room sensors must have detected the change in the air, that's all."

"It's still not right," said McCoy. "There must be a million Vraxar in here and I don't want to be turned into one."

"You are not going to be turned into a Vraxar," snapped McKinney. "Now shut up and wait here while I see how easy it'll be to get one of these bastards down from its rack."

He reached the closest Vraxar. It had once been Estral and was almost fresh. Two entry wounds in its chest told the story of how it had originally died. McKinney prodded it with the end of his gauss rifle. It didn't move or speak and he poked it again, trying to avoid looking at the agonised expression on its face. Part of the original Estral still lived within and was fully aware of what it had become. Even though the Estral had been no friends of the Confederation, it was heart-wrenching to see.

"What are you doing, Lieutenant?" asked Clifton.

"I want to see if its arms are fastened."

"It doesn't look happy."

"Nope. I'll bet it's praying to whichever god it believes in that we'll shoot it."

"*Are* you going to shoot it?" asked Roldan.

"No."

McKinney was unable to provoke a response from the alien, so he took a gamble and looked around its fastening post. Its wrists were held in place by two metal cuffs, which were attached to the main post. The Vraxar didn't make any attempt to break free.

McKinney had no desire to try and carry an Estral-sized Vraxar all the way to the shuttle, so he hunted for one of the smaller ones. He had to go through several rows, unwillingly brushing against the aliens, until he found what he wanted.

This Vraxar was less than six feet tall, with thin limbs and few alloy attachments embedded into its yellow-brown flesh. The creature's nose was gone, revealing oval holes which vanished into its skull. Its lips were thin and pulled back, revealing blackened teeth in receding grey gums. Its eyes were yellow and puckered, seemingly far too small for their sockets. Nevertheless, these eyes tracked McKinney as he came closer and then fixed on him when he stood in front of it. His reflective visor stopped it meeting his gaze and he tried to discern what it might be thinking. He'd expected there to be hatred and there was none. Whatever was going through its mind, he got no feeling for it.

Contrary to McKinney's first thoughts, the alien wasn't only held in place by the thick metal collar and the wristbands. There was also a rod jutting from the main support pillar which entered the mid-point of the Vraxar's back, just off to the side of its spine.

He could see an inch or two of it protruding and shook his head in absolute disgust. With careful hands, he gave the neck collar a pull. It was solid and with no indication of how to release it.

"Medic Grover, get yourself here and bring your med-box. Garcia and Whitlock, you're the next volunteers."

Grover left the doorway, lugging the medical box with him. His revulsion was clear and he struggled to reach McKinney without touching any of the Vraxar.

"I thought you'd be used to this kind of thing."

"No, sir. There were no rooms filled with living corpses in the training I went through. What do you want me to do?"

"Plug that med-box into this Vraxar and put it to sleep."

"It's an ugly bastard."

"It probably thinks the same of you. Now get on with it."

Grover started to say something and thought better of it. McKinney knew what the objections were likely to be and he didn't want to hear them spelled out. If the med-box computer couldn't figure out how to put the Vraxar into a coma, he'd need to think of another plan.

With the med-box on the floor, Grover pulled out a wire with a fat needle attached to the end. Garcia and Whitlock watched intently, trying to pretend they weren't surrounded by so many Vraxar. Grover didn't spend any time looking for a good spot – he simply jabbed the needle towards the alien's chest, aiming for the gap between its narrow ribs. The four-inch needle punctured its skin with a faint popping sound and Grover pushed until it was fully inside.

"It'll be easier if I got its heart on the first go."

The squad medic checked the display on the med-box.

"The needle-probe went into something similar to heart tissue, but there's no sign of a beat."

"It's dead?"

"Wait up, there it goes. There's a beat so slow it may as well be dead."

"Can you put it to sleep?"

"I'm going to try a couple of things."

The words hadn't fully left Grover's mouth when the green light in the room darkened, fading rapidly until the entire room was hardly lit.

McKinney whirled around, expecting the worse. His visor sensor adjusted, showing the room to be exactly as it was before. The lights strengthened again, brightening and then immediately cycling back to near-darkness. There was a booming from elsewhere in the Neutraliser – it was a hollow, echoing sound which might have emanated from above or below.

Grover was on one knee, tweaking the settings on his med-box. He paused to look upwards at McKinney and his voice was utterly calm. "I don't care how many times the sensor scans tell Captain Blake this spaceship is safe, we have the proof right here it isn't."

It was time for McKinney to confront the same truth. "I agree. And it's waking up."

"Yes, Lieutenant. I think it is."

"We're not leaving without this one."

"It doesn't want to fall asleep. It's either resistant or immune to the drugs the med-box is pumping into it. I think its circulatory system is so slow everything is taking time to work."

"Keep on it."

"How are you going to get it off this post?"

"I'm going to shoot through its restraints."

"That's more likely to..."

"Yes, I know."

If the squad had been jumpy before, the booming noise and the changes to the lighting in the room had left them close to breaking point. McKinney warned them again to hold steady and hoped his words would be sufficient.

"I think that's done it," said Grover.

The Vraxar's eyes changed from open and alert, to closed, over the course of two or three seconds. It was enough for McKinney.

"Stand back," he said.

He aimed his gauss rifle at the band around the alien's neck, doing his best to ensure any unwanted ricochets would fire off deeper into the room.

"Come on," said Roldan over the comms. "Do it."

McKinney fired from point-blank range. The gauss slug pinged off into the distance, leaving the collar damaged. He fired again and this time the alloy collar split close to where it joined the pillar. McKinney dropped his rifle, pushed his fingers between the collar and the Vraxar's thin neck, and pulled.

The metal was strong, but so was McKinney. The muscles on his arms bunched and he twisted the metal of the collar until it was bent right back. The Vraxar sagged forward and only the post embedded in its back prevented it from sliding to the floor.

McKinney picked up his rifle and took the two paces which brought him to the far side of the support post. The wristbands were adjustable and they'd been drawn tight against the alien's flesh. It was going to be messy.

A couple of shots got the first arm free. The second cuff wasn't so forthcoming and it required four shots from the gauss rifle to fracture the metal. One of the shots ricocheted into the Vraxar's flesh, taking off three of its fingers. A green fluid dripped slowly onto the floor – whether it was blood or something from the conversion process, McKinney didn't want to guess. He tore its arms free from the restraints, at which point it fell off the post and landed face-down on the floor with a crack.

"Why didn't you catch it?" McKinney demanded.

"Sorry, Lieutenant," said Whitlock.

"We want it alive."

"It'll have a sore head when it comes around," said Garcia.

"Shut up, you idiot! Pick it up and get it into the conversion room."

Neither of the two soldiers wanted to touch the Vraxar. Their fear of McKinney's likely response was greater and they put their arms beneath its shoulders and dragged it towards the rest of the squad. Grover hurried after them, keen that the needle from his med-box remain in the alien's heart.

McKinney came out last, sparing one final glance around this room. He wondered if he should ask Clifton to leave a few explosive charges behind. He dismissed the idea – the room was far too large for anything the squad's boom man was carrying. He sincerely hoped Captain Blake would destroy the Neutraliser from orbit when he heard what it was carrying.

He was just entering the conversion room when he heard a crackling on the comms channel. It wasn't coming from his own squad. The sound came again and he made out a voice so faint the words were unrecognizable.

"Repeat!" he shouted into the channel.

The words were repeated, stronger this time, though still not clear enough to understand.

"That's Corporal Evans!" said Garcia.

"We shouldn't be able to hear him from here," said McCoy.

"No, we shouldn't," said McKinney.

"Well, what's he..."

"Shhh!" said McKinney, straining to hear. If Corporal Evans was audible on the comms, that meant he was close by. And if he was close by, he'd come looking for McKinney and his squad. Whatever the reason for Corporal Evans' actions, it didn't seem likely to be good news.

The distraction caused McKinney to slow in his stride and he berated himself for it. "Come on," he urged. "We're heading to the shuttle."

At that moment, Corporal Evans burst through the opposite entrance into the conversion room, at the head of his squad. They slid to a halt and McKinney could imagine exactly what they were thinking.

"Lieutenant?" stammered Evans, his breathing heavy from running.

"Try to pretend you haven't seen this room. We're leaving."

"You know about the ship?"

"What?"

"Captain Blake sent us. This whole Neutraliser is going to blow and we don't want to be near when it happens."

"Damnit, how long?"

"I'm not sure, sir. The *Abyss* is working on an estimation. It could be anything between one hour and three. Maybe more, maybe less."

"Don't you just love the precision of science?" said Vega.

"You got exactly five fingers on your new hand, didn't you?" asked Garcia. "How much more precise do you want it?"

"Shut the hell up! This whole ship is going to explode and you *still* can't stop pissing about," snarled McKinney. "Just for that, you get to carry this Vraxar all the way out."

"Just me?"

"No, but you've got the left arm for the whole way, while the rest of us get to swap out. I'd suggest you get boosting."

"His suit probably ran dry before we left the *Abyss*."

"Is that you volunteering as well, McCoy?"

"No, sir."

"You still get first shift, along with Roldan and Munoz. Right, you four - pick up our alien friend and don't drop him. We've got a long distance to run and not a lot of time to do it in."

It was clear when McKinney wasn't in the mood for wisecracks and the four men stooped to pick up the unconscious Vraxar. Grover remained close, anxiously watching his med-box for signs of the alien coming out of its induced coma.

They headed across the conversion room, starting slowly in case they fell on the blood-slick floor. Corporal Evans and his men were still in a state of shock, the feeling compounded for those curious enough to look into the room filled with Vraxar.

It was Elias Mack who saw the impending problem. He walked cautiously through the conversion room, until he was facing directly into the *storage* room.

"Lieutenant? There's something moving in there."

Within the anonymity of his reflective visor, McKinney closed his eyes. "You're shitting me? What sort of movement?"

"I'm definitely not shitting you, Lieutenant. There's movement from about a hundred sources."

The sound of Mack's plasma repeater brought the seriousness of it home and tracers of white-hot plasma slugs streaked away. A large shape thumped to the floor near the doorway.

"We need to get out of here," said Mack in the no-nonsense tones of a man with twenty years of frontline experience. His confidence was astounding given that he was only twenty-six years old. "We're going to be overrun in about one minute."

McKinney stared in horror as he saw what was coming.

CHAPTER NINE

"CLOSE THE DAMN DOOR!" McKinney shouted.

"How do I do that?" asked Mack, turning his head to the left and right to see if he could figure out what he needed to do.

"Just stick your hand on the panel!"

"There's a panel on the opposite side in the other room," said Grover. "As soon as it's closed, they'll be able to open it again."

Mack wasn't a man to hang about. While Grover was speaking, he found the panel and smacked his hand against it like he was giving a high-five to his Friday night drinking partner. The door dropped like a stone, fast enough to crush anything caught underneath.

"What now, sir?"

McKinney had a flash of inspiration. More or less every Space Corps door was controlled by a pair of access panels – one on each side of the door. There was always one panel which had priority over the other and it was usually the panel that allowed people out of a room, presumably so no jokers could keep people trapped in a meeting room by leaving their hand planted on the access panel.

"Leave your hand on it!" he yelled. "The rest of you, cover that door!"

"Yes, sir."

Mack thumped his palm to the access panel again and held it there.

"Keep your fingers crossed that's the primary panel."

"I'm not sure I want to cross them while my hand is pressed here, sir."

"What do we do now?" asked Evans.

"You aren't planning to leave me here are you?" asked Mack.

"No," said McKinney. "We need to seal that door and we need to do it quickly. Clifton, do you have anything that can burn it shut?"

"You only have to ask and its done, sir."

"I'm asking. Do it."

Clifton made his way quickly over the bloody floor, using one hand to steady himself on the biers. He had a pack filled with charges and further explosives attached to a specially-designed belt slung across his chest. While the other soldiers carried grenades, Clifton had a different explosive for every day of the week. He reached the door and knelt, rummaging through his pack with one hand whilst the other pulled at the charges on his bandolier.

"You're doing a fine job, Mack," he said.

"Standing with my hand on a panel is exactly they trained me for."

A couple of men from Evans' squad were near to the window and they did their best to wipe clean an area through which they could see. Ronnie Horton produced a cloth from somewhere and cleared a gleaming arc through the dirt. There was movement on the other side – lots of movement. An object thumped against the window and Horton flinched.

"This is really not good," he stammered.

"Horton, Guzman, get back here," said McKinney.

Meanwhile, Clifton fixed his plasma charges around the edge of the door. He could be fastidious when it suited him, but not today – he stuck a dozen tiny limpet charges in apparently random places. Each time he activated one, a bright blue light illuminated on the explosive.

"Done," he said, retreating a few metres from the door.

"What about me?" asked Mack.

"It was nice knowing you, kid. When these charges go off, you'll die. We'll raise a glass in your memory."

"You bastards!"

"Clifton, pack it in!" roared McKinney. The last thing he wanted was for Mack to lose his bottle and run away from the access panel.

"Sorry, Lieutenant – I thought he might appreciate the joke."

McKinney clenched his hands tightly, wondering what it would feel like to wring Clifton's neck. He was saved from the temptation when the charges went off. They didn't explode as such; rather, they detonated with a low, angry fizzing sound, accompanied by a bright blue flaring light. The light remained for fifteen or twenty long seconds before it burned out. The soldiers fidgeted while they waited, anxious to be going, yet unwilling to leave anyone behind. The Vraxar continued pounding on the window and everyone was glad to see it had been built to withstand this level of physical punishment.

"Done?" asked McKinney.

Clifton hurried to check over the results of his handiwork. There were numerous patches on the door where the alloy had melted and dripped, joining the door with the frame.

"Might be enough," he said.

"Can I take my hand off this panel?"

"The metal needs to cool and harden."

"How long will that take?"

It was obvious Clifton wanted to continue his one-sided joke with Mack, but he didn't want a kick in the balls from McKinney and kept his answer straight.

"Not long. It's hardening already."

"Whatever they use to lift that door it has a lot of grunt," said McKinney.

"If it's strong enough to rip the door open, we'll die," Clifton replied with a shrug. "There's no way I can kill everything in that room with the stuff I'm carrying." He stooped and thrust one of his fingers at the reformed metal. "Done."

"Does that mean I can...?"

"Yup."

Mack pulled his hand off the access panel and aimed a mock-cuff at Clifton's head. Then, the two of them began jogging across the room.

There were occasions when it was best to speak the obvious, for the absolute avoidance of doubt. "We are going to get out of here as quickly as possible," said McKinney, urging the men towards the conversion room doorway. "We have no idea how many exits there are from that other room and it makes sense for there to be more than one. If anything moves, shoot it."

"I would highly recommend everyone utilises their spacesuit emergency boosters," said Grover.

The response to the medic's suggestion was muted – a few of the soldiers gave an acknowledgement, whilst the rest said nothing. McKinney suspected most of them had already taken the maximum dose of battlefield adrenaline which the suits would permit them to inject.

Once the squads were on the move and he was assured the sealed door wasn't about to open, McKinney pushed his way to the front of the group in order to lead. He'd always considered himself to have a fully-functioning sense of direction, but there was a brief moment when his brain did a mental fumble and he couldn't recall the way they'd come. Then, everything clicked into place and he was able to visualise the return route to the entry point.

He led them away at a jog, looking for the set of steps downwards. It was by necessity a rapid pace and he was relieved that the four men carrying the Vraxar were able to keep up. The group reached the steps – from the top they appeared much steeper than they had on the way up and much more dangerous.

I'm in the middle of a Neutraliser filled with hostile aliens and I'm getting worried about stairs, he chided himself.

"Be careful," he said.

Sometimes it was the mundane things which could be the most dangerous and as McKinney stepped downwards, he felt a weight hit him in the back. He stumbled, his left hand reaching out automatically for the railing which wasn't there. As McKinney recovered, a soldier fell past him. His visor informed him it was Woodrow Hughes and the man's fall was already out of control. McKinney whipped his hand out in a futile attempt to grab the soldier's arm. It was too late and even if he'd been successful, it was likely they'd have both fallen.

"No!"

Hughes frantically attempted to run with the momentum by trying to get his feet onto the treads. It looked as if he'd pull off an astounding recovery, but then he tripped and went into a headlong roll. The others could only watch in dumbfounded silence as Hughes clattered away into the distance.

Amy Sandoval, the medic who'd been with Corporal Evans, attempted to get past McKinney. He took hold of her upper arm in a crushing grip.

"Don't be stupid!" he shouted at her. "Let's not make it two, eh?"

"But..."

"Wait, damnit!"

Sandoval nodded her agreement and kept pace with McKinney when he set off again.

"Hughes, please report."

"There're no life signs from his suit, sir."

"I know. Hughes, please report."

There was no response from the soldier and, in spite of his warnings, McKinney found himself descending faster than was advisable. He held his gauss rifle in one hand and found it actually helped him with balance. With each new step, his anger grew. He had no idea why anyone – human or Vraxar – would think it a good idea to make steps so steep that it was necessary to turn sideways in order to traverse them.

The rest of the squad came with exaggerated care and they dropped rapidly behind. There was a continuous stream of expletives from those assigned to carry the Vraxar, particularly from Garcia. McKinney was in a foul mood and he set a mental note to have a quiet word with the man at a more appropriate moment.

Hughes had come to a halt more than halfway down. To McKinney's untrained eye, he looked in one piece. Sandoval wasn't so easily fooled.

"Dead," she said.

McKinney kept a respectful distance while Sandoval balanced across two steps near to the body and pulled the probe out from her med-box. From this close range, he could see the cracks across Hughes' visor. It took a significant force to make a scratch on the lenses, let alone shatter them.

The bottom wasn't too far away and McKinney kept a watchful eye for movement. There'd only been light for part of the journey here and he couldn't remember exactly when the darkness had ended. The steps were sufficiently illuminated that he didn't require his image intensifiers or his movement sensors. He listened, trying to detect anything which might indicate the

Vraxar were trying to head them off. The soldiers made some noise; other than that, there was nothing.

Sandoval removed the probe after less than five seconds. She pushed herself wearily to her feet – this was her first combat mission and she gave every indication that each death on her watch was going to leave a permanent imprint.

"Broken neck, skull and four smashed ribs. Somehow this feels worse than the shuttle crash. More personal," she said in answer to McKinney's unspoken question. "I hope it gets easier."

"Pray that it doesn't."

McKinney left her to mull over the words while he descended to the bottom. He looked out carefully into the passageway and was relieved to see it was clear. He was convinced there was more than one way from the Vraxar troop storage room to this area of the ship – it was absurd to think otherwise. Unfortunately, it was down to pure guesswork trying to estimate how long it would take the freed soldiers to catch up to the fleeing squad. There were other details about which he was more certain – the main passage from the entry point was four thousand metres long and it was approximately eight hundred metres until they reached that passage. It was a long, long way to run when they were burdened with the unconscious Vraxar. Even if they made it to the entry point, it wasn't an easy sprint to the shuttle and it would be near-impossible if there were thousands of alien soldiers at their heels.

It's going to be one hell of an escape if we can make it, he thought grimly.

The rest of the squad reached the end of the steps and McKinney once again took point, with Ricky Vega beside him and Dex Webb behind. The corridor was long and Webb's plasma tube would certainly come in handy against a packed group of Vraxar.

"They're going to find us long before we get away," said Vega.

"Yes."

"If they manage to get tooled up, we're screwed."

"Only if we stick around and let them take pot shots at us."

"Ever the optimist, Lieutenant."

"Someone has to be."

McKinney remembered this area of the Neutraliser – there were rooms joined by long corridors with many branches. The soldiers carrying the Vraxar had got into a routine and they were able to keep up with the increased pace, rotating in a new man or woman when someone became too tired to continue with the lifting. Even Garcia's grumbling died off and the open channel was mostly quiet.

"That door wasn't open when we came this way the first time," said Vega.

"I didn't see it," said McKinney, realising he was keeping his gaze locked in front and missing other important details.

"I didn't get a good look through, Lieutenant. I think it led to another passage like this one."

It was enough of a warning to McKinney and he made sure to look out for any changes since their initial march along here. His earlier words *waking up* spun around in his head, tormenting him with the endless unknowns such a thing entailed. The Neutraliser had crashed and suffered apparently terminal damage, yet there was enough of it working to preserve the lives of thousands of those onboard. Now here it was, returning to a partially operational state, with McKinney and his squad stuck deep inside. Worst of all was his suspicion that his actions or those of his men had somehow begun the process of the warship's awakening.

"Did Captain Blake express any doubt about this Neutraliser going critical?"

"No, sir, he did not. I spoke to Lieutenant Pointer and she

told me we needed to get the hell off this ship as quickly as possible, else it was going to blow."

McKinney wanted to keep on at Evans, to ask if he'd overlooked a detail or a word which might give a clue as to exactly what the crew on the *Abyss* thought was going to happen. There was no need – Evans was repeating what he'd been told and nothing more.

A few seconds later, two events happened in very close proximity, neither of which was in any way welcome.

The first event was the appearance of a large Vraxar of a type McKinney hadn't seen before. It walked calmly into sight where the corridor entered an open space up ahead. With a dreamlike feeling of being in slow-motion, McKinney treated it to a short burst from his plasma repeater. Even a slight tap on the weapon's activation switch was enough to send a few dozen white-hot metal slugs spewing from the barrel. The bullets punched into the alien, ripping off one arm and half of its shoulder, as well as shattering its skull in many places.

It fell without a sound, and in ten long strides McKinney was there. He hurdled its body and looked for more of the enemy. This room was a few metres across and with two additional exits leading away. It was empty, leaving McKinney mystified as to how the alien had got here ahead of them.

"Clear!"

The worrying conclusion from this briefest of engagements was that the Neutraliser's life support was beginning to revive pockets of Vraxar in several different locations in the spaceship and this specimen had simply wandered into his line of fire.

The second event was considerably more worrying than the first. The rest of the squad were halfway across the room with the dead Vraxar, when they both heard and felt a sound. It began as a groaning shriek of tortured metal which came through the walls, the ceiling and the floor. The sound was replaced by a metallic creaking, as if the hull of the spaceship was being subjected to immense pressure or stress. It faded, leaving a rough, lumpy vibration behind.

McKinney held his breath to see if silence would return. It did not and the vibration continued.

Several of the soldiers asked the exact same question at the exact same moment. "What's the hell is going on?"

"That's their engines," McKinney said. "They've started up their gravity engines."

This new development threw everything out of the window. There was no chance of survival if the Neutraliser managed to take off with them still onboard. That wasn't the worst part – there was absolutely no way the crew on the ES *Abyss* would permit the Neutraliser to escape from Vanistar and there was only one way they could prevent it happening.

CHAPTER TEN

THERE WAS intense consternation and anger on the bridge of the ES *Abyss*.

"Can someone tell me *exactly* what is happening?" demanded Captain Charlie Blake.

"They've got their engines online, sir," said Quinn. "I have no idea how they managed it."

"I thought they were all meant to be *dead*? How did they manage that when they were dead?"

"It could be they have a few active processing cores and their computers managed to tap into a source of power."

"Do they have weapons? Can they get power into those massive particle beams they have running along the top of their central section?"

"Those remain powered down," said Lieutenant Hawkins. "I'd guess their weapons control systems are still offline."

Blake stalked the length of the bridge. "Our guesswork hasn't proved too reliable up until now, has it?" He expected no answer and Hawkins didn't provide one. Blake continued. "What about that nullification sphere? Is it going to explode or did we get that one wrong as well?"

"It's becoming progressively more unstable," said Quinn. "The simulator is predicting sixty minutes from now as being the most likely time for its self-destruction."

"Is that a definite?"

"It'll definitely explode."

"What if they manage to contain it? What if they contain it, get power into their weapons and start taking pot shots at us?"

"You don't need us to tell you the answer to that one, sir," said Hawkins.

"We'd be forced to launch our weapons at them. With our soldiers still onboard."

"That's the logical conclusion."

"I know it's the logical damned conclusion!" Blake took several deep breaths and calmed himself. "We need to think of something and we need to do it fast."

"We've got everyone onboard apart from Lieutenant McKinney and Corporal Evans' squads," said Lieutenant Pointer. "They've been gone a long time, so they've got to be due back."

Pointer was trying to be helpful, though had managed to be anything but. They had no idea where the remaining soldiers were and no way to predict their return.

"I hope Lieutenant McKinney has managed to find something more useful than this other…" He struggled to articulate the word he was looking for.

"Crap?"

"Yes, this other crap the rest of the soldiers brought back with them. They need to pull something good out of the hat, else this will have been a high risk, ultra-low reward mission."

"There's another thing, sir," said Cruz tentatively.

"What is it?"

"At this altitude, it's a long shuttle ride to get from the surface to the *Abyss*. If Lieutenant McKinney escapes, his shuttle will be in the air for fifteen or twenty minutes. That's plenty of time." She didn't want to say the words.

Blake nodded. "Yes, I know. They'll be an easy target if the Neutraliser gets even a single particle beam working. And a long shuttle flight puts both our troops and the *Abyss* at risk if the enemy spaceship explodes."

"You could speak to Fleet Admiral Duggan, sir?" said Hawkins. "He has a lot of experience when it comes to combat situations."

It was tempting and Blake heard the insidious cajoling of an inner voice, telling him how comforting it would be to simply hand over the decision making for this difficult situation to another.

"No!" he said, with more force than intended. "We can't look for guidance every time there's a difficult choice ahead. Imagine the burden we'd be shifting on to the Fleet Admiral if he decided the only course of action was for us to destroy the Neutraliser immediately. I joined the Space Corps to make my own destiny, not to have someone else pick it for me!" He seethed with a fury that was directed at whatever capricious twists of fate had placed him in this position.

"What are we going to do?" asked Quinn.

"We're going towards Vanistar again. Closer this time – much closer. In fact, we're going to sit right on top of that Neutraliser."

Lieutenant Hawkins lifted a finger as if in admonishment. Suddenly, the furrows in her forehead smoothed out and she lowered her hand.

"Let's do it," she said.

The ES *Abyss*'s engines had an infinitely greater output than that of the last shuttle remaining on Vanistar's surface. Under maximum thrust and with guidance from the autopilot, its gravity drive only needed fifty seconds to bring the heavy cruiser to a position where it was less than two thousand metres above the Neutraliser. Blake gave the instruction for the energy shield to be kept active – not that Lieutenant Quinn needed telling – and also for two of the spaceship's main processing cores to be kept ready for a lightspeed transit.

"They've been churning through the computations for a while, sir," said Quinn. "Core #7 is hotter than I'd like."

"Can't you switch to another core to give that one a time to cool down?"

"The manual recommends holding the core until burnout. If you don't, there's an increased chance the next core will experience a premature failure."

"Really?"

"Really."

"Fine, I'm sure someone's done the research. Don't make any changes."

"Yes, sir."

With the *ES Abyss* dangerously close to the damaged Neutraliser, Blake prepared himself for an unpleasant wait. He felt a bond with Lieutenant McKinney and wanted to give him every opportunity to escape from the enemy vessel. On the other hand, Blake was fully aware he'd be derelict in his duty if he permitted his spaceship to be destroyed in the process. Trying to second guess the possibilities was going to be like a tightrope walk in a strong, blustery crosswind. Only a fool would attempt it, but the feeling of accomplishment at the end might just be worthwhile.

Blake smiled to himself. *Who am I trying to kid? A brave man would destroy the Neutraliser and live with the consequences.* He ignored the thought and stuck to his chosen course.

MCKINNEY and his squad reached the top of the long stairway without encountering more of the Vraxar. He'd been dreading this moment, with the unfortunate death of Hughes being so recent. The steps went steeply downwards, their end visible five hundred metres away. It was going to be a long, difficult descent.

"Listen up!" he shouted. "We've lost one of our number already. If any of you *dares* to fall down these stairs, I promise you I will do whatever it takes to bring you back to life so that you are able to feel my fist breaking your nose. Is there anyone who doesn't understand?"

"What about this Vraxar, sir?" asked Mack. "What if he falls?"

McKinney fought down a smile at the cheekiness of the question. "That *alien bastard* is the most important member of our team. If you drop him, you had better damn well make sure you throw yourselves after him. Do I make myself clear?"

"Yes, sir!"

"Keep your weapons ready – I've got a feeling things are going to heat up before we get out of this place."

With a glance over his shoulder to check everything was clear behind, McKinney began his descent. The steps were absolutely not designed for humans and he felt the muscles in his legs burn beneath the thick, comforting veneer of battlefield adrenaline. In his wake, the soldiers followed in the peculiar sideways gait they'd adopted to try and make the steps easier. The four carrying the Vraxar didn't have the luxury of being able to adjust their stride and they struggled to achieve a good pace. One of the men stumbled and nearly fell. McKinney took pity.

"Garcia, it's your lucky day. You're relieved until I tell you otherwise."

With that, McKinney took Garcia's place and carried his share of the unconscious Vraxar. It felt comparatively light at first. He wasn't deceived and knew it would feel like a dead weight before he was halfway to the bottom.

They didn't quite reach the end without incident. With one hundred metres to go, McKinney heard something crack off the ceiling overhead. Roldan and McCoy had the rear and they opened up with their repeaters. In the confines of the stairwell, the sound was tremendous.

"Report!"

"Movement, sir. Three, maybe four."

The two men fired again.

"More than four," said Roldan. "Lots."

McKinney heard further shots from the Vraxar and their projectiles pinged away from the walls a few metres behind. Shooting down or upslope wasn't quite so straightforward as firing flat and it seemed as if the Vraxar hadn't been taught how to adjust their aim.

"Caldwell, take over my position," said McKinney.

Bradley Caldwell was nearby and the two men swapped places smoothly. McKinney dropped to one knee and brought his gauss rifle to his shoulder. The repeaters were awe-inspiring weapons, but they lost their accuracy over longer distances and in truth, he felt the greatest affinity to the Space Corps rifle.

With one eye looking along the barrel, he felt his breathing deepen. A Vraxar head appeared at the top of the steps and he put a bullet through it. Then came another and another. With utter calm, McKinney shot them dead. Roldan and McCoy kept firing their repeaters, and their projectiles created overlapping cones of blazing white light. They were likely hitting the enemy, just not with anything like the same finesse.

"We should fall back, sir," said Roldan. "We're easy targets here."

"Agreed. Take it slowly, and don't take your eyes off those Vraxar up there."

McKinney took his first step back and then another. The movement of his feet took him out of his firing trance and though he kept shooting, he lost the certainty of knowing whether he was scoring one-shot kills.

"It's not like the Vraxar to have an interest in their own survival," said Roldan. "Why are they hanging back?"

McKinney didn't know. He'd been involved in engagements where the Vraxar threw themselves into the firing line without apparent care and then there were other times when they'd fought with tactics. *Like humans,* he thought. *If they have no motivation, they'll take no risks until an officer forces them.*

He didn't want to turn in order to see how close the rest of the squad were to the end of the stairs. "How are you getting on with our prisoner?" he asked.

"A few more steps," grunted Caldwell.

"We'll need to hightail it along this corridor," said Roldan. "Four klicks is a lot of running when we're carrying a body."

The fact wasn't lost on McKinney. It wasn't simply their reduced pace he was concerned about – the corridor was utterly straight, which would make the retreating soldiers an easy target once the Vraxar reached the bottom of the stairs. They'd be able to shoot freely from the cover of the stairwell.

"There's no way we'll make it," McKinney said. "We'll be killed before we get halfway along." He made a snap decision. "Garcia, Roldan, Webb, you're staying with me. We'll hold the stairwell to give the others time to escape."

It likely wasn't what these three wanted to hear, but they gave no argument. Step by step, McKinney, Roldan and McCoy backed down the steps. The Vraxar above didn't go away, nor did they make a concerted effort to kill the escaping soldiers. Whenever one of the aliens became too bold, McKinney hit it with a gauss slug. He was fully aware it was only a matter of time until the enemy rallied and made a concerted effort to flush the soldiers from the stairwell.

The three of them reached the bottom without injury and hid to one side of the opening. Webb and Garcia were waiting at the bottom, whilst the other fifteen had covered a respectable distance along the corridor towards the entry point. There were few motivations as effective as the threat of death to put speed into tired legs.

"McCoy, you go with them," said McKinney. "We'll hold the stairwell. Keep on your guard. With any luck the comms will remain active since we'll have a line of sight."

McCoy didn't ask to stay and sprinted after the others. The first transit of this corridor had been in the dark, now the lights were on and McKinney wasn't sure if he was happy about the change.

He filled Garcia, Roldan and Webb in with the details of his plan.

"We kill any of the bastards that try to come down the stairs."

"That's it?"

"What were you expecting? Webb, we'll be relying on your plasma tube to clear them out if they come down in force."

"Say the word, sir."

"Don't wait for the word – fire it when you need to."

The Vraxar had already become emboldened at the sight of the empty stairwell. A group of them advanced with speed, their long legs much more adapted to the height of the risers. McKinney stuck his head around the corner and shot a couple.

"Roldan, you're coming with me across to the far side." He pointed to the blank wall where the corridor ended. It continued for a metre past the stairwell, giving them somewhere to take cover.

Webb knew his stuff. "Get back," he said.

Without waiting for an acknowledgement, he stepped out

with the plasma tube warming up. The rocket sped away and exploded against the uppermost stairs. Without adequate room for the plasma blast to expand, it roared through the stairwell, casting bright light on the walls.

McKinney didn't hesitate. "Go!" he urged, pushing himself away from cover.

Roldan followed a split second later and the two of them made it to the opposite side of the stairwell without being hurt. A glance upwards told McKinney that anything on the stairs when the rocket came had been completely incinerated.

The two men arranged themselves awkwardly. Roldan remained in a crouch and McKinney leaned over him. Across from them, Garcia kept low and Webb leaned casually on the upright tube of his plasma launcher, like he was propping the bar up at his favourite watering hole.

"Incoming," said McKinney.

More Vraxar appeared to replace those killed in the explosion. With assistance from the zoom on his visor sensor, McKinney saw these ones were more Estral. What was presumably once a noble, if bloodthirsty, race, was now reduced to acting as suicide troops for the Vraxar.

The sadness of it wasn't lost on McKinney, though it didn't distract him from the task. The Vraxar came and he did his best to shoot as many of them as possible. They carried their usual stubby hand cannons, which they weren't able to fire accurately from the stairs. Consequently, a great number of the aliens died without offering a meaningful response. After three or four minutes, their bodies crowded the stairs and fouled the legs of the others.

"If they get their hands on any explosives, we're screwed," said Garcia.

It was an obvious fact, but Garcia was the first person willing to say it out loud.

"Just keep shooting," said McKinney. "We'll worry about explosives when they come."

The Vraxar adapted. Where they'd started out with a full-frontal assault on the stairs, now they stayed in cover at the top and attempted to pick off the soldiers. Their aim was little better than earlier and most of their slugs struck the ceiling fifty metres from the bottom. Nevertheless, McKinney found it harder to score kills with the Vraxar darting in and out of cover.

In a way, it was a good thing, since McKinney was looking to buy time for the others to escape. He was aware that the chances of his own escape were considerably diminished by staying here, though he hadn't entirely given up on life. He didn't dwell on it and focused his mind and aim. With a series of perfectly-directed shots, he killed a couple of Vraxar and drove others back into cover.

The standoff continued for a few minutes. The retreating soldiers were less than two thousand metres from the entry point and McKinney dared to think they might escape. Webb was getting bored with his lack of involvement and he fired two further rockets up the stairs. There was no way to be sure if it was an effective use of the rocket tube or not, though McKinney didn't ask him to hold fire.

It was inevitable the Vraxar would eventually bring their own explosives to the engagement. McKinney was in the process of leaning out to take a shot when he caught a glimpse of something coming in fast. He threw himself away from the edge, pulling Roldan with him.

"Incoming!" he shouted.

Garcia and Webb also tried to shield themselves. There was no way any of them could act quickly enough to avoid a rocket and McKinney expected to die in the coming blast. Luckily, the Vraxar with the rocket launcher was no better an aim than those with the guns. The weapon struck the ceiling and its dirty flames roiled downwards, spilling around the corners and engulfing the four soldiers. At this distance from the blast, the force of the explosion was lessened significantly and although it was sufficient to damage the protective surface polymers on the spacesuits, the men survived.

McKinney lifted his head, ignoring the warnings on his visor HUD. His spacesuit was blackened and it smoked in places, but it was holding together. One thing he couldn't be sure of was whether or not it would survive another close-range explosion. The odds weren't good.

"Webb, give us some cover!"

"On its way."

The rocket from Webb's launcher flew off in response. McKinney didn't spend time gawping and ran across the opening, Roldan two steps behind.

"Move!" he shouted, dragging Garcia roughly to his feet.

Garcia got the message and broke into a sprint with the others. Webb took one final look into the stairwell and then followed. The floor was solid and their footsteps thudded hard off the surface. McKinney experienced a feeling of exhilaration as the air filled his lungs and his body responded to his command that it run ever faster.

"We ain't gonna make it," panted Roldan.

"Yes, we are," said Garcia, his legs pumping and his rifle clunking off his repeater with each stride.

McKinney tried to guess at their chances. If the Vraxar came down the stairs at their fastest speed, they would be at the bottom long before the four soldiers reached safety. Even if they approached tentatively, they would still reach the bottom long before the soldiers reached safety. At that stage, it would be easy enough for them to shoot the fleeing men in the back.

"Corporal Evans, please report."

"We're making good progress, sir."

"We're retreating. At speed."

"Yes, sir – I can hear that."

"How long until you reach the entry point?"

"Four minutes. The comedown off this adrenaline is going to be a killer."

"You're not going to make it, Corporal."

"We can't move any faster than we are."

How much longer until they reach the bottom of those steps? McKinney asked himself. *Two minutes, three tops.*

He swore. "We'll cover you, Corporal."

"Yes, sir."

Without slowing his pace, McKinney spoke to the men with him. He panted the words out, though the high dose of battlefield adrenaline he'd taken provided near-unlimited stamina. "I'm going to count down three minutes. When the time runs out, we'll stop where we are and hold position."

"There's no cover, sir," said Roldan.

"The rest of the men haven't made it yet."

"Have they stopped to take a crap or something? They should've been on the shuttle by now."

"We can ask them about it later. One hundred and seventy seconds and then we stop."

"The recruitment officer never told me about this when I signed on the line," said Garcia.

"Let me guess? He told you women love a man in uniform?"

"How did you know?"

With the adrenaline burning like an unquenchable fire in his veins, McKinney still had the energy to laugh. The sound hadn't faded from his lips when Evans' words about the aftereffects came back to him. When the drugs wore off, they'd feel like crap and it would take a week of bedrest to recover. If he was still alive, he swore he'd welcome the pain.

CHAPTER ELEVEN

THE COUNTER TICKING down in one corner of McKinney's HUD reached zero. The three minutes felt like an eternity during which the end of the corridor came no closer, as though they were running on a conveyor belt designed to match their exact speed and ensure they made no progress towards their goal.

"Time's up," said McKinney.

He stopped running and wheeled around, raising his gauss rifle as he did so. It wasn't a moment too soon – his movement sensors highlighted a shape emerging from the bottom of the stairs. McKinney took aim and fired. There was a slight tremble in his muscles and the first volley of three bullets missed. Garcia helped him out and the Vraxar was thrown to the floor.

With nothing to hide behind, the four men stayed prone near to the walls in the hope it would make them less visible. Another Vraxar appeared. This time McKinney's aim was better and he put two slugs into its chest and another through its skull. He struggled to bring his breathing under control and waited for the onslaught.

The anticipated flood didn't happen at once and for a few seconds, no more Vraxar emerged into sight.

"Maybe they've gone a different way," said Webb.

"Yeah, right."

Then, they came. At first, a head appeared around the edge of the stairwell. The soldiers fired a fusillade of bullets towards it. Somehow, the Vraxar survived and it retreated into cover. McKinney's movement sensors illuminated other shapes, clustering near to the bottom of the steps. He fired and thought he'd caught one of the aliens in the arm or shoulder.

Three Vraxar jumped across the corridor and laid themselves flat on the floor. They fired at the soldiers and McKinney sensed a projectile passing through the air an inch from his face. He swore and returned fire. Garcia and Roldan rose to a crouch and used their repeaters in alternating bursts to kill any Vraxar who showed themselves.

More gathered on the stairwell. Webb launched a rocket towards them with perfect aim. The explosion scattered the burning bodies of the Vraxar, hurling their charred bodies violently against the walls.

"We're at the entry point now, sir," said Evans.

"Get on the shuttle!"

"What about you?"

"There's nothing you can do. We'll have to get ourselves out of this."

"Sir, I..."

"Go!"

The four men were in an exceptionally bad position. The entry point was a long way distant and there was no way they'd reach it without being killed. There was an effectively unlimited number of enemy soldiers coming for them and this was only the vanguard. Once the Vraxar got their act together, they would crush this tiny resistance. It was a miracle they'd not been more organised and McKinney assumed it was because their officers were dead or elsewhere on the ship. A slug hit the wall near his head and whined past his ear. Webb fired again and the Vraxar were once more reduced to ash by a detonating plasma rocket.

"I hope they hang the medal on my grave," said Roldan. "My repeater ammo's down to 30%."

"Mine's below 10%," said Garcia.

We're really going to die, thought McKinney. *Just when I was beginning to think I was immune to it.*

He smiled bitterly at this evaluation. McKinney wasn't a man who worried about death and now he was confronted by the inevitability, he discovered he really didn't want to give himself up to it. He expected to feel anger; instead there was calmness and a lack of fear.

Webb fired again and again. As soon as the tube recharged he fired, driving the Vraxar deeper into the stairwell. Since there was nothing to hide behind, it was only the plasma launcher keeping the men alive and the weapon held a limited number of projectiles. Once it ran out, it was game over.

Something caught McKinney's eye – there was a groove in the opposite wall, near to where Garcia crouched with his almost-depleted repeater. Above this groove was another and another, leading up to the ceiling.

He dashed across and sprang at the wall, putting his hand into the highest alcove he could reach. With an enormous effort, he hauled himself up with only his arms, while his toes scrabbled to find purchase. There was a hidden lever to one side of the ladder, exactly where he expected to find it. He jammed his fingers in and pulled. A hatch opened above his head and he climbed into the opening.

"What are you doing?" asked Garcia.

McKinney braced himself and leaned over the corridor below, with his arm outstretched. "Garcia, you're next. Quickly!"

The men were well-enough trained to figure out when was the best time to move under fire. Webb launched one of his rockets and Garcia acted. With desperate strength, he climbed the wall. Near the top, he reached out for McKinney's hand. His other hand slipped and he began to fall. McKinney's hand met Garcia's and gripped it tightly. With a snarl of effort, he pulled, feeling his bicep and shoulder scream with the effort of lifting a fully-kitted soldier. Garcia didn't hang passively in the air and he slapped his free hand over the lip. His legs kicked in space for a moment and then he was in.

"Roldan, your turn."

The soldier released an extended spray of burning hot slugs from his repeater. McKinney heard it click when its ammo well ran dry.

"Now!"

Webb fired another rocket. "I've only got one more left."

Roldan practically ran up the wall, betraying the climbing skills of a man either born in the mountains or one who was skilled at breaking and entering. He reached the top in moments and it was easy for McKinney and Garcia to drag him inside.

"Up you come," said Garcia encouragingly.

The final rocket whistled from the end of Webb's launcher. He threw it to the ground like it meant nothing to him and began hauling himself up the wall. Unlike Roldan, Webb was a poor climber and he fought his way up one rung at a time.

"Stop pissing around," said Roldan.

"I can't deal with heights."

McKinney gritted his teeth in frustration. Of all times to worry over a few metres of ladder, this wasn't the best one. "Come on," he growled.

Webb lacked the coordination to climb and look upwards simultaneously, so he kept his gaze pointed straight at the corridor wall. Consequently, when he reached up for the first time, he wasn't close enough for the others to grab him.

"One more rung!" said Garcia. "How the hell did you get through basic training?"

Webb twisted his head to one side. "They're coming again."

"Don't look, climb!"

With a laborious heave, Webb got himself onto the next rung and swung one arm up in a wide, aimless arc. It was his lucky day and McKinney's adrenaline-enhanced reactions allowed him to grab the soldier's wrist.

"Up you come," he said.

With a monumental effort, McKinney crooked his arm and then forced his powerful leg muscles to push him into a standing position, bringing Webb up with him.

"Thanks, Lieutenant," said Webb.

"Thanks for the good shooting," said Garcia in an unusual show of gratitude.

"No worries, man."

It was dark in the room, and with barely enough room for the four of them. McKinney couldn't recall if this was the same ladder he'd climbed last time and didn't care one way or another. What he did care about was the passage leading through the interior of the Neutraliser towards the central conduit. He squeezed between the three men and began walking. There was a moment of time during which realisation sunk into the consciousness of the soldiers.

"Are we going to that place you nearly died?"

"Yes."

"But you nearly died, Lieutenant."

"The suit brought me round." McKinney switched on his visor torch and turned to face the men. They milled uncertainly in the space over the still-open hatch. "The way I see it, if we stay down there, we'll *definitely* die. If we go this way, the suits might be able to keep us going."

"Shit, man, this is no good," said Roldan.

"I'm not leaving any of you behind and if that means we wait here to die, that's what it means. However, the way I see it is you've got to follow or you'll be responsible for killing your superior officer. They don't give out medals for that."

"He's clever," said Roldan grudgingly.

"That's why he's lieutenant and we're still R1Ts," said Garcia.

McKinney resumed his walk and grinned when he heard the others hurrying after him. The smile faded quickly – in reality he hated the thought of what was coming. He'd always been strong and fit, so the thought of his body failing scared him. He distracted himself by talking.

"I reckon we're eight hundred metres from the entry point room," he said. "Once we get into the conduit, there's a walkway – we're going to run along it as quickly as we can. When we're two hundred metres away from our goal, we'll start looking for another one of these passages. We'll drop back into the main corridor and hope we manage to surprise the Vraxar enough that we can escape."

"Do you think we're far enough ahead of them?" asked Roldan. "What if they're running along that corridor already?"

"Stop worrying about what might go wrong," said Garcia. "You need to look on the bright side, like I do."

There were some statements which were so unjust it was hard to come up with a coherent response. Roldan snorted and didn't say anything else.

"What's that buzzing?" asked Webb.

"It's coming from the central area and I have no idea what's generating it. It gets a lot louder."

The short conversation was enough to fill in the time it took to reach the end of the tight passage. Again, there was a small room identical to the last and with another lever in the same place.

"We help each other, right?" said McKinney. "We either all make it or none of us."

"Agreed," said Garcia.

Roldan and Webb nodded their own acceptance.

"If your repeaters are dry, this would be a good time to dump them."

The two men shrugged out of their repeater harnesses and dropped the weapons to the ground. There was no need for them to carry the extra weight if they were out of ammunition.

"It served me well," said Garcia, giving the discarded gun a poke with his foot.

"You can mourn it later. Now, get ready to run," said McKinney. "It's an impressive sight. Don't stop to gawp."

With that, he hooked his fingers over the top of the lever and dragged it down. The door leading to the Neutraliser's central conduit slid aside quietly and without fuss, allowing the sickly green light to enter. The buzzing increased in volume until it was painful to hear.

McKinney really didn't want to enter the conduit and every fibre of his being screamed at him to close the door again. He refused to listen to his fears and stepped through.

The central area was exactly as he remembered it – a cylindrical room with a ceiling a thousand or more metres above and an entwined bundle of black metal threads running from one end to another, alive with sparks of filthy Vraxar energy. The pressure in the air felt much greater than last time and it pressed against the material of his suit. *There must be even more power running through here now,* he thought.

The walkway was only about a metre wide, with a railing and grated floor he hadn't noticed last time. He began to run along it, checking once over his shoulder to see if his men followed. They were close behind and each had his neck craned to see the sights of the conduit.

They'd covered fifty metres or so when McKinney felt his heart thump wildly in his chest. He roared out a bestial sound of anger, as if his fury and the strength of his will could impose a rhythm onto the beating of his heart.

"Urgh," said Roldan behind.

The man stumbled and fell forward, with one arm clutching his chest. McKinney spun around and caught him, putting his hands beneath Roldan's arms. Garcia was also struggling and he wheezed out a panicked cry for help into the comms channel. Webb was the last man - he put both arms around Garcia's chest and arched his back as he squeezed once, twice, three times.

"Come on," gasped McKinney. His HUD beeped, the noise almost lost in the background droning buzz. He didn't need to read the medical computer's report to know that his heartbeat was dangerously irregular. The suit defibrillator gave him a shock. The electrical charge felt like the punch from a champion boxer in his chest and he thumped his ribcage repeatedly with his palm to try and lessen the pain.

Roldan fell from McKinney's grasp and dropped to all fours, with his head bowed and his life signs winking out.

"No!" shouted McKinney.

He planted his feet on the floor and pulled at Roldan's arm. The soldier's body stiffened and then spasmed violently. He coughed and his vital signs reappeared on the local network.

"I can walk," he said.

McKinney let go and tried to get his bearings. He was suddenly confused and couldn't figure out which was he was meant to be going.

"That way!" said Webb, his arm raised to point.

With a feeling of intense weariness, McKinney turned and

staggered off. He was already running above the maximum permitted dose of battlefield adrenaline, but his spacesuit medical computer was able to take whatever steps it thought necessary to preserve his life. It squirted him with a colossal dose of the stuff, along with a vast quantity of nausea suppressants to stop him from retching up his guts inside his visor.

Through it all, a number on his HUD taunted him, telling the tale of how little progress they'd managed.

500 metres to go. Surely we've come further than that?

The fresh dose of adrenaline kicked in. His body was far past the point where more of the drug would give him a significant boost. He experienced a faint surge, which allowed him to press on at a staggering run. There were access doors in the wall at regular intervals, each one giving false promises of safety.

Every ten metres, he turned to see how the others were getting on. Roldan was keeping up, though he wasn't managing to run in a straight line. At the back, Webb had Garcia over his shoulder and he strode after the others, the set of his shoulders indicating he had no intention of stopping for anything.

The inexorable approach of the soldier gave McKinney impetus to stay ahead and he found new strength in his legs. It became a competition in which they all either won or lost, but within the competition itself was an individual need to keep going so that everyone could take hope from the display of certainty and push themselves to the limit and beyond.

"How far?" asked Roldan, his voice hardly more than a whisper.

"Two hundred metres. Nearly there."

McKinney's breathing became ragged, and he drew in painful, shuddering gulps of air that never seemed enough to feed the demands of his body. He heard the thud of a falling body. He turned, dazed, and saw Roldan had fallen face-down onto the grating, with one arm caught on the railing.

"I can't get past," said Webb, sounding lost.

McKinney stooped and grabbed Roldan's arm. "Up you get," he said.

Roldan was past the point of getting his feet under him. "Sorry, Lieutenant," he mumbled. "Leave me here."

"Everyone lives or everyone dies."

With those words, McKinney drew on the last vestiges of his energy and hauled Roldan upwards. The soldier tried to straighten his legs but flopped down. McKinney didn't let go and began walking backwards, pulling Roldan with him.

A hair-thin thread of green energy flicked between McKinney and the central conduit bundle. His heart missed one beat, two and then kicked in again. He gritted his teeth and did his best to ignore it.

"Come on, sir," said Webb.

McKinney raised his head slightly, wondering how the soldier remained so strong that he was able to carry Garcia over his shoulder and keep walking.

"If there's one thing going to keep me running away," McKinney gasped, "it's the sight of your ugly face and Garcia's backside."

Step by step, they continued. With his reserves spent, McKinney saw that the distance counter had dropped to minus fifty metres. They'd travelled further than expected, yet there'd been no exit door for a longer interval than normal. He was still walking backwards and did his best to look behind. There was no sign of the conduit's end and he guessed it continued into the middle of the nullification sphere.

"Where's the next damn door?" he said.

"I see one!" said Webb. "Fifty metres!"

It was the longest, hardest fifty metres of McKinney's life, but he made it. Roldan felt like he weighed a thousand pounds and the soldier's lower body scraped and bumped over the flooring.

As soon as he came within five metres of the door, McKinney dropped Roldan and dashed for the flat section of the wall. These few paces were enough for him to obtain a better view along the conduit. It appeared to end after another thousand metres or so and opened into an even larger space, where the bundle of metal formed a different, more spherical shape. The front nullification sphere was extensively damaged and the interior was badly malformed as a result. The green light flickered, producing countless shadows onto the warped metal.

McKinney found the lever and pulled. The door moved aside, offering sanctuary within the darkened interior. Webb squeezed past the fallen Roldan and was dutiful enough to wait for instruction.

"In!"

Webb didn't need to be told twice and he hurried past into the small room beyond. There wasn't enough room to keep Garcia over his shoulder and he dropped to one knee in order to lower the soldier onto the floor.

Meanwhile, Roldan had tapped into his own final reserves and he half-walked, half-crawled towards the opening. McKinney put an arm across the man's shoulders and assisted him for the final few steps.

With the four men inside, Webb pulled the lever and the door closed behind, leaving them in a darkness so complete that McKinney's scrambled brain wondered if he was dead.

CHAPTER TWELVE

MCKINNEY WAS NOT DEAD, nor were the men with him.

"We can't sit here, Lieutenant," said Webb. "We've got to move."

Now he was away from the energy-draining aura of the conduit, with its grating, persistent buzzing, McKinney felt something return to him. *Strength* wasn't the correct word to use, since he knew he was as weak as a kitten. Nevertheless, the conduit's suppression of his body was gone and the battlefield adrenaline reasserted a tiny measure of control, urging him to rise and start shooting some Vraxar.

He tried to smile at this sudden understanding – how obvious the drug's manipulation of his thoughts was becoming. The spacesuit and the adrenaline had saved his life and he wasn't about to criticise. He switched on his visor torch and its light illuminated the three men squashed into the space. They looked spent.

"Roldan, are you ready to face the enemy?"

"Ready when you are, sir."

"You sound like shit."

"I feel a whole lot worse."

"Garcia?"

"What?"

"Are you awake yet?"

Garcia mumbled something which may have been *piss off* but McKinney gave him the benefit of the doubt and assumed the words were *Wide awake and raring to go, Lieutenant!*

"There are four heartbeats on the suit medical network. That means it's time to move."

"Can't we wait here for a while? To gather our strength?"

"Negative. We went through that crap to get a lead on the Vraxar. If we wait here, we're going to give them a chance to get ahead of us. Then we'll die and next thing you know you'll find you've been converted and all you'll want is to shoot the soldiers who were once your friends."

McKinney led the way, climbing over the exhausted limbs of his fellows in order to reach the exit passage. There were no complaints, only weary sighs of men who wanted nothing more than to be gone from this place and never return. It was a motivation of sorts.

"Think of your beds," said McKinney. "I'll ensure you get a private room and seventy-two hours of undisturbed sleep on the *Abyss*."

"There are no private rooms on the *Abyss*," said Roldan. "Except for the crew and I doubt they'll be giving them up for unwashed grunts like us."

"I'll have a word with Captain Blake. I promise."

"I'm going to hold you to your word, Lieutenant."

"I always keep my promises, you know that Garcia."

The conversation was enough to distract the men from their physical pain and it rallied them a little. McKinney had no idea if the *Abyss*'s crew would give up their cabins but in reality, it wouldn't come to that since there were a few spare rooms in the officer's quarters for the times when the heavy cruiser had a larger contingent on the bridge. The soldiers would get their three days of rest, though it was more likely to be spent in the medical bay.

They reached the hatch above the main corridor which led to the entry point.

"Get ready," said McKinney. "I estimate there could be anything up to one hundred metres of running until we reach the way out. If there are lots of Vraxar, we're screwed."

"You've got your repeater, sir."

"It's not going to kill them all."

He pulled the lever and the hatch slid quietly into its recess. McKinney felt despair when his visor earpiece picked up the sound of footsteps, somewhere ahead.

"We were too slow."

He tried to work out how long they'd been in the conduit and came up blank. It had felt like forever but wasn't anything more than a few minutes. Evidently it was sufficient for the Vraxar to either overtake them along this corridor or find another way around.

"What now?" asked Roldan.

"We've come this far," said Garcia. "Why don't we take a few down with us?"

Against any other opponent, the idea of going out in a blaze of glory might have been tempting – to whittle away at the enemy in order to give your fellows a greater chance in the future. With the Vraxar, every corpse could simply be added to their numbers.

Unless we blow ourselves up with grenades, thought McKinney.

He wasn't ready for suicide. "Hold my legs," he said.

With Roldan and Webb sitting on his upper legs, McKinney leaned carefully out through the hatch. They were tantalisingly close to the entry point room – only a few metres away, in fact.

There were Vraxar inside the room and he tried to count the numbers.

"Maybe twenty or thirty of them in the entry point room," he said. "It's hard to be certain."

McKinney twisted until he could see in the other direction. His movement sensor picked up shapes a few hundred metres towards the steps.

"There's a group of six coming from the other way," he said. "I can't make out if there are any more coming after them."

McKinney attempted to curl himself back up through the hatch and found his stomach muscles unwilling to comply.

"Pull me up."

Roldan and Webb dragged him unceremoniously into the room and McKinney lay panting and waiting for the blood flow through his brain to normalise.

"Can we make it?" asked Garcia.

"It's going to be tough. We'll need to get through this hatch fast, clear out the smaller group and then make a run for the entry point room." He eyed up their grenade bandoliers and noted that each man had plenty spare.

"It's a long way down," said Webb.

"Hang and drop. It's not far," said Garcia.

"We can't wait any longer," said McKinney. "I'll drop first, then Roldan, Garcia, Webb."

He didn't give them a chance to ask any further questions. He stood over the hatch and looked down – it seemed much further to the bottom when he was on his feet. He dropped into a crouch and turned around so that his back was to the opening. He used his right hand to pull his gauss rifle free and kept a tight grip on it, leaving his left hand to deal with slowing his fall.

"Here goes."

McKinney slid backwards into the hatch opening. His shins scraped painfully on the metal lip and he dropped through. As he fell into space, he grabbed at the rim with his left hand. His fingers gripped for just long enough to snap him to a brief halt and then his weight tore them free. He fell the final two metres and the high gravity of Vanistar caused him to hit the floor with a heavy, painful thump. He bent his knees to reduce the impact, which helped only a little.

With the wind knocked out of him, McKinney took a hurried stride forward to clear the area beneath the hatch and lay flat on the floor. He pulled the gauss rifle tight against his shoulder and took aim at the group of six Vraxar coming towards him. The lights were on, but the enemy showed no signs of recognition and McKinney was glad they were too far away to realise he was human instead of Vraxar.

His first three shots were accurate, each one striking a vital area. He fired again, this second volley not so effective. The survivors of his ambush fell flat to the floor, using their fallen as cover.

Roldan landed next to McKinney with a crunch and stumbled into the wall. He recovered quickly and lay prone. The two men fired another couple of bursts. The gauss rounds had enough power to penetrate several opponents before they were spent and the Vraxar discovered that the bodies of their fellows were ineffective protection. The remainder of the aliens died quickly, though the two men fired several more times to ensure the job was done.

With the first group defeated, McKinney spun around to look into the entry point room. It had been a gamble to take out the rear group first, but the few seconds spent were intended to allow everyone time to reach the floor so they could make a combined assault on the larger group of Vraxar. The gauss rifles killed in near-silence and so far, there was no sign the aliens had detected anything was wrong.

Garcia dropped from the ceiling. He got his timing wrong

and landed awkwardly, twisting his ankle. McKinney heard the sickening pop of breaking bones.

"That is going to hurt like a bastard when these drugs wear off," said Garcia happily.

McKinney rose into a crouch, keeping himself pressed close to the wall. He slung his gauss rifle and lowered the barrel of his repeater. The enemy were in groups in the entry point room, though they had set no guard and showed no signs they were interested in their surroundings. It was like they'd chased the fleeing soldiers off the Neutraliser and now they didn't have a clue what they were going to do. McKinney was more than pleased to take advantage and crept along the corridor towards them, with Roldan following and Garcia limping.

Webb arrived, plummeting from the ceiling with the grace of a hippo. His landing was more successful than Garcia's and he righted himself quickly and hugged the wall. This time, the movement caught the eye of one of the Vraxar soldiers. It didn't make a sound, but the other aliens in the room responded immediately by reaching for their guns.

"Time to move," said McKinney.

The closest group of Vraxar was thirty metres away – near enough for the plasma repeater to chew them up in less than a second. McKinney gave them a long burst and the glowing arc of projectiles ripped them to pieces, hurling chunks of flesh and armour across the floor. The standard repeaters were enormously effective shock weapons and the plasma versions were a step up. The Vraxar fell, given no chance to respond with fire of their own.

With grim satisfaction, McKinney turned the weapon onto the next group. The aliens had already started to spread themselves out. Some dropped prone, whilst others tried to cut off McKinney's angle by moving away from his line of sight. The repeater ploughed through many more, churning up flesh and bones, spitting the pieces dozens of metres to collide with the walls and the floor.

"Holy shit!" laughed Roldan. "Look at them fall!"

When it came to the Vraxar there was none of the sympathy one soldier might feel for another. Instead there was a hungering lust to destroy as many of these abominations as possible. McKinney felt the craving and kept the trigger on his repeater held tightly against the barrel. Its ammunition reserves dropped rapidly, but so too did the enemy fall.

A few Vraxar survived the withering hail of plasma slugs and made it out McKinney's line of sight.

"Go!" he shouted.

Roldan and Garcia needed no more encouragement. They stepped clear of the wall and pitched grenades one after the other into the room, doing their best to catch the enemy in the blasts. Webb crossed to the opposite wall of the corridor and tried to get a firing angle. The coils on his rifle whined again and again.

"Got three!" he shouted.

"Don't stop!"

McKinney inched forward while Webb maintained his suppressing fire and the others continued to throw grenades.

The Vraxar had grenades of their own. One of them landed on the floor fifteen metres away, bounced once and then exploded. The dark, corrosive flames licked against the four men, before receding as quickly as they came. McKinney was unhurt, but his suit was damaged and he saw that most of Webb's spacesuit was left blistered by the explosion. The soldier kept firing.

"Got the bastard!" he shouted.

"Are we clear?"

"Negative, Lieutenant. We are not clear," said Webb.

"What numbers and where are they?"

"They're tight to the walls, sir – to the right of the corridor exit."

"I see at least two more in the closest side passage," said Garcia.

"Get a grenade in there!"

With a mighty heavy, Garcia threw one of his remaining grenades into the room. McKinney was too close to the wall to see where it landed. The side passages were wide and he hoped Garcia's aim wasn't terrible.

"Well?"

"Not sure, sir."

McKinney grimaced and chanced a look behind. The corridor was still empty, though he was sure time was running out to resolve this stalemate. He checked his repeater magazine: 35%.

"Roldan, Garcia, keep throwing grenades into that side passage. I'm going in."

The two soldiers pitched their grenades and reached for more.

"Webb, hold fire!"

Webb held fire at once and McKinney made a crouch-sprint for the room. With a burst of speed he didn't think he had left in him, McKinney charged into the room. He didn't wait for his brain to catch up with what his eyes saw and he opened fire with his repeater, raking the walls and corner with a thousand slugs. There were four Vraxar, standing several metres apart and with their guns ready. McKinney's brain dimly recognized that one had its arm raised to throw a grenade.

The repeater tore them to pieces in moments. One of the Vraxar was fast enough to get a shot off at McKinney. It missed and that was all he cared about. The alien holding the grenade toppled over, much of its body shredded and unrecognizable. The grenade went off with a heavy percussive thump and McKinney turned his back to the blast, dropping into a crouch at the same time. He was far enough away and his spacesuit suffered little damage.

Roldan appeared next to him, his face surveying the room for any more Vraxar.

"Clear!" he shouted.

"We did it?" said Webb.

McKinney was already on the move. "Looks like."

The hull breach was an area of brightness against the gloom of the interior. He knew how bad it was outside, yet the sight of it was as welcome as a holidaymaker's first view across the perfect white beaches of an Atlantis holiday resort. He waved the soldiers towards it. "Move!"

The four of them made haste across the room, with Garcia leaning on Roldan. McKinney dared to hope he'd once more escaped against the odds. Then, he saw a body on the floor with blood crusting around several bullet wounds. There was no way to guess who was inside the suit and the sight was a reminder that not everyone got lucky.

They reached the hull breach and McKinney waited for the men to get through. The Vraxar life support systems were clearly more advanced than those of the Space Corps if they could maintain the internal pressure of the Neutraliser even with this big hole through the armour. It was one for the scientists to puzzle over. Without further pause, he stepped into the breach.

The Vraxar had one more nasty surprise for him. McKinney felt a thump on his back. Before he had time to wonder what it was, his shoulder detonated outwards in a spray of blood. From his periphery, he saw movement far along the main corridor. He couldn't make out the details, but it seemed like one of the Vraxar had finally managed to land a shot on him.

He nearly fell. Strong hands took hold of him and he found himself dragged out of the Neutraliser and into the biting winds of Vanistar. The howling gale showed no mercy and battered him with its fury. He tried to drop into a huddle to protect himself from the pinpricks of dust which was carried along in the storm. The hands lifted him up and wouldn't let him fall.

"I've got you, Lieutenant," said Webb.

McKinney's brain swam and he looked at the exit wound on his chest. It seemed like such a little thing and the suit had already formed a thin skin over it, sealing the wound and keeping him safe from the low-pressure of the atmosphere.

With Webb providing support, McKinney walked through the Neutraliser's damaged armour. The skies of Vanistar were darker than before and he wondered if this was dawn or dusk. He couldn't quite remember how long they'd been inside.

"Where's the shuttle?" he asked.

Roldan sprinted ahead and up the slope of the impact crater, with Garcia limping afterwards. They turned this way and that, trying to find where the escape craft was waiting.

"They've left us! They've damned well abandoned us here!"

McKinney checked the comms – there were no receptors available except those representing the other three soldiers. He bent his neck and saw he was still sheltered within the Neutraliser's hull and it was likely blocking his signal. There should have been a beacon. *Where's the damned beacon?* he thought.

Hopelessness washed over McKinney. It was an emotion he was a stranger to and it made him feel weaker than he had done even in the conduit. A question came to him, pointless in the circumstances, though one which he somehow found important.

"How did you manage so well in the conduit?" he mumbled. "I mean, we all nearly died, except you. You just kept on going."

Webb gave a short laugh. "You remember when I got shot up on the *Juniper* and I spent weeks in that medical place?" He banged his chest with his spare hand. "They fitted me with some kind of new heart. The doctors said it would never stop ticking, even long after I died. One little piece of Obsidiar is all it needs to run for a hundred thousand years."

"You've been augmented, soldier. How does it feel?"

"Feel? I don't know if I feel anything special, Lieutenant. I'm alive the same way I always was and that's what matters, eh?"

"Yeah, that's what matters. You did good, soldier."

As McKinney's eyes closed, the last thing he remembered seeing was the *ES Abyss*'s fourth shuttle drop like a stone from the sky. It decelerated at the very last moment, coming to a halt just above the ground a couple of hundred metres away. After that, he knew no more.

CHAPTER THIRTEEN

THE INTERIOR of the central medical facility on the New Earth Tucson military base wasn't much different to every other medical facility Fleet Admiral Duggan had ever visited. The truth was, he hadn't seen more than a handful of such places, owing to the fact that they made him feel uncomfortable. This effect was something he'd experienced ever since he was a young man and while it wasn't quite *fear,* it wasn't too far removed from it.

Duggan walked at the head of the small team of his personal staff who were there to relay his orders and also to offer advice where necessary. In addition, eight heavily-armed soldiers followed in their wake, each one dressed in protective body armour and wearing a specially-adapted version of a spacesuit visor, which kept them safe from gas attacks. Not that Duggan expected to run into assassins, but it seemed a wise and easily-enacted precaution against the vagaries of the unknown.

The corridors of the facility stretched on interminably, as though the entire building was nothing more than a series of interconnected passages with nowhere for research or treatment to take place. As was common in such places, the air was chilled to an uncomfortable level and Duggan found himself longing to be on the hot, stifling bridge of an ancient Vincent class fighter. His piloting days were long gone and of all things, it was this loss he felt keenly, almost as much as the deaths of those who'd served with him during the Estral and Ghast wars.

Duggan set a fast pace and Dr Faith Clarke walked alongside him. Duggan wasn't fond of Clarke's defensiveness when it came to her work and she was equally unhappy at having to answer to a military man, even though her department was entirely funded from the Space Corps' budget. Consequently, they only spoke when absolutely necessary.

Their destination was six levels below ground, though such was the identical nature of each floor it wasn't obvious and only a lack of windows on the perimeter corridors gave the game away. Not even the signs dangling at regular intervals from the stark white ceilings alluded to the subterranean nature of level DF-17.

"In here," said Dr Clarke, offering with ill-grace to let Duggan go first through a set of double-doors.

He pressed his fingers to the access panel and a red light appeared, to indicate his entry was denied.

"Override code: Duggan," he said without hesitation. The red light turned green and the doors slid open. "That will be fixed today."

"Yes, Fleet Admiral," said Clarke.

He went through and his entourage followed. Clarke gave the impression she wanted to object to their presence; luckily for her, she was wise enough to keep her mouth closed.

The room beyond the doors was large and with a high ceiling. The walls were white, the floor was covered in white tiles and the overhead lights were white. There were several white-coloured consoles arranged along the walls and teams of scientists and other medical staff, again dressed in white, talked in hushed tones.

Only two things broke up the monotony of colour. The first was a hulking military robot, which was grey. This robot looked nothing like a human – it was part cube, part cylinder, covered in screens and equipped with an array of hidden defensive weaponry and a tiny Obsidiar power source to keep its gravity drive running in the event of a Neutraliser attack. Inside, was more Obsidiar, this in the form of a number-crunching processing cluster designed to do all manner of tricks when it came to encryption.

A thick, flexible cable emerged from midway up the robot's central section and descended through the empty eye socket of a Vraxar on the table, which was the second intruder upon the preponderance of whiteness. This Vraxar was held completely immobile by a combination of drugs and numerous grey metal straps which held it in a semi-upright position on a slanted examination table.

Duggan stepped closer to the alien – the light of the room made the creature's skin appear nearly translucent and he saw bones and organs where they came close to the surface. This room carried the odour of powerful cleaning solutions in the same way as the other parts of the facility. However, there was another smell, which caused Duggan to wrinkle his nose. The Vraxar exuded the stench of rotting flesh and harsh preservative fluids. When he came even closer, the alien's second eye opened and it looked at him steadily.

With an infinite array of possible questions open to him, Duggan asked one to which he knew the answer.

"Why have you attacked us?"

The Vraxar's mouth moved in what might have been a grin, giving Duggan an unwanted view of its decaying teeth. A pallid, green-tinged tongue slipped into view and briefly touched against lips before vanishing once more. When the alien spoke, its voice was a hollow, whispering sound and it was difficult to make out the words clearly.

"We come where there is life."

"Why do you need to kill in order to prosper? I am not aware of any other species that requires the extinction of others."

"We are what we are."

"What sort of an answer is that?"

"It's the only answer I have."

"Do you follow willingly? Is this what you wished for when you were alive?"

The Vraxar closed its eye. "This is not what any of us wished for. Not the Estral, not the Rilq, nor the Fuabnar, the Grax'd or the Fade before them. A hundred thousand years of misery. We are unwilling soldiers fighting for the species which defeated us."

"Who are the originals? Who started this?"

"I don't know. Perhaps they have turned to dust, or perhaps they direct their fleet from a place I shall never learn."

"What compels you to fight for them? You are not under duress to talk, yet you answer my questions."

"Do you understand what it is like to lose your soul, human? We have had ours stolen and replaced with embalming fluids and command processors."

"We have studied the processing unit embedded in your brain and there is nothing there which forces you to act with hostility."

The Vraxar showed its teeth again. "It is more than the Fior implant. The conversion takes everything and leaves behind only a corrupt version of what there was."

Duggan struggled to understand. The Vraxar was telling only partial truths or perhaps the truths as it knew them. Believing either could be equally dangerous.

"If you are corrupted, does that mean you are acting of your own free will? Have your morals been subverted and changed to something else?"

A soft whoosh of breath escaped the Vraxar's mouth and Duggan realised it was laughing. "We Rilq are unimportant and so too are the Estral, though they fought the hardest. All we have left is existence. We are left with a memory of life and a desire to continue living. We are children and each new Vraxar is welcomed like a child amongst us."

Duggan was horrified at these words and at that moment he knew there was no way to fully understand the Vraxar and it was the final confirmation that there would be no negotiating with them, nor ever a settlement reached.

"If I let you free from these bonds, what would you do?"

"I don't know. I might try to work out what those consoles over there are for. I might speak to these scientists. I believe I once learned about things. More likely, I would try to kill everyone here and attempt to make a connection with Ix-Gorghal."

The name was something new.

"What is *Ix-Gorghal*? A commander of the Vraxar?"

"I don't know who commands the Vraxar."

"Then what is *Ix-Gorghal*?"

"It is one of the Vraxar capital ships. You humans destroyed much of the local fleet with your bomb, so they have summoned *Ix-Gorghal*."

"What do you mean by *summoned*?"

"I will assume you do not have the technological capabilities to do the same. The Ir-Klion can produce power in such quantities that they can *reach* through barriers of mere distance. They can pull vessels through space from anywhere in the universe. It is how fleets are brought once we have found new children."

Duggan felt giddy with the stream of new names, ideas and technologies the Vraxar was telling him about. Partial truths or not, he was certain he was on the brink of learning something of absolutely vital importance.

"Are these Ir-Klion the vessels with nullification spheres? We know them as Neutralisers."

"The descriptive name is fitting. We Vraxar have conquered civilisation after civilisation with the Ir-Klion. The only significant power source they are ineffective against is what you call Obsidiar."

"And they have brought *Ix-Gorghal* into Confederation Space?"

"That was the purpose of the spaceship your soldiers took me from. After *Ix-Gorghal*, we were to summon *Ix-Gastiol*, but we had insufficient Ir-Klion to accomplish both summons."

"Is that what damaged your vessel?"

"It was. Ten others were destroyed in the chain reaction. Only the *Ir-Klion-32* and the *Ir-Klion-6* escaped annihilation. We were too badly damaged for the *Ir-Klion-6* to assist."

"The Vraxar make no attempt to save their children?"

"There will always be more. What happened to the *Ir-Klion-32* after I was taken away?"

"Your Neutraliser attempted lift off and its rear nullification sphere was close to exploding. One of our heavy cruisers destroyed your vessel to prevent both its escape and detonation."

"A shame."

"That is in the eye of the beholder. What can we expect from this *Ix-Gorghal*?"

"You can expect death, human, followed by new life amongst us."

The words caused a few of Duggan's staff to mutter and his armed guard shifted uneasily. He gave a look which told them he'd brook no more interruptions and the whispering abruptly ceased. He continued speaking to the captive Vraxar.

"What capabilities does this capital ship have?"

"I do not know. It was not required to defeat the Rilq. I know it exists, without knowing how it is used."

"What about the Estral? Was it deployed against them?"

"It destroyed many of their spaceships towards the end of the war and ensured their final defeat. They had opportunities and they failed to take them."

"What about *Ix-Gastiol*? Is it similarly powerful?"

"I do not know. We Vraxar are many and it does not generally require our entire fleet to conquer a new species. It is likely that other civilisations than your own are currently at war with us. I do not know why we were instructed to summon both of our capital ships, since one is more than sufficient for a civilisation as limited in its expansion as yours."

"Why don't you know?"

"I do not know everything."

Duggan remained silent for a time, with his mind trying to sift the nuggets of truth from the hints and suggestions. The Vraxar stated that its Neutraliser had been *instructed* to summon the *Ix-Gorghal*. On the one hand, it gave the impression there were no commanders and then it suggested exactly the opposite. It wasn't a necessity for Duggan to know his enemy, but it was always best to have an idea of their motives and their command structure. His conversation with the Vraxar left him no more enlightened than he had been when they first attacked Atlantis.

The real concern he had from the conversation was the mention of *Ix-Gorghal*. If it was a Vraxar capital ship, then it was likely to be an exceptionally powerful opponent. Even worse was the Vraxar's assertion that it had been successfully summoned into Confederation Space. It wasn't as though the Confederation's territory was so compact that there were only a hundred planets to explore – in fact there were many thousands. The worry was that the Vraxar were unlikely to have brought one of their most powerful warships if there was no hope of forcing an engagement of some type. It didn't seem likely that *Ix-Gorghal* would jump happily from place to place in a random search for human worlds, which suggested they knew where they were going or soon would.

During the attack on Atlantis the Vraxar had stolen a fleet warship, from the databanks of which it was certain they'd try to extract the location of the Confederation worlds. Duggan's various forecasting and predictions teams had told him it was probable that the *ES Determinant* had been destroyed in the Obsidiar bomb blast on the Cheops-A system. In fact, they'd handed him a sheet of paper with an exact percentage on it, that percentage being 73.271%.

"The Vraxar captured one of our warships during the attack on our planet Atlantis. Was it in the hold of one of the ships destroyed near Cheops-A?"

The Vraxar was evidently intelligent enough to guess why the question was important and it gave the same rustling laugh. There was no mockery and no humour in the sound, as though the once-living part of its brain remembered laughter, yet without knowing how to enjoy it. The laughter stopped and the Vraxar gave the answer Duggan was expecting.

"I do not know."

Sometimes even an expected answer is a cause for anger and Duggan swore loudly. He spun on his heel and strode towards his personal staff.

"Lieutenant Jacobs," he said in a low voice, directing his gaze towards a slim, mousey-haired woman in her late thirties. "I want you to gather the best people from your team. Get them here as soon as possible and have them question this Vraxar at length. Record everything it says and analyse every word and sentence for repetition or contradiction. Find out what it knows and separate that from what it thinks it knows."

Allison Jacobs was one of the brightest people in the entire

Confederation and her blue eyes gleamed with eagerness at this challenge.

"Do you think it's lying, sir?"

"I'd say it's not capable of lying and that's what makes it so valuable to us. It clearly doesn't know everything and I'm certain it takes no enjoyment from misleading us – this creature is simply different to us."

"I know just the people to deal with what you ask, sir."

Duggan had no appetite for further conversation with the Vraxar and he began walking towards the exit door, with his staff and escort falling in behind and Jacobs walking alongside. The door wouldn't open again and Duggan suppressed his anger at the temerity of whoever had thought it a good idea to try and prevent the Admiral of the whole damned fleet from getting into this room.

"Override code: Duggan." The door opened again. "Lieutenant Jacobs - if anyone here gives you trouble or does anything whatsoever to impede you or your team, come to me immediately."

"I absolutely will do that, sir."

The group retraced their steps through the medical facility and this time the predictable monotony of the walls was a welcome change from the capriciousness of doctors and aliens. They entered one of the huge airlifts and returned to the surface. Fifteen minutes later, Duggan was in the comfortable surroundings of his office once more, where he found a new potted plant on the corner of his desk, no doubt placed there by his wife.

He turned the plant to a more agreeable angle and sat in his chair, mulling over what he'd learned.

CHAPTER FOURTEEN

DUGGAN WAS BLESSED or cursed with a brain that never ran short of practical ideas about how to solve a problem. The snippets divulged by the captive Vraxar made him think the aliens either realised they'd bitten off more than they could chew when they lost a big chunk of their fleet at Cheops-A and had sent this *Ix-Gorghal* to bolster their remaining forces, or they'd found a new species elsewhere and wished to overcome the Confederation as quickly as possible in order to move on to the next target. It might be that neither was correct, yet he felt confident he was thinking along the right lines. It was also becoming apparent that the Vraxar were voracious in their appetite for war, and, rather than taking tentative steps, they gathered intelligence and then attacked quickly.

"Cerys, please scan our data archives for any mention of a vessel called *Ix-Gorghal*."

The answer came back immediately and was spoken in a voice so sultry it made Duggan wonder what on earth his computer-generated personal assistant was playing at. "There is no mention of those words in our archives, nor anything which probability suggests may have been derived from those words."

"Please access the records we extracted from the *Valpian* and scan for any mention of a large-scale engagement between the Estral and the Vraxar."

The *Valpian* was an Estral cruiser which Duggan and his squad had captured on a hard-fought mission several decades before. It was during this mission he'd first started to suspect that the Estral were fighting on too many fronts. At the time, the *Valpian* was one of the Estral's newest, most advanced warships and likely a prototype designed specifically to combat the Vraxar. Now, the fully-intact and operational cruiser sat on a disused part of the Tucson base. Duggan visited it often, if just to sit on the bridge and think about his past.

Detriment, Crimson, Valpian, Rampage, Ransor-D. Tybalt. The names rolled through his head, each one tied to memories of success, failure and endless death.

"Fleet Admiral Duggan?"

He shook his head clear and realised Cerys was waiting for his input.

"Please excuse me. What did you say?"

"No excuses necessary, Fleet Admiral." The voice oozed with seduction, leaving Duggan flummoxed as to what was going on. "I simply reminded you that we were only able to break the encryption on 83.439% of the *Valpian*'s data cores and that the results will therefore be incomplete."

The process of cracking into the Estral arrays was a slow one and it had taken years to achieve 83.439%. Eventually it reached the point where one of Duggan's predecessors had called it off in order to utilise the processing resources elsewhere. The Estral hadn't returned and the operation had simply never resumed.

"Fine, please give me a summary of your findings."

"Very well. The *Valpian*'s databanks record 1638 engagements between Estral warships and Vraxar. Most were sightings or encounters involving a single ship on each side."

"How many involving twenty warships or more on the Estral side?"

"There were 210 such engagements."

The size of the number reminded Duggan how extensive the Estral Empire was compared to the Confederation. They had enough spaceships to fight at least three wars simultaneously and still field twenty or more vessels against the Vraxar on more than two hundred occasions. Not for the first time, Duggan experienced a creeping admiration for the Estral. *Even though they were just as murderous as every other alien species in the universe.*

"Is there any mention of the Estral facing a warship that was particularly large in size?"

"They mention only one vessel larger than a Neutraliser, Fleet Admiral. The Estral fought what they describe as a Class 1 Battleship, which measured twenty-five thousand metres from nose to stern."

"That might be it."

"This Class 1 Battleship was destroyed by the Estral."

"Anything else?"

"I already told you there was only one mention of a spaceship larger than a Neutraliser, Fleet Admiral," Cerys admonished.

"It is not wise to bring the Fleet Admiral's frailties to the Fleet Admiral's attention!" he replied.

"Your wife will be amused to hear you have been referring to yourself in the third person," said Cerys primly.

Duggan's jaw dropped open and he determined to speak to one of the tech guys later to find out what had got into Cerys lately. It was a distraction, though not a priority and he put the issue to one side for the moment.

"How many Obsidiar clusters do we have on the Tucson base?"

"There are five clusters of twenty within the central administration building, as well as two portable clusters of twenty-four, one currently being used by the Fission Prediction project and the other..."

"Yes, I know. That one's in the central medical facility connected to a Vraxar's processor through its eye socket."

The Fission Prediction project was currently at a critical phase, whilst the clusters in the administration building were fixed in place and not straightforward to move. They could connect remotely to the *Valpian*, though with a significantly reduced bandwidth.

"The medical facility can do without the portable cluster. The Vraxar processing units aren't sophisticated enough to need a dedicated resource. Please have the cluster robot moved to the *Valpian* as a highest-priority. I want to find out what remains undiscovered in that spaceship's memory arrays."

"Certainly, Fleet Admiral. I have chosen the appropriate personnel and alerted them to your orders."

"Send an officer of suitable rank to the medical facility, just in case the staff there find a sudden, urgent use for the robot that might result in a delay."

Cerys was good for many things. "Already done," she said.

"Provide me with a time estimate."

"I estimate it will take not more than three hours for the portable cluster to reach the *Valpian*, plus a further ten minutes for it to reach the bridge and interface."

"How long until I see results?"

The latest Obsidiar clusters were worlds faster than the old cores they'd used to dissect the *Valpian*'s arrays all those years ago and Duggan was hopeful he'd get quick answers.

"I estimate it will take in excess of a week until extraction of the remaining data on the *Valpian* is completed. There will be a linear supply of new information beginning within moments of the cluster robot's interface."

"With no guarantee it'll be what I want," said Duggan.

"No, Fleet Admiral. Would you like to hear a list of calculated percentages?"

"No."

"Very well."

Duggan was aware that Cerys was also becoming increasingly eager to get in the last word and he chuckled suddenly at the notion that it was striving to become more human. Perhaps the tech guys had updated the software recently to try and give him a more natural experience.

The delay in decrypting the *Valpian*'s data stores was an unwanted one and Duggan had no intention of twiddling his thumbs while he waited for answers that might not even exist. *Ix-Gorghal* was somewhere in Confederation Space and he needed to take action in order to locate it. Once he knew where and what it was, he could attempt to counter this new threat.

"Show me a list of significant resources in the Hyptron Sector," he said.

His desk console lit up and a list appeared on one of the screens. He scanned it carefully, each name familiar to him.

"What is Monitoring Station Sigma's current focus?"

"They are performing random deep space scans in the Garon Sector, in anticipation of a Vraxar return to Atlantis or their discovery of Overtide."

"Provide new orders – they are to aim their lenses towards the area surrounding Vanistar. Assign a team to provide them with a list of possibilities as to where *Ix-Gorghal* might be headed."

"What sort of possibilities, Fleet Admiral?"

"I don't know – that's what we pay these bright minds for. To find order in chaos and to second-guess our enemies."

"The orders have been made."

"I want Monitoring Station Tau assigned to the same duties."

"That will leave us blind in a number of significant areas, Fleet Admiral. Specifically, there will be gaps in our deep space sensor sight on Zircon and Hope."

"Step up security on those planets. Cancel shore leave where necessary and get every ship in space. How many from our Obsidiar Fleet do we have in the vicinity?"

"There are six within a day's travel of Hope and seven the same distance from Zircon."

"Recall them and have them stationed appropriately in case we have any surprises."

"Done."

Duggan tapped his fingers on his desk in thought. "Captain Blake discovered an anomaly near to Vanistar."

"It was investigated."

"And?"

"It was classified as a *semi-stable fission cloud* and assigned to a primary research team."

"What is a semi-stable fission cloud?"

"An unexplained result from a lightspeed arrival, where the fission energy lingers for an extended period instead of dissipating. It's a theoretical possibility."

"Why wasn't I told? I asked for a thorough report on every aspect of that mission."

"A failure of communications, Fleet Admiral. Would you like me to issue a standard reprimand to the officer who made the final decision?"

Duggan was angry, though much of it was directed towards his own forgetfulness. His personal medical team informed him it was an inevitable symptom of his brain's gradual decay, though they hadn't yet detected any measurable evidence to suggest he was afflicted.

"No, get me through to the officer in question."

"Awaiting connection to Research Lead Joel Breeze. Connection established."

"Joel?" Duggan's anger faded when he heard the name. "Bring him through."

"Hello?" said a voice, clearly not yet recovered from the surprise of this unexpected comms call.

"How are you doing RL Breeze?"

"Very well, sir."

"I'll cut to the chase – a recent mission to Vanistar found evidence of a semi-stable fission cloud."

"Yes, sir," said Breeze, his voice warming up with immediate enthusiasm. "An exceptionally interesting possibility has almost been proven. We have verified the *ES Abyss*'s sensor data and now we are attempting to unravel the nature of the anomaly itself."

"You assigned the research to your own team?"

"Most definitely, sir! This is extremely exciting for all of us."

Duggan found that if he closed his eyes, he could almost be speaking to the man's grandfather, such was the similarity in both tone and enthusiasm.

"Joel, the Vraxar have sent something into Confederation Space. A potential game-changer, not that they needed one."

"And you believe the semi-stable fission cloud is evidence of it, sir?"

"It could be. The engine man on the *ES Abyss* detected similarities with a wormhole, though he lacked the time to do a full analysis. I have received information which suggests the Vraxar can summon their warships across vast distances of space."

"Through a temporary wormhole?" RL Breeze sounded momentarily puzzled. "You can't make a wormhole without access to an almost infinite power source. And then to hold the wormhole open…"

"It took twelve Neutralisers and ten of them were destroyed in the process."

Breeze was quiet and Duggan could just about hear the cogs in the man's brain turning as he added up the numbers. "Twelve Neutralisers can generate a lot of power."

"I would like you to change the direction of your investigation. I would like you to assume that the Vraxar were able to generate a wormhole and I would like you to assume that something came through it."

"You can't work backwards like that, sir! It would be a scientific calamity!"

"If anyone ridicules your end report, I will be very pleased to speak to them personally."

"What exactly are you hoping to find?"

"Something I can work with. There is something called *Ix-Gorghal* in the Hyptron Sector and I want to know what it is. More importantly, I want to find out where it is. The Vraxar believe we warrant the attention of one of their capital ships and I would like to know what we're up against."

"I was running through some numbers when you called, sir. I'll get on with it."

"This is top priority. Do you need any help?"

"I've got a good team, sir. You remember what they say about too many cooks."

"Yes."

"Will there be anything else, sir?"

Duggan hesitated. "How's your grandmother getting along?"

"I haven't seen her for a few days, sir. She likes getting the flowers."

"It's the least we can do."

The conversation tailed off and Duggan let Breeze return to his number crunching. He dragged himself from his reverie and picked up the next item on his agenda.

CHAPTER FIFTEEN

THE NEXT FEW days were more than frustrating for Fleet Admiral Duggan. The mobile processing robot gradually decrypted the contents of the *Valpian*'s memory banks and while the new information was of great interest to those Space Corps teams dedicated to the study of alien history, there were no clues as to the nature of *Ix-Gorghal*. There was a chance the Vraxar capital ship appeared in Estral Space after the theft of the *Valpian*, in which case there'd be no records whatsoever.

The second frustrating event was the death of the Vraxar captive. One morning, it simply died and no amount of medical intervention was sufficient to bring it back to life. Duggan wanted to shout at someone, but he had no excuse to do so. For all he found Dr Faith Clarke annoying she was also excellent at her job, which was why the Space Corps employed her.

The report into the Vraxar's death wasn't long in forthcoming. Like the other - dead - specimens they'd studied, this alien was filled with cancers and also many drugs to suppress the disease. Its cells were turgid with a preservative fluid which was unknown to the medical staff. There was every indication it lived in constant, terrible pain and Duggan had no doubt the creature was happier dead than it was alive. That didn't mean *he* was happier to have it dead, but his anger wasn't going to bring it back to life.

He had Cerys check on the two deep space monitoring stations regularly to see if there was anything for him to work on – even the smallest of clues might enable him to take direct action and send out a ship to investigate. The monitoring stations were both new and filled with so many Obsidiar processors and bristled with so many Hynus sensor arrays it seemed inconceivable they could turn up with blanks. However, blanks were what Duggan got.

It wasn't only *Ix-Gorghal* which was a cause for worry. The Vraxar had lost many ships at Cheops-A and it was surely a sizable percentage of what they had in Confederation Space. The trouble was, the Vraxar fleet had so many warships it was certain enough remained to for these remnants to present a grave threat in themselves.

During these few days, Duggan spoke regularly to his various teams and also to the Ghosts. The aliens hadn't detected anything unusual, nor taken part in any engagements. The leader of the Ghost navy – Subjos Kion-Tur - seemed to be rather more dejected than usual, which Duggan put down to the lack of action. If there was one thing about the Ghosts which wasn't in doubt, it was their wholehearted commitment to a cause.

In the end, someone came through for Duggan, albeit in a slightly different manner to what he was expecting.

"I have a request from Research Lead Joel Breeze to speak to you, Fleet Admiral," said Cerys.

"Bring him through."

"Hello, sir," said Breeze.

"What can I do for you, RL Breeze? Please tell me you have some positive news."

"I've got something, sir, though I don't know if it's exactly what you want. You asked me to contact you with any developments."

"That I did. What have you found?"

"Well, I did as you asked and accepted several assumptions as truth. The fewer unknowns you have, the easier it is to fill in the other missing pieces."

Duggan sat up straight. "You've learned something about the Vraxar ship?"

"The direction of its travel."

"Where's it going?"

Like all researchers, Breeze liked to tell the story of how he got to his conclusion. Duggan didn't mind a good story when he had the time, though he was feeling somewhat agitated at the moment. Even so, he sat patiently and listened.

"We took a look at the sensor data the ES *Abyss* captured on the Vanistar anomaly and compared it to old data from the Helius Blackstar."

"That data is *very* old."

"And very rudimentary, sir. We were stumped for a while, but when you took the ESS *Crimson* through the wormhole, it left a wave pattern of disturbed energy. We compared that pattern with the ripples in the Vraxar wormhole and tried to work out an exit vector."

"And?"

"At first, it didn't work – there was no commonality between them. We assumed different shapes and sizes for the Vraxar ship and eventually we got a kind of match."

"What probability did the computer give you?"

"We don't work off computer probabilities here, sir. We work off our own data and..."

"Gut feeling?"

"Don't tell anyone, will you? We've been keeping a record for the last two years called *hunch versus computer*. At the moment, *hunch* is ten points in the lead."

Duggan roared with laughter. "I might have known!" he said. "All these years we've been relying on computers and they still can't beat gut instinct!"

"It's uplifting, isn't it? Humanity is not redundant yet, no matter how much people grumble about being replaced by a computer."

"When we've sent the Vraxar packing, you can write me a paper on that one. The Space Corps will give you whatever funding you need and I'll personally fix the medal to your chest."

"It's not quite that easy, sir. You see, some people are absolutely terrible when it comes to hunches. Others? Well, they can beat the odds every time. It's a fascinating subject."

It was indeed a subject close to Duggan's heart and he would have enjoyed talking at greater length about this hunch versus computer chart. He knew it would have to wait. "Where did the Vraxar go?"

"We believe they came out of the temporary wormhole at a sub-light speed following a trajectory I am just offering to your personal assistant."

"Cerys, accept that data and show it on my screen."

His personal assistant knew when to stay quiet. It accepted the inbound data packet and fed it through to his console. A star chart appeared on Duggan's right-hand console screen, with Vanistar to one side and a line tracing through the solar system.

"I gave you details of when the *ES Abyss* arrived in the locality, didn't I?"

"Yes, sir."

"How long after these events did the *Abyss* reach Vanistar?"

"Somewhere between eighteen and twenty hours."

Duggan was impressed – the personnel on Monitoring Station Delta had located the crashed Neutraliser a mere six to eight hours after it came down on Vanistar. He zoomed out his view of the chart and the computer obligingly extended the trajectory line for him. He zoomed out again until Vanistar was a tiny dot. The line continued into empty space.

"Eighteen to twenty hours at sub light speed leads nowhere," he said.

"I agree, sir. The summoned spaceship certainly went to lightspeed shortly after it came through the wormhole."

Duggan zoomed out his display once more, assuming the Vraxar ship could travel as fast as anything in the Space Corps. The line intersected a number of solar systems and represented a huge area of space.

"If it continues on this predicted course it will never reach a Confederation Planet," he mused. "It will exit the Hyptron Sector and eventually pass by Ghast occupied space, again without intersecting one of their planets. Where the hell are they going?"

RL Breeze cleared his throat. "Well, sir, I've had some thoughts on that."

"I'm all ears."

"This is both good news and bad news. It's good because the Vraxar don't know where we are, but it's bad because they've been forced to send one of their most powerful vessels. I can't imagine they'd send what we assume is an exceptionally significant resource just to have it float around waiting to learn its final target location."

"We're working on the belief that the *ES Determinant* is their sole way of finding out where our planets are."

"Yes, sir. It may be they wish to transfer the Determinant's memory array from the Atlantis Neutraliser to *Ix-Gorghal*. It's probably not too much of a stretch to expect the Vraxar's main ship will have the processing clout to pull what it needs from the static array."

"If that was the case, we'd need to accept that the remains of the Determinant weren't destroyed at Cheops-A." He grimaced. "The cynic in me was never in doubt."

"The trajectory line passes through more than thirty solar systems, as well as vast areas of emptiness. They'd need to meet somewhere along there, with a solar system making a good point of reference for them if their navigational systems haven't plotted a full map of Confederation Space."

"So the question is, how do we predict the rendezvous point on this line?"

"When there are unknowns, you need to use whatever data-point is available to you, sir."

"The Determinant was taken from Atlantis twelve months ago, RL Breeze."

"It's all we have to work with."

"If we assume they left Atlantis without knowing their vector, they could intersect this line at any point." He thought for a moment. "Unless..."

"Unless we join a line between Atlantis and Cheops-A!" said Breeze, interrupting in his excitement.

Duggan spent a moment adding a connecting line on his display which joined Atlantis to Cheops-A. The line diverged from the predicted course of *Ix-Gorghal*. He changed it slightly, this time joining a line from the Vraxar departure point in the skies of Atlantis, to the place where Captain Blake had detonated the Inferno Sphere device.

"Almost a perfect match," he said. "Right in the middle of this solar system here."

"The chances of that are slim to say the least, sir!"

"I agree. Before we found the crashed Neutraliser on Vanistar, there was a gap of twelve months since we last saw a Vraxar spaceship. It's still a bit of a long shot to expect everything to drop into place."

"They may have taken the Determinant to this new solar system right after they left Atlantis, sir. It may be that *Ix-Gorghal* is going to a place where the Neutraliser has been waiting for a year, rather than the two ships being on a converging heading."

Duggan remembered a question which he hadn't yet been able to ask. "You mentioned having to play with different shapes and sizes of the Vraxar ship in order to predict its arrival trajectory."

"Yes, I did say that."

Duggan detected the reluctance at once. "How big did you have to go in order for your numbers to work?"

"That's the thing, sir. It's the one weakness in our conclusion."

"Tell me."

RL Breeze told him.

"What's the variation?" asked Duggan.

"If you go plus or minus three percent everything still sort of fits."

"I was hoping for a greater variance."

"So were we."

The last piece of information was like a punch to the stomach and Duggan felt queasy with the news. Only a couple of minutes ago he'd felt invigorated to have a new plan. It had been taken away from him by three words. *Fifty thousand metres.* It was bigger than the Vraxar spaceship which had carried off the *Juniper*. It was awful news, but he could only work with what he was given and until he had confirmation, he was going to hope Breeze's estimate was wildly wrong.

"Thank you very much for your work and that of your team, RL Breeze," said Duggan.

"It's what we're here for."

"Your grandfather would have been proud, Joel. You've got his love of solving problems."

Breeze sounded embarrassed. "Thank you, sir."

Duggan ended the comms channel, wondering if he was becoming too sentimental.

For the next few minutes, he looked at the two converging lines on the star chart and he found it hard to wrench his gaze away from the intersection point. It was surely too much to expect year-old data to show the location of the Vraxar. There again, the lines met perfectly and the chances of that were too small to measure.

"Cerys, please give me a list of assets within twenty-four hours of maximum lightspeed travel from the Dranmir system."

The answer wasn't long in coming and it was no surprise. "There is only a single ship within twenty-four hours of Dranmir. The Galactic class ES *Abyss* is currently seventeen hours from the sun."

"He's always there," said Duggan to himself. "Just like I was always there."

He knew this assessment wasn't quite correct. While Duggan had been actively chosen for the hard missions when he was a serving captain, it was pure chance which kept putting Blake in the thick of things. *I wonder if he's regretting his luck.* He laughed to himself. *I bet he loves it, the same way a part of me used to love it.*

"The ES *Abyss* is not at lightspeed. Would you like me to send a message to Captain Blake informing him of his new destination?" asked Cerys.

"Hold, please. I can't send him in alone. Do we have any other resources which may be a little further afield?"

"The next closest Space Corps vessel is a Crimson class destroyer which is escorting a prospector towards a potential new Gallenium-bearing moon. The ES *Jouster* is thirty-three hours away."

"I wanted a little more than a destroyer," said Duggan.

"What about the Ghasts? Do they have anything we can call upon?"

"The Ghasts have two significant warships within twenty-four hours of Dranmir."

Duggan checked the details. Under the terms of their alliance, the Ghasts were not only permitted in Confederation Space, but actively encouraged to patrol it. The Vraxar would need to fly through human territory in order to reach the Ghasts and both parties agreed this was the most appropriate way to try and counter the enemy threat.

"Get me a channel through to Subjos Kion-Tur," he said.

"I am attempting the connection."

It took fifteen minutes to get Kion-Tur into the comms channel and when he appeared, he was the same hulking figure of muscle and grey flesh, dressed in a blue uniform. The Ghast's face was surprisingly human and he didn't look happy.

"You look upset, Subjos Kion-Tur."

"I am not upset, Fleet Admiral." The Ghast laughed suddenly. "Perhaps a little upset."

It didn't take much to guess what the matter was. The Ghasts had committed to a military alliance expecting to face immediate and continuous action. They were a martial race and were more afraid of peace than they were of war.

"I might have something to cheer you up."

"The deaths of our enemies will cheer me up."

"Perhaps that is what I have for you. You have two warships stationed within our Hyptron sector."

Kion-Tur furrowed his brow in thought. "The Oblivion class *Sciontrar* and the Cadaveron class *Kalon-T7*."

"Are they Obsidiar equipped?"

"They are. What do you need them for?"

"We recently captured a live Vraxar from a crashed Neutraliser."

"Yes, you informed us of it."

"What we haven't yet informed you of is the possible presence of a Vraxar capital ship in Confederation Space."

Kion-Tur rubbed his hands together. "What do you know of its capabilities?"

"Absolutely nothing. We know its name – *Ix-Gorghal* – and we believe it to be in the region of fifty thousand metres long, with proportional volume."

"Fifty thousand?" said the Ghost. "That would be a deadly opponent."

"We believe it finished off the final Estral resistance."

"That was forty years ago! This *Ix-Gorghal* must be covered in rust and useful for nothing other than spare parts!"

The Ghost talked a good fight and Duggan didn't doubt his bravery. He also knew that Kion-Tur was fiercely intelligent and that his words were little more than blowing off steam.

"We think we have located it, Subjos, in the Dranmir solar system."

Kion-Tur nodded. "What spaceships of your own will you send?"

"We have only one – a Galactic class heavy cruiser."

"It will have to suffice. You have my approval for this venture, Fleet Admiral. Have your Cerys send the details to the *Sciontrar* and the *Kalon-T7*. Their commanding officers will be expecting to hear."

"Thank you."

"I would like to have those warships back if possible, Fleet Admiral. The *Sciontrar* is the pride of the Ghost navy. You will be impressed when you see what it can do."

"This isn't to be a suicide mission, Kion-Tur. I don't believe in them."

"But you are a man who always finds a path to victory. I can see it in your face and I have read it in our reports of your past engagements."

The Ghost had a good eye and Duggan couldn't deny the words. He'd lived through many situations where anyone else would have died. Perhaps he was so far along the probability curve he'd survived on luck rather than by application of skill. It made him different – he couldn't accept defeat and he carried an underlying certainty that winning was an option available to everyone. *Maybe it isn't,* he thought.

"We must find out what we are up against, Kion-Tur, and destroy it if possible."

"Three ships won't be enough if it is as big as you say."

"I know but having three will maximise the chance we gather useful intelligence. Or land a lucky strike and make the Vraxar run."

"I am not giving you an argument!" said the Ghost. "Our ships will rendezvous with your heavy cruiser and together we will see what there is to be seen."

With the agreement made, Duggan ended the connection. He had misgivings about the mission so he made direct contact with Captain Blake to pass on the orders. When it was done, he spent some time looking out of his window. It was gloomy and a steady drizzle shrouded the nearby buildings and trees.

"Cerys, what is the estimated completion time for Desolation and Falsehood?"

"Desolation will be prepared within nineteen days and Falsehood within seventeen. The other three are complete."

"I signed off ten more."

"Your orders have been received by the factory, Fleet Admiral. The construction will take time."

He nodded in response and continued staring outside.

CHAPTER SIXTEEN

ONE PART of Captain Charlie Blake – the part which was capable of childlike joy at the overcoming of minor obstacles – was ecstatic. Another, larger, part of Captain Charlie Blake was distinctly concerned.

On the one hand, he'd tracked down the source of the smell on the *Abyss*'s bridge to a malfunctioning replicator and put in place a temporary fix by shutting the machine off. On the other hand, he'd been given the details of his latest mission.

"Fifty thousand metres! How the hell are we expected to beat something like that?"

"I was listening to the same conversation as you were, sir, and there was no mention of beating anything," said Lieutenant Dixie Hawkins. "In fact, I distinctly recall hearing Fleet Admiral Duggan using the words *don't do anything rash*."

"And then he said *gather intel and get the hell out of there*," said Lieutenant Caz Pointer.

Blake stopped pacing and faced his crew. "You appear to have the impression that I'm some kind of gung-ho rookie," he said.

There was silence and Blake could see this was important to them. *They think I'm going to kill them in some insane hunt for glory,* he realised.

"We've been given another dangerous mission," he said. "Based on size alone this *Ix-Gorghal* sounds like it could destroy fifty ships without breaking a sweat and I'm not going to throw the ES *Abyss* at it. I take risks only where necessary."

"I think we were just getting used to the idea that the Vraxar might have something bigger than the last big one we faced," said Lieutenant Maria Cruz. "That other vessel – the one we thought was a mothership – was more than big enough and we had a super-stealth craft and an Obsidiar bomb. What do we have now? Missiles."

"We have a lot more than missiles, Lieutenant. Plus, the Ghasts are sending two of their newest vessels. I'm sure they have something up their sleeves."

"The *Sciontrar* is pushing six thousand metres long," said Lieutenant Jake Quinn. "It has an estimated displacement of thirty billion tonnes and could wipe out a dozen less advanced civilisations before lunch and without breaking a sweat. Since we don't know the precise dimensions of *Ix-Gorghal*, we can't estimate its displacement, but we can be sure the Ghasts' latest battleship is a minnow in comparison."

"Thank you, Lieutenant, now can we have less of the pessimism from everyone? We're going to find out what we can and then we're going to escape. Fleet Admiral Duggan believes there may be a Neutraliser at our destination, along with one or two smaller ships. My personal vision of outstanding success for this mission sees us locating *Ix-Gorghal* and destroying some of the accompanying vessels. I do not, I repeat *not*, want us to throw ourselves against what is certainly a vastly superior foe."

"It might not even be there," said Ensign Charlotte Bailey.

"Good luck believing that," said Pointer.

Blake had given them plenty of latitude to air their feelings and it was time to put an end to it. "Enough talk, it's time to get down to business. We've got a job to do and I don't want everyone to think the mission has failed before we begin."

The crew didn't push it.

"We'll rendezvous with the Ghosts in twenty minutes," said Quinn. "We'll tie up our navigational systems and be on our way. I assume you have a plan, sir?"

"We're going to play it more or less by the book. The Dranmir system has only four planets and six moons. We're going to enter local space sixteen million klicks from the most distant planet."

"Raxion."

"Yes, Raxion. From there, we're going to take it slow and steady, moving inwards until we've swept up to Dranmir itself."

"The Ghosts don't have stealth technology yet, sir," said Quinn. "At sixteen million klicks they should be safe from detection, but as we move in, they'll become increasingly vulnerable to a short-range transition attack from the Vraxar."

"In which case they'll have to SRT out of there. The three of us have the firepower to knock out a single Neutraliser as well as support ships. If this *Ix-Gorghal* decides to show its face, we only need to escape with the knowledge."

"I could set up a stream of our sensor data to the New Earth Central Command Station, sir?" said Cruz.

"Don't bother. The Vraxar will knock out our primary comms immediately they detect us and the backups are too slow and lack the bandwidth to do a stream."

"I didn't mean a full-resolution stream."

"Do what you think will work for us, Lieutenant Cruz."

"Who has command of this mission?" asked Hawkins.

It was an excellent question, though the answer was not quite so sparkling. "I command the *Abyss*, whilst Tarjos Nil-Tras of the battleship *Sciontrar* commands the Ghosts."

"Split command. Super."

"We have an alliance. The Ghosts aren't a vassal race and the trust will come in time." Blake thought for a moment, asking himself if he should say something else. "I've read a redacted version of Admiral Talley's report concerning his experiences with the Oblivion *Gallatrin-9*. He was exceptionally complimentary about the Ghosts' bravery and skill. He did, however, raise minor concerns about their headstrong approach to combat."

"It's what makes them such good allies, sir, and why they were so hard to beat in the Human-Ghost war," said Pointer.

"What makes you say that?"

"It's an opinion I've formed through my own research on the subject," she replied airily.

There was more to Caz Pointer than met the eye and Blake was starting to think he'd got her wrong from the outset. Perhaps it was his own failings which had made him think of her as an untrustworthy ladder-climber. Sometimes a reputation was unfairly won. *Bah!* he thought, without knowing why he did so.

A short while later, the *ES Abyss* entered local space in a part of the Hyptron Sector which was nowhere close to anything significant. Bad luck saw a couple of slow-moving rocks clatter off their hull before Quinn could activate the energy shield. The operational damage was insignificant, though it would take a few billion dollars' worth of spit and polish to get the hull looking pristine again.

Blake wasn't overly concerned about this tiny slice of bad luck. "Are our friends here, yet? They didn't have so far to travel."

Pointer and Cruz worked hard on the sensors. "We've got two vessels within half a million klicks of our current location, sir," said Pointer. "I'm bringing them up on the main screen."

The *Sciontrar* was every bit as impressive as Blake was expecting. It looked even longer than six thousand metres and its shape was far more hulking than sleek. In addition to its dozen particle beam domes, there was something else which Blake didn't recognize – there was a four-hundred-metre wide narrow oval slot at the front of the battleship with a maximum height of about fifty metres. It reminded him of a very early exhaust system, yet it was clearly nothing of the sort.

"We're being hailed," said Cruz. "I have Tarjos Nil-Tras of the *Sciontrar* waiting to speak with you."

Blake's eyes lingered on the screen for a moment longer. The Cadaveron heavy cruiser *Kalon-T7* looked like a smaller version of the battleship – advanced, mean and afraid of nothing.

"Bring him through."

The Ghost captain's voice was particularly harsh and the translation modules worked overtime to add a human touch to his words. Blake had no idea if cigars were commonly smoked by the Ghosts. Certainly, Nil-Tras sounded like he had a twenty-a-day habit.

"Captain Charles Blake."

Blake winced. "Tarjos Nil-Tras. The *Sciontrar* is an impressive warship."

The Ghost roared with laughter. "It will be a [translation uncertainty: *bastard*] for our enemies."

"I'm sure you're right. I assume you have been fully briefed on what we might find?"

"If it's a Neutraliser, we are going to destroy it and then I am going to take a shuttle to the wreckage so that I might piss on the pieces!"

"And if it's *Ix-Gorghal*?"

The Ghost's voice changed at once, betraying the intelligence required to command such an important warship. "If it's *Ix-Gorghal*, we will probe it for weaknesses and then we will leave it for our fleet to counter."

"We can work with that. Once the navigational tie-in is

complete we will head to Dranmir. I propose sixteen million klicks from the furthest planet."

"Agreed."

There was little more to discuss and Blake shut off the channel. A few minutes later, the three warships entered high lightspeed.

"We aren't running at 100% on the deep fission drives," said Quinn. "We're either a shade faster than them or they don't wish to show their available output. It'll be nine hours until we exit lightspeed."

"We might be faster than the *Kalon-T7*. I'm not so sure about the battleship," Blake replied.

"I got a couple of quick scans of their engine mass and efficiency," Quinn replied. "You're almost certainly correct."

"If we go by appearances alone, the Ghasts haven't been standing still when it comes to their spaceships, have they? Both of those make the *ES Abyss* look old and we're not long out of the yard."

"You can be sure our next generation is underway, sir," said Hawkins. "I hear we have almost a hundred spaceships in production."

"It's one hundred and twelve," Blake said. "And they're all bigger than destroyers and we have Obsidiar cores for each one."

"There you have it. I wager we'll be trialling a few new weapons systems amongst that lot."

"We are." Blake shrugged to show he wasn't able to divulge specifics. "They aren't up in the skies yet, whilst those two Ghast vessels are battle ready."

"It's a good thing they're our allies," said Cruz. "That Nil-Tras sounded like he was up for a fight."

"Any idea what that slot on the front of the *Sciontrar* is meant to deliver?" asked Blake.

"We have no record of it," said Pointer. "Do you remember those plasma incendiaries the Ghasts used against the Vraxar battleship at Cheops-A? I suspect the *Sciontrar* is equipped with an advanced version of the same weapon."

Blake nodded. "Could be. Perhaps we'll get to see what it can do."

The journey was only nine hours long, though the time didn't pass with sympathetic speed. The crew were allocated short sleep breaks, to ensure they were fully alert when they arrived into what was likely to be a hostile situation. Blake had never adapted to the little and often method of sleep and he napped fitfully. When he awoke, his tongue was dry and his mouth felt parched. He stumbled towards the mess hall in search of sustenance and company.

The main mess hall was fairly busy with groups of soldiers, laughing and joking amongst themselves in the carefree manner of those content to live for the day. Blake stood at one of the replicators and watched a man who was as broad as an ox lift a tray loaded with fried chicken and a single tomato.

"Replicator broke when you asked for a full salad?"

"Anything that comes from the ground goes straight through me, sir, but the doctor said I should keep trying to see if my body gets used to it."

Blake got himself an orange juice, a coffee and a grilled chicken sandwich. *I might be dead in a few hours,* he thought. *What the hell am I playing at?* Allowing this rebellious idea to control his fingers, he ordered three cheeseburgers and a piece of cake.

He looked around for someone to talk to and saw Caz Pointer, laughing and joking with a couple of the men. He felt a surge of something in his chest, the existence of which he unsuccessfully tried to deny. *Jealousy. It's jealousy, you idiot.*

He didn't know anyone else well enough to make conversation with and he had no intention of eating alone, so he made his way across.

"Mind if I sit?" he asked

"You don't need to ask," said Caz Pointer, nursing a coffee.

"Catch you around, Lieutenant," said one of the men. The pair of them rose.

"Stay," said Blake.

"Our time's up, sir."

The two left the room and Pointer twisted her head to follow their progress. Blake felt the twinge again.

"Six hours until we exit lightspeed," he said.

"Come on, sir, this is break time."

He blinked. "You're quite right. Work talk for the bridge only. Who are those guys?"

"You mean you don't know them all by name yet?"

She was teasing.

"I haven't had the chance," he replied.

"You don't really mix with the soldiers." This was closer to an accusation.

"There's no need to tread on the toes of their COs."

"I doubt they'd mind."

"You think it's a problem? My not mixing?"

"It's not my place to say."

"Since you've pretty much told me it's a problem, you can't deliver the message and then run away."

She laughed. "Fleet Admiral Duggan got the best out of his soldiers because they knew him. They fought for each other and they kept on winning."

"I didn't know you were such a history buff."

"What do you know about me, sir?"

"I..."

"I know what people say – spoilt girl, ambitious."

"I've heard those things."

"And?"

"I believed them. Not anymore."

"What do you believe now?"

"I couldn't want a better comms officer."

"That's it?"

"Isn't it enough?"

She finished her coffee. "My break is over. Got to get back to the bridge before the scheduling computer puts a demerit against my timekeeping."

"We should meet up sometime."

"Like a date, you mean?"

"Yes. Like date, once we're back on land."

"I'm not sure that would be appropriate, sir," she said. "And furthermore, cheeseburgers aren't good for you."

With that, she was gone, leaving Blake puzzled and faintly embarrassed. Relationships between Space Corps personnel were discouraged, but not forbidden, so it wasn't as if he'd broken the rules. It wasn't the first time he'd misjudged Caz Pointer and he guessed it wouldn't be the last.

He killed an hour by eating his food slowly and making sure he left not a single crumb from his cheeseburgers. Afterwards, he returned to the bridge feeling slightly lethargic from the quantity of food he'd consumed. He was relieved to find the only coldness on the bridge was from the air conditioning, rather than from his comms lieutenant. He dropped into his seat.

"Anything to report?"

"No, sir," said Hawkins. "There have been no alerts while you were away."

"Good."

With nothing better to do, Blake found himself poking around in the history archives. He knew the basics – it was taught in every school and expanded upon during officer training. When it came to some of the details, his knowledge was lacking and soon he found himself engrossed. It therefore came as a surprise when Lieutenant Quinn announced there were ten minutes until arrival in the Dranmir system.

CHAPTER SEVENTEEN

"TELL ME WHAT WE'VE GOT," said Blake, the second he felt the shuddering transition from lightspeed.

"The *Sciontrar* and *Kalon-T7* arrived at the precise moment we did, sir," said Pointer.

"I've activated our energy shield and stealth modules," said Quinn.

A series of gauges on Blake's console swung around crazily before the Obsidiar core stabilised and everything settled.

"There are no hostile forces in the immediate vicinity," said Cruz. "Commencing far scan."

"I'm bringing planet Raxion onto the main screen," said Pointer. "Not that there's anything to see."

She was right – Raxion was the same kind of medium-sized ice-clad ball that appeared in practically every single solar system Blake had ever visited. It had a lone, equally cold, moon which travelled an exceptionally slow orbit of its parent.

"The two Ghost vessels have activated their energy shields as well, sir. I'd say they're packing a lot of Obsidiar from the power readings. And the *Sciontrar* has just this moment activated its own stealth modules."

"What?" asked Blake in shock.

"It was inevitable they'd crack it eventually."

"This is really important, Lieutenant. It was humanity's biggest advantage."

"Not anymore."

"Lieutenant Cruz, let command and control know the good news."

"It *is* good news," said Pointer hotly. "We should be sharing this technology with our allies anyway! The only important thing is that the Vraxar don't have stealth modules."

"In principle I agree. Now is not the time to talk about it."

With the three warships prepared for combat, they spread out into a line with ten thousand kilometres between each vessel. The journey to Raxion would take two hours if they remained on gravity engines only. It was time Blake was willing to invest to ensure they didn't encounter any nasty surprises.

"Load up cores #7 and #8 for short range transits," he said. "Inform me at once if they look like burning out."

"Done."

The far scans came back clear on both human and Ghast spaceships. It wasn't unexpected.

"The super-fars are going to take longer than usual with cores seven and eight loaded," said Pointer.

"I'm sure that Oblivion has a hundred cores working on it," said Quinn.

There was a lot of area to cover – Blake wasn't specifically interested in Raxion and he wanted as much of the solar system checked as possible, all the way to Dranmir and the two planets currently on the far side of the sun. The sensors took snapshots and the ship's cores pulled apart the data, searching for anything which wasn't vacuum. It was time consuming and a good comms officer could speed up the task significantly by directing the processing cores to focus on certain areas before others.

The *Sciontrar* reported first.

"The Ghasts have completed their first super-far scan," said Cruz. "They have not detected anything."

Blake drummed his fingers. "Tondar is completely out of sight around the sun and we're blind when it comes to what's behind Raxion, Mavlon and Pels. What about our own scan?"

"Just finishing now, sir," said Pointer. "We've got the same result as the Ghasts."

"The *Kalon-T7*'s comms team concur," added Cruz.

"Let's commence the search," said Blake. "Lieutenant Cruz, please calculate an efficient course which will allow us to fill in the blanks. When you've finished your workings, send the details to the Ghasts."

Cruz was fast. "That's finished and the Ghasts have accepted our recommendation."

The three ships travelled onwards. From a distance, their journey appeared serene and effortless. In reality, it took huge gravity engines to keep them going at speeds in excess of two thousand kilometres per second.

"The *Sciontrar* is holding back," said Quinn. "I'm sure of it."

"What do you think they've got?"

"Two-and-a-half thousand klicks per second. Possibly more."

"We can't be envious, Lieutenant."

"I'm not – I'm speaking as an interested observer."

The three warships came ever closer to Raxion and remained in formation. Sticking together was going to slow the hunt, but it was infinitely better than being picked off one-by-one.

Is it a hunt? wondered Blake. *Or are we deer in the tall grass walking into the rifle's sights?*

It only required two orbits of Raxion and its moon until a consensus was reached – the Vraxar were elsewhere.

"It's a big jump to Mavlon," said Pointer. "Four hundred million klicks."

"That's more than two days on gravity engines," said Quinn.

"Something makes me think the Ghosts lack the patience for such a long journey," said Blake. "We'll make the jump."

The Ghosts didn't give an argument. The three vessels entered a short lightspeed jump, emerging sixteen million kilometres from Mavlon. There was a considerable amount of debris in the area they arrived and the ES *Abyss*'s energy shield deflected several uneven lumps of rock. In other circumstances, Blake would have used missiles to clear a path, or simply divert elsewhere. With the presence of hostiles likely, he didn't wish to draw attention.

"Sorry, sir, I missed those," said Pointer.

"No matter. They not going to bring our shield down. Keep your eyes on the planet and the area around."

"With a few changes, Mavlon could support life," said Cruz. "Maybe in a few million years there'll be amoebae."

"Something to look forward to," laughed Hawkins.

"It's bigger than anything in the Confederation," said Quinn. "Room enough for a hundred billion."

"History is beginning to teach that we should spread ourselves far and wide," said Blake. "The more of us there are in one place, the more vulnerable we become."

Mavlon had two moons and it took several frustrating circuits before the comms teams were able to say for certain there was nothing to be found.

"The more uneven the surface, the longer it takes," Pointer explained. "Mavlon has lots of mountains and it's heavily pitted, presumably from these stupid asteroids which keep hitting our shield."

"Pels and Tondar are way beyond Dranmir," said Blake.

"Each time we do a fission jump there's a chance we'll be seen and I'd far rather stay hidden for now."

"I think I've located something," said Cruz. "I'm not sure if it's Vraxar."

"Show me."

"There's a fluctuation of some kind running across Dranmir's corona. I thought it was natural for a moment, but it's actually moving in a dead straight line."

Cruz used the data to generate a graphic to show what she'd found. Blake watched what appeared to be a tiny V-shaped ripple moving above the corona. It travelled with unhurried interest, like a shark on the lookout for prey.

"Is that what I think it is?"

"I think that's the effect of a Neutraliser's suppression field," she said. "I estimate they're at an altitude of about sixty million klicks – hot enough to warm their toes but not enough to burn up."

"That's twice we've caught them skimming over a sun. It's enough to be interesting, if not yet enough to call it their method."

"I'm more astounded they've had an observable effect on a body as large as a star," said Quinn. "Even if it is only a tiny, tiny fraction of the whole."

"We still don't know what material they use in those Neutralisers. The Space Corps' scientists assume it's a type of Obsidiar but they have no idea how to replicate the effect," said Blake. "Therefore, we only have guesses about what they can do with it."

"Want me to transmit our findings to the Ghasts?" asked Cruz.

"Yes, with a strong recommendation we wait before taking action."

"The Ghasts acknowledge and they are holding position."

"I want to know if it's just a Neutraliser we're seeing, or if it's got an escort."

"It's going to be difficult to get you a definite answer, sir. It's easier for our sensors to pick up the suppression effect on the corona than it is for them to see what's causing it."

"I don't want to get any closer until I have a better idea what we're facing. If it's a lone Neutraliser, we're going to blow the crap out of it. If it's in formation with a dozen battleships we're going to watch them for a while and then say goodbye to the Dranmir system."

It wasn't an easy job for the human or Ghast sensors. They observed the Neutraliser across a great distance, trying to piece together snippets of data into something resembling certainty.

"There's a single Neutraliser, along with two of their light cruisers that we fought above Atlantis," concluded Pointer.

"There's a fourth spaceship as well," said Cruz. "It's bulky and approximately four thousand metres in length, of a type unknown."

"It's the only one not flying in formation," said Pointer.

Blake frowned. "Explain."

"The other Vraxar ships are maintaining an exact formation. This fourth one is behind and to one side. It's gradually falling back from the others."

"Can we destroy it separately?"

"Not yet. It will be an option in the near future if it remains on its divergent course."

There wasn't much information on this unknown fourth vessel, other than its dimensions. It was too far away to determine its offensive capabilities, if any.

"On proportions alone, it's like a much smaller version of the main Vraxar ship which took the *Juniper*."

"Fleet Admiral Duggan said he expected the Vraxar to transfer the Determinant's memory arrays onto *Ix-Gorghal*, didn't he?" said Hawkins. "Maybe that's a carrier of some kind with the wreckage loaded into its hold."

"Just waiting for us to drop in and destroy it," said Blake, rubbing his chin in thought.

He was momentarily lost for what to do. Faced with an opposing fleet of spacecraft it was best to focus fire on the greatest threat, that being the Neutraliser. Afterwards, the mopping up could begin. In this situation, Blake was very interested in the fourth Vraxar vessel – if it was indeed carrying the *ES Determinant*, that made it the primary target. He didn't want to pick the wrong opponent and have the other Vraxar vanish into lightspeed, whereupon they might be lost until they chose to show their faces again.

"The Ghasts are becoming impatient, sir," said Cruz. "I think they want to get in there and start shooting."

"Hold them off," said Blake. "It's important we pick the best target."

Blake was shortly given a reminder that he wasn't in overall charge of the mission.

"Tarjos Nil-Tras wants to speak, sir."

"Bring him in."

The Ghast didn't mince words.

"Captain Charles Blake, why are we sitting out here [translation ambiguous: *scratching our behinds*] while the enemy continue unmolested on their course?"

"I believe the fourth Vraxar spaceship may be carrying the remains of the Space Corps vessel *ES Determinant*. If we destroy it, there is a chance the Vraxar will no longer be able to locate our planets."

"What evidence do you have for this?"

Blake didn't enjoy lying. "No direct evidence."

"Then we destroy the Neutraliser."

"What if I'm right?"

"Then you cannot berate yourself for choosing incorrectly between two guesses."

"The Neutraliser, then."

"Yes, Captain Blake. We will exit lightspeed right on top of it and punch a way through its energy shield. When it is destroyed, we will finish off the little ones."

"Those little ones can fight."

"Against the *Sciontrar* they are nothing."

There was no sign of boasting in the Ghast's words, only total confidence in the capabilities of his battleship.

"Very well. I would like the fourth vessel to be the secondary target."

"Agreed. Once we defeat the Neutraliser, we will concentrate our efforts on this fourth vessel."

The channel went dead.

"Please coordinate with the Ghast ships," said Blake.

"Our comms are going to get a bit flaky once we get close to Dranmir," said Cruz.

"They'll disable the primary comms anyway. What about the backups?"

"It's the backups I was talking about."

"Fine, we'll send a message to New Earth Central Command before we commence engagement."

The preparations didn't take long – the *Abyss* was a battle-ready warship and the crew were well trained, if lacking in extensive experience. With a rumble of overlapping fission clouds the three ships hurtled into lightspeed, aiming directly for the Neutraliser.

CHAPTER EIGHTEEN

AT HIGH LIGHTSPEED, it took less than a single second for the ES *Abyss* to leave Mavlon orbit and cross the distance towards the sun Dranmir. The moment the heavy cruiser re-entered local space, the crew began shouting out their status updates for Blake to unravel and act upon. The information came thick and fast.

"Enemy Neutraliser visible to sensor sight – twenty thousand klicks," said Pointer.

"Our energy shield is online. The stealth modules don't like the interference," said Quinn. "Our Gallenium power is shutting down. We'll be on the Obsidiar backup core within five seconds."

"The *Sciontrar* and *Kalon-T7* are in their expected positions," said Cruz. "I'm coordinating with their comms teams."

"Fire overcharged front particle beam," said Blake. "Give them a full salvo from our Lambdas, Shatterers and Shimmers. Launch eight nukes with proximity detection and fire standard particle beams at will."

"Front particle beam has discharged," said Hawkins. "I'm reading a minor attenuation from the sun's corona. Missiles launched. Our particle beam strike hit them dead centre, straight through their energy shield."

"The view is on the bulkhead screen," said Cruz. "They're burning bright."

Blake sat in his chair and switched his attention between the bulkhead view of the Neutraliser and his tactical screen. The overcharged particle beam had heated a large section of the enemy vessel's central structure, turning the black metal into mixed oranges and whites. Against the background of Dranmir, the colossal Vraxar ship appeared tiny and insignificant.

Meanwhile, the tactical display showed eight hundred green specks, fired from the *Abyss* and converging on the Neutraliser. The Space Corps had spent the last year working to overcome the targeting problems their missiles experienced when they were fired at Vraxar spaceships. The improvements were mostly software and this was the first time they were being live tested. Appearances were hopeful in that the missiles had actually fired, instead of remaining in their tubes.

"The *Sciontrar* has fired missiles, as well as six particle beams," said Hawkins. "The *Kalon-T7* has also unloaded. Looks like we caught the Neutraliser by surprise."

"There's a power build up from the *Sciontrar*," said Quinn. "Something's going to happen. The *Kalon-T7* is charging up as well."

A sphere of energy thumped away from the Neutraliser, expanding for thousands of kilometres. It engulfed three thousand inbound missiles, wrecking their targeting systems and rendering them useless.

"There go their countermeasures. Shatterers and Shimmers got through. So did the nukes."

The Neutraliser's shield was struck by nearly fifty high-yield plasma warheads. Such was the combined ferocity, it was momentarily lost from sight on the viewscreen and Blake squinted at the brightness.

"The two Vraxar light cruisers are moving to intercept," said Cruz. "Looks like we're the target."

"What about the fourth spaceship?"

"It has dropped back and is lost from sight."

"Lost from sight or *temporarily* lost from sight?"

"I can't give you an answer, sir."

"Here come the nukes," said Hawkins. "Six gigatons of fun and games."

The nuclear warheads – back in service at Fleet Admiral Duggan's insistence – were mounted on the slowest, largest and most robust propulsion sections. They sailed through the Vraxar countermeasures and detonated when they came within a few hundred kilometres of the enemy shields. Without a supply of oxygen, there was no extensive explosion, however they weren't employed for the power of their blast. The detonations produced an intense sphere of gamma radiation, with a radius of several thousand kilometres. The technology which generated the energy shields was susceptible to the radiation from these crudest of weapons and nuclear warheads had been employed successfully in the brief war against the Estral.

"Got them!"

"Is their shield down?"

"Not sure," said Quinn. "There's a fluctuation from their front nullification sphere."

"They're breaking away from the blast zone," said Pointer.

Blake grabbed the control bars and turned the *ES Abyss* onto a parallel course, five thousand kilometres away. "Let's stay close so they have less chance to knock out our missiles. Keep firing everything we've got."

"We've got an angle for the rear overcharge. Firing. Direct hit."

"Their shields have stabilised."

The combat progressed rapidly. Particle beams leapt between the spaceships, projected from their generators and crossing thousands of kilometres instantly. The Vraxar used their dark energy beams as well and these proved more effective at draining the power reserves of an energy shield.

"The Neutraliser has decided we're a good target as well, sir," said Hawkins. "We've taken six beam hits already."

The Obsidiar power bar dropped in erratic chunks with each strike of the Vraxar weapons. Missiles spilled from the *Sciontrar* and *Kalon-T7* in staggered waves and Blake ordered Hawkins to copy the technique. The Vraxar could only use their countermeasures every few seconds and he hoped this method would flood their anti-missile system.

"Why did I forget what tough bastards these Neutralisers are?" Blake said bitterly.

"The *Sciontrar* requests that we increase our distance from the enemy," said Pointer. "Immediately."

Blake didn't hesitate and pulled the warship away, whilst maintaining the same speed as the Neutraliser. When the *Abyss* was eight thousand kilometres from the Vraxar ship, the Ghasts fired.

"What the hell?" said Hawkins.

A thick beam of blue light jumped from the front port on the *Sciontrar* and connected with the Neutraliser's shield. A split second later, a similar, smaller beam sprang from the *Kalon-T7*. These beams remained in existence for less than a second, but where they landed on the Vraxar's energy shield, they erupted into a torrent of blue-white plasma flames. These flames spread rapidly outwards from the two impact points, until the Neutraliser was completely encased. It remained on course, leaving a fading trail of plasma behind.

"Their energy shield is failing, sir!" shouted Quinn in excitement.

"So is ours," Blake replied, with one eye on the ES *Abyss*'s rapidly-depleting Obsidiar power reserves.

"Firing the front overcharge," said Hawkins. "Their countermeasures have disabled two of our missile waves. Launching more."

"The Ghasts are taking damage!" said Ensign Bailey.

"How? They've hardly taken a hit on their shields," said Blake.

"Whatever they just fired, it's either drained everything they've got or it's interfered with their shields," said Quinn.

"We'd best finish the job soon, Lieutenant."

The Ghast weapon took out the Neutraliser's shield. The next two waves of missiles plunged into the enemy's hull, illuminating its eighteen thousand metre length with fire.

"Break up, you bastard," said Hawkins.

Two of the *Abyss*'s Shimmer missiles exploded against the central section of the Vraxar ship, visible amongst the chaos. The flames faded in places, allowing the crew to see the extensive damage inflicted upon the enemy spaceship. Still it continued firing and its particle beams flickered through the flames like the sharp, deadly point of a rapier.

Another salvo of missiles struck the Neutraliser in near-unison, along with the rear overcharge from the ES *Abyss*. Finally, the Neutraliser began to break up. The front connecting strut separated completely from the central section and it began spiralling wildly as if it was generating thrust from one end only. The attached nullification sphere sparked violently, throwing green bolts of energy far into space.

"Is it going to explode?" asked Blake.

"It's unstable..." said Quinn.

"Do we need to transit out? Lieutenant, I need an answer."

Blake hadn't finished speaking when the next wave of missiles crashed into both sections of the Neutraliser, along with six particle beam strikes in quick succession.

"No, sir. It's shutting down. Both parts will burn up in Dranmir's corona at some point in the next sixty minutes."

The Neutraliser was out of the fight, but the two Vraxar cruisers showed no signs of giving up. Pointer switched the main bulkhead view to show the closest one – it was the same tapered cylinder of black metal that Blake remembered from his encounter near Atlantis. The enemy ships jumped across space, each leap taking them a few thousand kilometres from their previous position. They were also aware of the capabilities of an overcharged particle beam and they wheeled and spun, never quite coming within range and with each passing second, they whittled away the heavy cruiser's shield. Finally, two of the Vraxar disintegration beams completely depleted the *Abyss*'s Obsidiar core.

"That's knocked out our shield," said Quinn. "We're out of power and coasting towards Dranmir."

A particle beam hit the *Abyss* on the nose and a second struck it nearby. The hull plating smouldered and glowed, but this was exactly the sort of weapon the heavy cruiser was designed to soak and the damage was minimal. Blake's console was alive with warnings from the various onboard systems affected by the attack. Elsewhere on his console, the tactical screen was acting up. Objects it was tracking vanished from existence as the sensors lacked the power to track them accurately and with any sort of definition.

"The Neutraliser's gone, where are our Gallenium engines?" Blake asked.

"Coming online, sir. Slowly."

"Speed them up, Lieutenant. We can't even do a transit out of here and I do not want to die in the fires of a star."

"They'll be ready within the minute."

"Is there enough power to target and launch ballistic weapons?"

"No, sir, we've got nothing. The life support will shut off in seconds."

It was a worrying few moments. In his mind, Blake told himself there was no need for concern – with the Neutraliser's suppression aura gone, the Gallenium engines would kick in soon and begin powering the rest of the warship again. In reality, those seconds passed slowly, whilst the pursuing Vraxar ships raked the heavy cruiser with particle beams.

"Here we go," said Quinn. "The engines are straight up to sixty percent. Now eighty."

The *Abyss* responded reluctantly to the controls at first. Then, the power climbed further and it regained some of the agility Blake was accustomed to.

"Find me those Vraxar and destroy them!" he shouted.

For once, there was some good news.

"There's only one enemy cruiser in the vicinity," said Pointer. "The other must have gone to lightspeed. No...wait...the Ghasts have destroyed it."

"Where's the other one?"

"Here."

The second Vraxar cruiser came onto the screen. It doggedly pursued the *ES Abyss*, its armour a ragged mess of missile craters and thousands of dents from the *Sciontrar*'s Vule cannons. Greasy smoke poured away from its hull and it was a miracle it was still functioning.

"It's got no shields left," said Quinn.

"Why haven't they gone to lightspeed?" asked Cruz in wonder.

"To give us one last chance to destroy them," said Blake. "Where are our weapons?"

"On it," said Hawkins. "They're just warming up. Firing Lambdas."

The motivations of the Vraxar were an enigma to Blake. There was no reason for them to continue this battle, yet here they were, plugging away without hope of a kill, let alone ensuring an overall victory, and at the same time ensuring their own destruction.

A swarm of missiles fired from the ES *Abyss* as well as the two Ghost warships, converged upon the smaller Vraxar cruiser. It was already badly damaged and there was no way it could survive against the hundreds of missiles which thundered into its hull. The resulting explosions ripped it into many pieces, many of which melted or were turned into flaming comets which dropped towards Dranmir.

There wasn't time for Blake to congratulate his crew, nor to ask where the fourth Vraxar ship was, before he received a comms request.

"I've got Tarjos Nil-Tras, sir," said Cruz.

Blake nodded to indicate he was ready.

"What do you think of that, Captain Blake?" said the Ghost. "A victory against our common enemy!"

"We only got three out of four, Tarjos – have you managed to keep track of the fourth vessel?"

"Our battle took us away from it. Perhaps it escaped into lightspeed."

"We didn't detect a fission signature," said Blake, unable to hide his disappointment. "The battle isn't over until they are all dead."

"Yes – we will seek this fourth Vraxar warship and send it to the same place as its fellows."

"My comms team are searching." He turned to face Pointer and Cruz for confirmation. They each nodded to indicate they were indeed looking for the missing Vraxar spaceship.

"Ours also. We should increase our distance from Dranmir. It is interfering with our comms and our sensors."

"I would prefer to stay at this altitude, since it is where we saw them last."

"Very well, we will search amongst the interference. I must warn you it will take some time for our shields to recharge."

The Ghost's words reminded Blake of the weapon he'd witnessed them use against the Neutraliser. "What did you fire against the enemy?"

"It is a recent addition to a select few warships in our fleet," said Nil-Tras. "It is an incendiary designed specifically to burn away an energy shield. I am giving you no secret when I tell you it has an extensive charge time and it also sucks an immense amount of power from our Obsidiar cores."

"Why don't your engines shut down?" asked Blake. "When our Obsidiar runs dry, we lose everything."

The Ghost sounded puzzled. "You don't equip your ships with two Obsidiar cores?"

The Ghosts were allies, yet Blake felt like he needed to paper over this obvious deficiency in the Space Corps fleet by giving a partial response. "This heavy cruiser has only one."

Nil-Tras didn't laugh, nor did he sound triumphant. "It is a failing in your design and one which you must overcome quickly."

"It would be a useful update," Blake admitted. "Have your comms teams had luck finding the fourth spaceship while we have been talking?"

"Not as yet. We have some predictions based on its last known trajectory. I will have them sent across to your ship. The enemy has definitely not overtaken us, so I suggest we double-back and begin the search. There is a large area to cover."

It was a great understatement. Dranmir wasn't especially large as far as suns went – compared to Cheops-A it was tiny.

Nevertheless, every second of every day for billions of years it had generated more power than any living species could even dream about. Searching for a single object in orbit was a potentially monumental task.

In this case, Blake knew they had something to go on. They had a sighting of their target, along with a possible vector. It limited the search area, without giving him either confidence or scepticism about the final outcome.

"The *Sciontrar* has provided details of the course they believe we should follow," said Cruz.

"How does it look?"

"It looks good."

"Very well, send it to my console."

The navigational system populated with the new details. It showed a yellow graphic representing Dranmir, overlaid with a line to indicate the most efficient course as plotted by the *Sciontrar*'s computers. There was other information such as places where the sun's corona reached higher temperatures, as well as possible other trajectories to explore. So far, the Ghasts were proving to be worthwhile companions on the mission and Blake made a mental note that he would carry this message back to his superiors.

"Have you provided an update to New Earth Central Command?" he asked.

"Yes, sir," said Pointer. "You're aware we're on the backups, so the news is going to take while to reach them. They can't contact us quickly either."

The three warships adopted the same formation as previously, which was a line with the *Sciontrar* central and the others ten thousand kilometres away from its flanks. The Oblivion battleship and the Space Corps heavy cruiser activated their stealth modules.

"Perhaps the *Kalon-T7* should drop back," said Blake. "I'd

prefer to surprise the enemy and that won't happen with the Cadaveron flying in full sight."

"Should I pass on your recommendation to Tarjos Nil-Tras?" asked Pointer.

"Please do. If the *Kalon-T7* keeps us in sensor sight, they will be able to do a short lightspeed transit to catch up if necessary."

The Ghosts were either remarkably amenable, or they possessed Blake's combat sense.

"The *Kalon-T7* will drop back and follow at a distance of half a million klicks."

"That should be enough."

With the arrangements in place the hunt resumed, though Blake wasn't able to shake off a sense of apprehension which persisted even after the victory over the Neutraliser.

CHAPTER NINETEEN

"THE GHASTS THINK the missing spaceship went lower towards Dranmir," said Blake, studying the projections sent over from the *Sciontrar*.

"That tallies with our findings," said Pointer.

"I'm worried," said Blake. "I know the Vraxar don't follow human logic, but this situation seems more unusual than normal."

"In what way?" asked Hawkins.

"I don't know," he admitted. "Is there any chance the final ship could have failed to spot our destruction of the other three?"

"Maybe," said Pointer. "At the start of the engagement it was a long distance back and our own sensors aren't working too well this close to Dranmir."

"They would have received a comms signal, surely?" said Cruz. "It's not like we blew up the Neutraliser in half a second. They had plenty of time to speak to each other."

"I agree," said Blake. "The fact that this fourth ship didn't come to assist suggests to me that it's not intended for combat, which is why it hasn't shown up yet. Lieutenant Hawkins, you mentioned the possibility it has the *ES Determinant* in its hold."

"It's one potential way of carrying a wrecked destroyer from one ship to another. If this *Ix-Gorghal* is fifty thousand metres long, it could likely fit a Neutraliser in its hold anyway, if it was designed to do so."

"We're speculating," said Blake. "I'm trying to gain some insight into why the fourth ship didn't join in the fight."

"It seems obvious enough to me," said Quinn. "If it was heading away from the Neutraliser, it was in the process of going somewhere else. If it was a non-combat ship, it was likely carrying something."

"With only one destination for it to carry this *something*," said Blake.

"There it is!" said Pointer. "Two hundred thousand klicks in front and half a million klicks closer towards Dranmir. From its shape, it's definitely a cargo vessel rather than a warship."

The Vraxar ship appeared on Blake's tactical display. The image wasn't perfect, but it was sufficient for him to make out the vessel's outline and enough for him to agree with Pointer's assessment that it wasn't intended to take a significant part in hostilities. One feature stood out more than any other. "It's stationary," he said.

"A sitting duck," said Hawkins.

"I don't like it."

"We're running cloaked, so they don't know we're here."

"There's nothing else on the scans, sir."

"Look again. You keep telling me there's a lot of interference, I don't want you to miss something important. Check with the Ghasts – this could be a rendezvous point and we may have a huge Vraxar warship inbound."

"The Ghasts are raring to go, sir. They see nothing untoward."

Even so, Blake was gripped by a deep unease. "This feels

wrong," he said. "If Dranmir is a Vraxar rendezvous point, why didn't the four ships simply stick together?"

"They didn't know we were here, nor had any reason to expect us come," said Hawkins.

"What if they detected us at the same time as we found them?"

"A remote chance," said Pointer.

"A chance nonetheless. And since the *Abyss* and the *Sciontrar* were running with their stealth modules, the Vraxar would have seen only the *Kalon-T7*."

"And the *Kalon-T7* would not have attacked a Neutraliser alone, but it might have attacked a lone ship," said Quinn.

"Which makes the vessel sitting out there..." continued Hawkins.

"Bait," said Blake. "That spaceship there is a juicy piece of bait."

Hawkins went through it again, as if trying to slot everything into place in her mind. "So they didn't realise we had three ships and they separated in the hope of luring us into combat, which has come back to bite them because we attacked elsewhere and they lost a Neutraliser."

"While the fourth ship is still here, waiting to see what we'll do," said Blake. "Their plan is blown, yet they don't know how to adapt."

"There's nothing at all on the scans, sir," Cruz said again. Her face was screwed up in concentration and her hands never stopped moving over her console.

"I recommend we approach with extreme caution," said Hawkins. "On second thoughts, I recommend we get the hell out of here."

"We can't, Lieutenant. We were sent to find information about a Vraxar capital ship and so far, we only have guesswork and supposition."

"If it's a trap, it seems unwise for us to stroll into it."

Blake made up his mind. "Message the Ghasts. Tell them we believe this is a trap and that we are going to commence bombardment of the enemy ship from a distance."

"Tarjos Nil-Tras responds with his agreement. If the enemy ship powers up its deep fission drive he says the *Sciontrar* and *Kalon-T7* will activate an SRT and will destroy the Vraxar from close range."

"Fine. Ask him how his energy shield is recharging."

"They're at fifty percent."

"About the same as us. We will commence firing in twenty seconds."

"Tarjos Nil-Tras acknowledges."

Blake gave out his last-minute instructions. "Hold cores #7 and #8 in case we need a short-range transit. Fire our Lambdas in staggered waves of two hundred, along with Shatterer and Shimmer full launches on the first wave."

"Nukes, sir?"

"They're too slow from this range."

"Ready whenever you are."

"Fire."

The *ES Abyss* unleashed a barrage of missiles from tubes positioned beneath armoured hatches in its hull. The Shimmers were the fastest and they flew ahead of the others.

"Two minutes until Shimmer impact," said Hawkins. "Another fifteen seconds for the Shatterers and fifteen more on top of that for the Lambdas."

The *Sciontrar* was rather less subtle and it fired more than a thousand missiles in a tightly-packed cluster.

"If they all hit, there's surely enough to take out a cargo ship's energy shield," said Blake.

"Firing second wave," said Hawkins.

"Keep watching for inbound fission signatures, Lieutenant Quinn."

"I am, sir."

"And make sure they aren't preparing to go to lightspeed."

"I am, sir."

There was a tiniest hitch in Quinn's voice when he said these last words and it was enough to make Blake turn. "What is it?"

"The Vraxar ship isn't preparing for lightspeed. The readings from its hull don't look right, though."

"Tell me what you mean."

"It's like there's something muffling its output."

"Is Dranmir causing it?"

"No, sir. The output from the sun is distinct."

"Do I need to be concerned? Ignore that question – I *am* concerned."

"It's as if I'm reading the hull output from the enemy vessel through a filter."

Blake's heart gave a single, heavy thump against the inside of his ribcage. "Like there's something in the way?"

"I'm not sure," said Quinn. Then, "Yes, there's something in the way."

"The sensors are clean," said Pointer, shaking her head in slowly-dawning realisation that her readings might be wrong.

"I don't care. Alert the Ghasts and tell them an unknown vessel is between us and that cargo ship!"

"Should I activate an SRT?" asked Quinn.

Blake was momentarily unsure what to do for the best. If they exited the Dranmir system now, they would have learned nothing at all about *Ix-Gorghal*, assuming that was what awaited them. On the other hand, it didn't seem likely the Vraxar would go to the trouble of setting a trap without having a way of destroying anything which stumbled into it.

In spite of his apparent reputation as a risk-taker, Blake cared deeply about his ship and his crew.

"Advise the Ghasts we're leaving. If they agree, activate the SRT," he ordered.

"I'm speaking to them now," said Cruz.

"Our Shimmer missiles have detonated early," said Hawkins. "Whatever it is they've hit, it's not that cargo carrier."

"I got a reading at the time of impact," said Quinn. "There was a surge of power about five thousand klicks in front of the Vraxar ship."

"What sort of reading?" asked Blake urgently.

"An energy shield, sir. It is my belief there is a cloaked ship between us and the cargo carrier."

"The Ghasts do not want to leave," said Cruz.

"In that case, tell them *Ix-Gorghal* is here and to prepare for an engagement."

"Two waves of Shatterers have exploded against the unknown vessel," said Hawkins.

Blake took the controls of the *ES Abyss* and hauled the ship onto a new heading. The stealth modules were still active, but launching missiles gave the enemy a head start when it came to pinpointing the heavy cruiser's location.

"The Ghasts are splitting off to our right," said Pointer.

Hawkins had her face glued to the weapons console. "Twelve hundred conventional missiles have exploded near to the visible ship. They have not made contact."

"Look!" said Cruz.

The forward sensor feed showed the extensive combined blast from twelve hundred plasma warheads. Roiling flame smeared thousands of metres in all directions. Blake immediately saw the problem – given the size of the blast, he'd expect to see the shape of a sphere defined by the plasma spill. There was no visible curve, like the missiles had struck a vertical wall that reached a huge distance upwards.

"Oh shit," said Quinn.

The man didn't swear often and it was concerning when he did.

"Speak up!" demanded Blake.

"There's been a surge of *something* coming from near to the Vraxar cargo ship. Whatever it is, it took a big step towards us."

"We have to leave," said Hawkins.

The Ghast captain, having previously thought otherwise, had evidently changed his mind. "Tarjos Nil-Tras recommends immediate withdrawal," said Cruz.

"Activate the SRT!" said Blake. "Take us anywhere."

"Activating. The Ghasts are doing likewise."

Blake unconsciously shifted his stance in preparation for the shift into lightspeed. The expected transition didn't happen.

"What's the matter?"

"The core must have burned out," said Quinn, his voice higher-pitched with the stress.

"Cores #7 and #8 are fully functional," said Ensign Bailey.

"Something must be wrong! Activating core #8."

Core #8 also failed to send the *ES Abyss* to lightspeed. Quinn thumped his seat in frustration.

"What's wrong? And where is the *Sciontrar*?" asked Blake.

"The Ghasts are eighteen thousand klicks to starboard, sir."

Without warning, the *Abyss*'s forward movement dropped to zero. There was no period of deceleration, the warship simply stopped. The life support systems were designed to cope with near-instant acceleration to lightspeed and their support field prevented all biological matter on the heavy cruiser being reduced to a microscopically-thin layer of sludge across the bulkhead walls.

"We're being held," said Quinn.

"By what?"

"I have no idea, sir."

Blake cast his eyes frantically across his console – the Gallenium engines were offering 99.99% of their theoretical maximum output and the Obsidiar core was still online. He rammed the left control bar forward. The *Abyss*'s walls ground out a deep, grating vibration so low it made Blake's jaw ache. Still he tried and the gravity engines strained against a much, much greater force.

"Keep firing!" he ordered.

"We can't see it to target!" said Hawkins.

"I think I've got a ping off it," said Pointer. Her next words were choked out through the shock. "I have no idea what we've found, sir."

With its prey caught, *Ix-Gorghal* dropped its sensor-deflecting shroud and appeared before them. The crew on the *Abyss* were dumbfounded and not one of them was able to find their tongue in order to put words to the sight before them.

It was Blake who broke the collective trance. He opened his mouth and swore loudly.

IT WAS LATE EVENING, though Fleet Admiral Duggan had many tasks to finish before he could contemplate sleep. With the Confederation spread over so many worlds, it was always daytime somewhere and while it was joked that members of the Council enjoyed a three-hour working day, the reality was that many of them worked hours as long as anyone. In general, the more important a person's job, the harder it was for them to find time for bed.

Duggan yawned and signed off a few orders for new warship parts, as well as giving his approval for work to begin on three new Hadrons. Cerys had been quiet for the last hour, and the computer's voice gave him a start.

"Fleet Admiral Duggan, I have a request from Research Leader Joel Breeze. He would like to speak with you."

Duggan frowned. "Is it urgent or can it wait until morning?"

There was a pause while Cerys obtained a response. "At first he said it is urgent and then he corrected himself and said it might be urgent."

"Bring him through."

The voice of Joel Breeze came from the room's speakers and he sounded uncertain, worried and outright scared. "Good evening, sir."

"It's quite late, Joel. What can I do for you?"

"Apologies for the late hour. I found something which I thought you ought to know."

Duggan had a certain prescience, though he tried to deny it. He felt the skin tightening across his chest. "What have you found?"

"Do you remember when I said we had to play around with the figures in order to get the energy readings from the Vraxar wormhole to match up with our own readings for the *ESS Crimson* and the *Helius Blackstar*?"

"I remember."

"And we increased our estimate of *Ix-Gorghal*'s size until we found something which fit."

"Fifty thousand metres, plus or minus three percent."

"Yes. There might be a problem, sir. We stopped at fifty thousand, thinking that was the only answer. I've taken another look at the figures and while fifty thousand metres remains correct, there's another number which also fits. In fact, it fits a lot better. After that, there are no other numbers which fit the equation, no matter how high you go."

"How big?"

"Well, if we ignore some of the inaccuracies in the…"

"How big?"

"Six hundred kilometres, sir."

Duggan bowed his head. "You're telling me *Ix-Gorghal* could be six *hundred* kilometres long?"

"Yes, sir, and with a colossal volume."

"And there's no error?"

"No, sir. Those are the two numbers which fit."

"Thank you, RL Breeze. Goodnight."

"Goodnight, sir."

Duggan wished more than anything he hadn't received this late-night call. There was nothing he could do to change the fact and there was no time to think of the ramifications.

"Cerys, please get me through to Captain Blake on the *ES Abyss*. Priority 1 message."

"There is no response from the *ES Abyss*, Fleet Admiral. They sent a message to command and control several minutes ago, informing us they were about to engage with a Vraxar Neutraliser and have detected no sign of *Ix-Gorghal*."

"Why didn't you tell me?"

"I judged your conversation with RL Breeze to be of equal importance."

"Try the *Abyss* again."

"Still no response."

Duggan put his head in his hands and wondered what to do.

CHAPTER TWENTY

"THAT'S WHAT WE FACE," said Blake.

"There's no way we're going to take that down," said Hawkins.

"*Ix-Gorghal*. No wonder the Estral lost their war."

"Still want me to launch those weapons, sir?"

"Hold for the moment."

The enormous craft was clad in the Vraxar's near-black alloy and measured slightly more than six hundred kilometres on its longest axis. Its vertical axis extended for three hundred kilometres at the front-centre part of the vessel. The *Sciontrar* and *ES Abyss* looked like insignificant specks of crude metal in comparison, pinned in place like insects.

Ix-Gorghal's ovoid form was covered in huge metal constructions of countless different shapes. There were towers, antennae arrays and squat domes forty kilometres or more in diameter. Blake found his eyes drawn to other places – elaborate, ugly and angular outcroppings of metal which were surely intended for destructive purposes. It was terrible and it had come to render humanity and Ghasts extinct.

"Why haven't they killed us?"

"I don't know. Speak to the *Sciontrar* and see what they're planning."

"There's something blocking our signal, sir. I imagine the Ghasts are unable to reach us for the same reason."

"Lieutenant Quinn, I would like you to find out what they are using to keep us in place and figure out a way we can escape."

"I'm trying, sir. It's something new."

"It's always something new. Work out what it is and tell me how to beat it."

"They are projecting some kind of stasis beam from that tower towards the front," said Quinn. "It's holding us and the *Sciontrar*."

"Any indication if it's feeling the strain or is it coasting?"

"I don't know, sir. Look at the size of the parent vessel – I bet it could hold a hundred warships in place."

Minutes went by, with Blake becoming increasingly concerned about what the Vraxar intended. He was tempted to start firing missiles, but he'd already witnessed *Ix-Gorghal* soak up a thousand plasma warheads without apparent strain and he was sure any offensive act would result in swift and terminal retribution.

A surprise was in store.

"Sir, there's an inbound comms request. It's coming from the enemy ship."

"Who is it?"

"There is no introduction."

"Make the connection."

The comms link was established. It hummed and droned with background noise, even though the distance between the two ships wasn't enormous.

"I am Captain Charlie Blake of the Space Corps ship *ES Abyss*. Who is this?" asked Blake, fumbling for what to say. There seemed little point asking the Vraxar why they'd chosen to capture the two warships. There was no answer for a short time and Blake repeated the words.

When the response came, the words were delivered by a voice that was powerful and undeniably ancient, as though the speaker had seen the birth of stars. The tones rumbled with the allure of an orator inviting an audience to eat meat laced with poison.

"My name is Tassin-Dak and I command *Ix-Gorghal*."

"What do you want from us, Tassin-Dak?"

The question generated an angry response. "Do not speak my name, human! It is not a privilege I have granted you."

Blake bit his tongue, wishing he could tell this Vraxar where he could stick his privilege and his enormous spaceship. Discretion seemed advisable. "What do you want from us?" he repeated.

"Our hunger grows and we must embrace new life forms. We do not have forever to search and each new species we find seems more ungrateful than the one preceding it. Nevertheless, I am here to welcome new children, whatever the tribulations. I see we have discovered a place where humans and near-Estral are in harmony." The Vraxar laughed nastily. "It will bring me great happiness to expunge the remaining Estral filth."

"You do not require more Estral?"

"Our ranks are bursting with their numbers, bringing imbalance to the Vraxar. I have with me in excess of one billion converted Estral and I will be sure to spend them without consideration. Those on *Ix-Gorghal* are only a fraction of the total."

"We call these Estral by a different name. We call them Ghasts."

"Call them what you will. We have no more need of their flesh and we will eliminate them."

"Why will you eliminate them if you have no need of them?"

asked Blake. He was certain Tassin-Dak was from the original species which had become Vraxar and was therefore likely to possess an invaluable insight into their motives and plans.

"It will be a fitting punishment for their unwillingness to capitulate."

"How will you find them? How will you find the worlds belonging to the human Confederation?"

"You will tell us, Captain Blake. And after you tell us, you will be converted to Vraxar."

"Why would I do that? What possible reason is there for me to voluntarily tell you where to find the Confederation's worlds?"

"It will not be voluntary. We have many different ways of finding out the truth. If we did not, how could we succeed in our goals?"

"There aren't many of us humans. Why make the effort? Why not go elsewhere and save us from having to destroy your precious *Ix-Gorghal* in the same way we destroyed your fleet?"

Tassin-Dak didn't provide an emotional reaction to the threat. "You destroyed a fraction of our spaceships and we will bring many more. Your Confederation is lucky to be in a place which provides a stepping stone to several, more populous, areas of this universe. We will pass through and we will take your bodies and your expertise. Eventually, we will move on and when we do, you will be part of us when we begin our assault on the Antaron. *That* will be a war to rival the one against the Estral."

A message appeared in the corner of one screen on Blake's console and he glanced at it.

Caz Pointer: We have established an ultra-low band connection to the Sciontrar. Shhhh!

Blake tapped out a quick response, whilst at the same time speaking to Tassin-Dak. "How do you plan to get onboard in order to make me divulge the information you crave?"

Charlie Blake: We need a plan. Find out what Nil-Tras is up to!

Caz Pointer: Aye aye, Captain!

The Vraxar responded, unaware Blake was juggling his attention between two conversations. "We have disabled your ability to escape. We will bring your spaceship into our hold and send our troops onboard."

"The *ES Abyss* is carrying an Obsidiar bomb," Blake lied. "By all means, bring us into your hold. Perhaps I will detonate it anyway if you do not release us."

"Go ahead, Captain Blake. The loss of your warship's memory arrays will slow us down and nothing more. I will, however advise you - even now, the near-Estral is bargaining for his life."

Caz Pointer: He's lying about the Ghasts. The Vraxar have not spoken to anyone on the Sciontrar.

Charlie Blake: Interesting.

Blake wasn't sure if Tassin-Dak was counter-bluffing by acting unconcerned about the possibility of the *Abyss* carrying an Obsidiar bomb. The thought that *Ix-Gorghal*'s energy shield was capable of withstanding the blast from such a bomb was something Blake did not wish to contemplate. The Vraxar talked with a high degree of intelligence, which meant he was probably capable of lies and deceit.

"You already have the memory arrays from one of our ships. Why do you need those on the *ES Abyss*?"

"The previously-captured arrays are on the smaller cargo vessel you were in the process of attacking. It would be destroyed if you detonated an Obsidiar bomb."

At that exact moment, the Vraxar cargo ship exited into light-speed, vanishing from the Dranmir system. Blake muted the comms immediately.

"Capture the details of its fission cloud. I want to find out where it's gone."

"We're too far away for comfort. The data might be patchy, sir," said Quinn.

"Do what you can."

He unmuted the comms and spoke to the Vraxar again.

"You said we are a stepping stone," said Blake, trying to buy some time as well as obtain information. "Your Neutralisers were destroyed when they summoned *Ix-Gorghal*. How do you plan to bring your ships into Confederation Space?"

The Vraxar appeared content to talk. "The Ir-Klion are a makeshift solution. We will make a gate and our fleet will come through. I am sure this technology is beyond your species."

"How do you make a gate?"

"Watch."

The connection went dead, leaving Blake asking himself if he'd done something wrong. The sensor feed of *Ix-Gorghal* remained as it was, unchanging except for the slow passage of the Vraxar vessel as it flew leisurely above Dranmir, bringing the *Sciontrar* and *Abyss* with it. Blake did his best to make efficient use of the time.

"Tassin-Dak has yet to admit it, but we're at a stalemate," he said. "He will not attempt to bring us within his shield now that he thinks there's a chance we're equipped with an Obsidiar bomb."

"I wonder why he's not scared of us launching our missiles within his shield," said Hawkins.

"They must have a way to counter them, or they're just willing to take a few hits in order to accomplish their aims."

"Or they can make a shield funnel," said Quinn. "And draw us in through that."

"The specifics don't matter. What's important is their reluctance to bring the *Abyss* into their hold. Tassin-Dak has just revealed that the *ES Determinant*'s arrays are intact and in the Vraxar's possession. That means they haven't cracked them open yet. It also means the only way they can speed up the process of finding our worlds is by getting us to volunteer the information."

"Which we aren't going to do," said Pointer.

"No. He'll likely try to persuade us. After that..."

"Boom!" said Hawkins. "He'll order our destruction."

"They don't seem too interested in the *Sciontrar*," said Cruz.

"It sounds like they've had enough of the Estral," Blake replied. "It's clouding their judgement."

"I doubt the Ghosts are any more willing to talk than we are," said Cruz.

Blake had a thought. "Where the hell is the *Kalon-T7*?"

There wasn't time to find an answer to the question.

"Look!" said Pointer, her finger aimed directly towards the bulkhead screen.

A set of hangar doors started to open on the side of *Ix-Gorghal*. The gap appeared small against the flank of the Vraxar ship, but Blake guessed the doors were in the region of ten thousand metres wide. The upper and lower doors vanished into recesses in the armoured walls, revealing green light within. There was no angle for Blake to see directly into the interior of the enemy ship and he tilted his head to one side, as though he could somehow improve his view by doing so.

"There's something coming out," said Hawkins.

The vessel which emerged was plain in appearance – it was a polished, featureless, perfect sphere of black alloy. It came out of the hangar rapidly, as though it was in a hurry to complete whatever mission it had been given.

"What is that?" asked Ensign Park.

"We probably don't want to find out," said Hawkins.

The new vessel maintained a parallel course to *Ix-Gorghal* for a short period and then it accelerated so rapidly it appeared for a moment as if it had gone to lightspeed.

"Got it!" said Cruz, focusing one of the sensors on the rapidly-diminishing spaceship. "It's moving fast."

"Warming up for a jump," said Quinn.

The spherical vessel went into lightspeed, leaving the invisible plume from its deep fission engine across a huge patch of space.

"Get a recording of that one as well!" shouted Blake.

"Already on with it, sir," said Quinn. "We've got a much better view of that cloud."

"Enough to find out where it's gone?"

"Given time and assuming we aren't hit by a disintegration cannon in the next two minutes."

As if responding to a prompt, Tassin-Dak returned to the comms. "The Gate Maker knows a suitable location to build its portal. Once complete, this area of space will become home to much of the Vraxar fleet."

"How does it work?"

Captain Blake: Ask Nil-Tras to launch his anti-shield incendiaries at Ix-Gorghal.

"How it functions is not important." The Vraxar's voice made it clear he was no longer interested in indulging his *children*. "You have likely already guessed that we have no easy way to entice you from your ship in order that I might extract information from you."

Caz Pointer: Nil-Tras says the weapon takes too long to charge – the Vraxar will detect the build-up.

Charlie Blake: We need a diversion. Where is the Kalon-T7?

Caz Pointer: Its coming. Nil-Tras suggests we stay on our toes.

"I couldn't tell you the details from the top of my head anyway, Tassin-Dak, my rotting friend," said Blake, deliberately using the Vraxar's name. "What are you going to do about it?"

The Vraxar didn't bother with verbal sparring. It cut the comms channel, leaving Blake in no doubt as to what it intended.

"Fire everything we've got!" he shouted. "Aim our particle beams at that stasis tower!"

The *Abyss* lacked the sheer grunt of the *Sciontrar*, but it was equipped with Estral-designed particle beams which were able to penetrate energy shields and Blake hoped they'd be enough to disable the hold on the two warships.

Hawkins clearly wasn't expecting the command but she reacted with admirable speed. "Front and rear overcharge firing. They have both struck the stasis generator. We've fired missiles from every single one of our launch tubes and the Bulwarks are set to auto."

On the sensor feed, the tower which was holding the *Sciontrar* and *Abyss* in place looked tiny in comparison to *Ix-Gorghal*. When the two overcharged particle beams struck its surface, they lit up only a fraction of the whole, indicating the tower was, in fact, huge.

Blake was ready and he pushed the heavy cruiser's gravity engines to full. The bridge walls shuddered as they had before and the ship remained trapped.

"That tower is massive," said Blake. "It's going to take more shots to knock it out."

"Its output fell twenty percent and then stabilised," said Quinn. "I have no idea how many times we'll need to hit it."

"The *Sciontrar* is launching," said Hawkins. "Let's see what they've got."

The Ghost battleship was a little newer than the *Abyss* and it was certainly more advanced. Missiles poured from its tubes, flooding the sky in their thousands. Its particle beams flashed in rapid succession, snaking across to *Ix-Gorghal*'s energy shield. Energy spikes from its disruptors triggered the instrumentation on Blake's console, even though the *Abyss* wasn't a target. On top of it all, two hundred or more Vule cannons sprayed white-hot streaks of metal onto the Vraxar shield.

"That's one mean bastard of a battleship," said Ensign Bailey in wonder.

"They're charging up their incendiary launcher," said Quinn.

"It needs to be quicker than last time."

The suddenness of the attack had evidently caught the Vraxar unawares and Blake guessed Tassin-Dak was accustomed to controlling affairs from his seat in what was certainly one of the most powerful spaceships in the universe. Even so, it didn't take long for *Ix-Gorghal* to offer a response and when it arrived, it came with expected brutality.

A pair of huge cannons were housed on the upper-front section of the Vraxar ship. There might have been more, but Blake didn't have time for a close inspection. The first cannon fired a massive projectile at near-lightspeed. A ball of hardened Gallenium crashed into the ES *Abyss*'s shield. At the time of impact, Blake's eye was on the power gauge for the energy shield. To his astonishment, the bar dropped from 95% straight to zero. He swore.

"That takes out our overcharge capability, sir," said Hawkins.

"I know, Lieutenant. That's a kick in the teeth for us."

It was grim news – Blake was relying on getting off a few more shots from the overcharged particle beams in order to shut down the Vraxar stasis tower. Now it was going to take miracle for them to escape.

"The *Sciontrar* took a hit from the second cannon, sir," said Quinn. "Their shield is holding."

"They've got more Obsidiar than us," muttered Blake.

His eyes flicked to a new sensor feed, this one showing an uncomfortably close view of the endless depths of a huge-bore cannon. He felt sure the Vraxar could have turned a thousand extra weapons onto the *Abyss*, yet they seemed content to take an unhurried approach. *Overconfident bastards,* he thought angrily.

"We can't take another hit," said Hawkins.

It seemed inevitable that her statement was about to be tested. Before the Vraxar cannon could fire for a second time, a third spaceship burst into local space, dropping out of lightspeed a few hundred kilometres away and carrying enough speed to cross the intervening space between itself and *Ix-Gorghal*'s shield in less than a second. The *Kalon-T7* crashed into the energy shield at an enormous speed. The Vraxar ship was huge, but the Cadaveron was dense and with incredible inertia. Where it struck the enemy shield blue-green zig-zags of energy burst away, crackling with fury.

"How on earth is their shield holding after that?" asked Hawkins.

"They're diverting power!" yelled Quinn.

Blake reached for the control bars and realised he hadn't relinquished his grip from the last time. At maximum thrust, the *ES Abyss* inched forward.

"Come on!" shouted Pointer.

It wasn't enough. *Ix-Gorghal* had so much power in reserve it was able to maintain its shield as well as keeping the human and Ghost ships locked in place, even with the cascade of missiles raining continuously upon it.

The *Kalon-T7* pulled away laboriously from its place of impact. The Cadaveron looked nothing like its previous form – its nose was flattened and spread, and the vessel was a thousand metres shorter than when it arrived in the Dranmir solar system. Its attack had angered the Vraxar and the two immense cannons rotated in their turrets, each one firing at the Ghost heavy cruiser. The first projectile crumpled against the Cadaveron's still-intact energy shield. The second broke through with scarcely-reduced velocity. The massive Gallenium slug punched a vast hole in the

Ghost spaceship, leaving a crater several hundred metres across and deep. Blake had no idea if the crew had survived and he had no time to investigate.

The two cannons rotated once more, one of them aimed at the *ES Abyss*.

Before the Vraxar could fire, the *Sciontrar* launched its plasma incendiaries. The familiar beam of pulsing blue light jumped across to the enemy's shield. The incendiary spread out rapidly from the point of contact, racing like an unstoppable tide until *Ix-Gorghal* was engulfed in the centre. Blake watched, one hand keeping the left control bar jammed at the far end of its runner. The shuddering of the engines became a howl and still the *Abyss* lacked the power to break free.

"Try the short-range transit again!" he shouted.

"That stasis beam is blocking the launch," said Quinn. "We're not going anywhere while it's operational."

Ix-Gorghal was now completely lost within the incendiary fires. The flames reached their peak and began to recede, dwindling slowly at first. Blake experienced a sensation of utter, helpless frustration when it appeared if the Vraxar would have enough in reserve to withstand the plasma clinging to their energy shield.

"They don't like it," said Quinn. "Something's happening to that tower – they're diverting power from it!"

Blake dared to hope. He closed his eyes and poured the strength of his will to the task of defeating fate. Freedom, when it came, was sudden and jarring. The *ES Abyss* didn't creep forward, tugging at the invisible shackles, rather, it burst free in a surge, accelerating with its usual vigour.

"Yes!" shouted Blake.

"The *Sciontrar* has broken away as well, sir!" said Cruz.

"Get us away from here!"

"Activating SRT," said Quinn.

At the exact moment of transition, a projectile from one of *Ix-Gorghal*'s cannons smashed into the rear section of the ES *Abyss*, ramming its way through fifteen hundred metres of solid Gallenium, before friction heat and the density of the spaceship brought its progress to a halt. The single shot caused enormous damage to the engines and missed the life support units by a short distance. It wasn't the harm done to the engines which was the most catastrophic result of the cannon strike. The last few metres the projectile travelled through the heavy cruiser's solid hull brought it into contact with the Obsidiar core which was hidden in a room deep inside. The massive slug crunched into the pitch-black cylinder of Obsidiar, shattering it and breaking its connection with the rest of the warship.

It wasn't enough to disable the heavy cruiser and the ES *Abyss* entered a reduced lightspeed state and limped its way to safety.

In the moments of realisation at what humanity faced and how lucky they'd been to escape this encounter, the crew said nothing. Blake remained in his chair, his hands still gripping the control rods even though the warship's processors now had complete charge of the journey. The mission had been a success of sorts, he reflected. Unfortunately, what they'd learned showed the depths of the challenge ahead. It wasn't going to get any easier.

CHAPTER TWENTY-ONE

AFTER TWO HOURS AT LIGHTSPEED, Blake ordered a switchover to the gravity engines. With noticeably more vibration than usual, the *ES Abyss* exited into an area of space which contained absolutely nothing. The heavy cruiser's rear quarter was a mess of crushed metal and there wasn't a single display on the bridge which didn't have some kind of warning light flashing.

The time since their escape had been filled with desperate efforts to establish some kind of connection with the Obsidiar core. In the end, the crew were forced to admit defeat – the *Abyss*'s backup power source was gone and they had no hope of fixing it themselves. It was a devastating blow.

With the entry into local space complete, Lieutenant Quinn activated the stealth modules. The energy shield wouldn't come online, no matter how hard he tried to tap into the main engines. The stealth modules alone took a vast amount of energy to maintain and the heavy cruiser's engines took a big hit in output, with some of the gauges stuck at seventy percent instead of one hundred percent. Blake ignored the mess on his console and explained the reasoning behind this unscheduled stop.

"If we can read a fission cloud, I wouldn't be surprised if *Ix-Gorghal* has a similar facility and I don't want to lead them straight to a Confederation planet," he said.

"What if they follow us to here?" asked Quinn.

"You will take us back to lightspeed the moment you detect an incoming fission signature, Lieutenant."

"Yes, sir."

"Do we have any idea what happened to the Ghosts?" asked Blake.

"I can't reach them, sir," said Cruz. "They're either at lightspeed or they didn't make it."

"We're still on backup comms?"

"Yes, and will be until we reach a shipyard able to complete a refit."

"The primary comms aren't robust enough," grumbled Blake. He couldn't do anything about it at the moment. "Can we reach Fleet Admiral Duggan? I want him to hear this directly."

"There'll be a long delay," said Pointer. "It'll work if you're patient."

"I think I have a better way," said Cruz. "We're close enough to Monitoring Station Sigma to use it as a comms booster. We give them our slow speed signal and they send it onwards using their fully-functioning main comms systems."

"Do it."

It didn't take long to establish a connection to New Earth Central Command Station. When Fleet Admiral Duggan spoke, he sounded dog-tired as though he'd denied himself sleep in case he missed any important news. The line clicked and hummed as the signal routed through Monitoring Station Sigma and there was a delay of a few seconds which took Blake a while to get used to.

"Captain Blake, I was beginning to worry," said Duggan.

"With good reason, sir. *Ix-Gorghal* is a lot bigger than you thought it was."

"I received an updated estimate. Tell me it isn't six hundred klicks from nose to tail."

"It's slightly more, sir, and it's going to take a lot of firepower to bring it down. I'm sending you the sensor recordings we took – I'm sure you've got hundreds of people ready to study the details."

"Did you suffer losses?"

"No losses, though we've taken extensive damage. The *Abyss* is still functioning, but it's not as fast as it was."

"You're operational?" pressed Duggan.

"Yes, sir. We're operational." Blake took a deep breath. "We've lost our Obsidiar core and the energy shield won't come online."

Duggan swore. He wasn't interested in the financial cost – it was the major reduction in the *ES Abyss*'s effectiveness that hurt. With an effort, he calmed himself.

"If it's gone, it's gone and we'll have to deal with it - the Galactics were built tough and the energy shield was just a bonus. Now, tell me what happened to the Ghasts in all this."

"We were lucky to have them and they performed admirably. I don't know if they escaped from the engagement with *Ix-Gorghal*. We didn't run out on them."

"I will speak to Subjos Kion-Tur and find out what he knows."

"They've got a weapon which is designed to knock out energy shields. It's slow to fire but it's what allowed us to escape."

"I'll make sure the Subjos is aware of its effectiveness."

"There is a lot more you need to know."

"A way forward?"

"If we can capitalise. There are two opportunities and I need your guidance on how to proceed, sir. The Vraxar still have the

ES *Determinant* – it's in the hold of a cargo vessel which went to lightspeed when I threatened *Ix-Gorghal* with an imaginary Obsidiar bomb."

"You captured a model of their fission cloud?"

"We did, sir. It's not a perfect copy, since we had sensor interference."

"Have you obtained an estimation of their destination?"

"Not yet, sir. We've been at lightspeed and haven't had many dedicated processing cycles to spare unravelling the fission cloud model, since we've been attempting to reconnect the Obsidiar core."

"What is the second opportunity?"

"There is a Vraxar called Tassin-Dak in command of *Ix-Gorghal* – I got the impression he might be one of the original race and he certainly talked with authority. He dispatched what he called a Gate Maker spaceship, which has the sole purpose of creating a portal for the remainder of the Vraxar fleet to come through. You're already aware the Neutralisers can do it at a pinch but I don't think they have many remaining in Confederation Space."

"I know of one."

"I have a feeling it's the last, sir. At least until this Gate Maker does its job and brings the rest of the fleet in. Apparently, we're a stepping stone to the Vraxar's real target, which is a species called Antaron. Tassin-Dak thinks they'll be as difficult to overcome as the Estral."

"He's already written us off as a challenge?" asked Duggan bitterly. "Even after you destroyed a hundred of their warships at Cheops-A?"

"I think we're small fry to them – an interesting diversion before the real fun starts."

"I suppose it doesn't matter what they think. If we kick them where it hurts often enough, the message will eventually get through."

"Which path would you like the ES *Abyss* to take, sir?"

"The *ES Determinant* holds details of our planets, whilst this Gate Maker you describe is the Vraxar's route to Confederation space."

"Yes, sir."

The channel went silent apart from the clicking and humming sounds. Blake waited patiently while Duggan worked through the possibilities.

"Captain Blake, how long will it take the *Abyss* to determine the destination of the two Vraxar ships?"

This was information Blake had already obtained in advance from Lieutenant Quinn. "We got the best look at the Gate Maker, sir. There's a chance we'll have a good enough idea of its destination in the next six to eight hours. Their cargo ship will be harder for us – my engine man believes we might require twenty-four hours or more. Perhaps significantly more."

"The problem I have is that the *ES Abyss* is once again the closest of our warships to the action."

"We want this, sir."

"Can you send your fission models to Monitoring Station Sigma? They have a lot of processing power which should cut hours off the modelling time."

Blake glanced over to his comms team to find both officers shaking their heads. *No chance,* mouthed Pointer.

"We lack the bandwidth," said Cruz in a loud whisper.

With a nod of his head, Blake relayed the news. "We can't transfer the data easily or quickly, sir."

"That leaves me in a very difficult position. I would like to bring you back home and extract the data into a dedicated processing unit. Unfortunately, you are several days from the closest facility, which is more time than I am willing to waste. All of this means I need to send the *ES Abyss* along one road or the other, with the knowledge that your heavy cruiser is the only repository for such valuable data."

"I have discussed this with my crew and we have not been able to come up with an adequate compromise, sir."

"Which way to proceed?" mused Duggan. "We know the least about this Gate Maker. If they have only one on *Ix-Gorghal* and we destroy it, we may slow down the Vraxar advance significantly while we build up our own forces. If, on the other hand, we find and destroy the wreckage of the *ES Determinant*, it will remove the enemy's ability to locate our planets."

"Delay their ability," said Blake. "They found us once and they'll find us again. They need a fleet to conquer and without anything to support *Ix-Gorghal* it will be more vulnerable to a strike using overwhelming numbers."

"It sounds as though you have already made your own mind up, Captain Blake."

"I think I have. If we find and destroy the Gate Maker, we cut *Ix-Gorghal* off from its support. If the Vraxar have only a handful of warships in Confederation Space, even with knowledge of our planets, they will find it harder to overcome us all."

"An optimist would tell you there are times when both answers are right, whilst a pessimist would say the opposite. Whichever side you fall it doesn't matter, since in both cases you need to make a choice. If you think the Gate Maker is a priority, please calculate where it has gone and, assuming the *ES Abyss* is the closest warship to the destination, pursue and destroy it."

"Yes, sir. And we'll get to work on finding out where they took the *ES Determinant* straight after."

"It's as much of a plan as could be expected. Please put it into action."

"Yes, sir."

With the most important details covered, Blake prepared to

spend a few additional minutes filling in the gaps, knowing there were people in the Space Corps who would pore over every word for clues and hints about the Vraxar's intentions. He didn't get the chance.

"Oh crap," said Lieutenant Quinn.

"What?" said Blake sharply.

The *ES Abyss* rumbled and core #7 triggered a transition to lightspeed. Caught off-guard, Blake stumbled and grabbed the edge of his console to steady himself.

"*Ix-Gorghal*," said Quinn. "It was doing something to suppress its inbound signature but I managed to spot it in time."

"You're sure it was the Vraxar?"

"Absolutely."

"In that case, good work, Lieutenant."

"Does that mean *Ix-Gorghal* can follow us through lightspeed?" asked Cruz.

"Looks like it."

"That's awful news," said Pointer.

"Let's not dwell on it," said Blake. "Lieutenant Quinn – what course have you set us along?"

"The very early calculations on the Gate Maker's destination gave a wide arc of possibilities. I've pointed us directly along the middle of that arc. We'll remain at lightspeed for sixty minutes unless we intervene and shut off the fission engines."

"Once again that's excellent thinking, Lieutenant. We might not be on the exact trail of the enemy, but we'll sure as hell not be going in the opposite direction."

"I take it from your conversation with the Fleet Admiral I'm dedicating every spare processing cycle to the task of finding their Gate Maker?"

"Yes, that's our target. We'll find it, destroy it and if we're lucky, still have a shot at the wreckage of the *ES Determinant*."

"You're definitely the optimist, sir," said Hawkins. "I approve."

Next was the question Blake knew the answer to, whilst still needing backup confirmation. "Did we leave enough of a mark behind for *Ix-Gorghal* to get a sighting of us?"

"If you're asking me whether the Vraxar will shortly be following us through lightspeed, I'd say you should make allowances for it."

"Which is a roundabout way of saying *yes*?"

"Yes, sir, it is."

Blake ran through the numbers. "Our previous time at lightspeed was two hours. On top of that, I spent fifteen minutes in conversation with Fleet Admiral Duggan."

"Which means that two hours fifteen minutes was sufficient time for *Ix-Gorghal* to calculate our destination and reach us," said Lieutenant Quinn. "We're substantially down on power, so we're not as fast as usual."

"Even so, the Vraxar caught up fast."

"Very fast."

"This presents a number of problems. How are we going to find the Gate Maker and destroy it before *Ix-Gorghal* shows up?"

"That's not the biggest problem," said Hawkins. "What if the Vraxar guess where we're going and decide to get there ahead of us? We're heading in approximately the right direction, so it may not be too hard to work out what we're up to."

"You raise a good point, Lieutenant, and one to which I have no answer." Blake scratched at the stubble he'd not found the time to shave off. "Lieutenant Quinn, what happens if we simply terminate our lightspeed run midway through? In other words, we set a course that will take us across half the universe, but exit lightspeed after a couple of hours."

"Well, sir, lightspeed travel in theory shouldn't be possible. When our navigational computer plots a course, it generates a graph of probabilities. The further the destination, the lower the probability and the more work it takes in predicting where the target spaceship is going. Therefore, once a course is set..."

Blake lifted a hand to interrupt. "This is very interesting, though not the appropriate time for the background, Lieutenant Quinn."

Quinn cleared his throat. "We leave a trail of positrons."

"As simple as that?"

"Yes, sir. If we abort mid-way through, the trail of positrons will end and the enemy ship will know what we've done."

"Does that mean they'll overshoot before they realise and have to backtrack?"

"I don't have the expertise to give you an exact answer. You'd need a team of skilled mathematicians and physicists."

The crew of a spaceship invariably had a strong background in maths and science. It didn't necessarily mean they were the most capable mathematicians in the Confederation, since it required many other skills to perform on-ship duties.

"I understand," said Blake. "Best guess?"

"Best guess is they're packing too much processing power to overshoot."

Cruz raised a hand.

"You're not at school, Lieutenant Cruz."

"No, sir. Isn't the solution for us to simply do a series of rapid lightspeed jumps in random directions? My understanding is that the fission cloud dissipates rapidly. If the enemy is required to spend time calculating our course, even a few minutes' delay should ensure they lose our trail because there'll be no fission signature to run the modelling."

Blake turned to Quinn. "Well?"

Quinn furrowed his brow. "What Lieutenant Cruz says is logical enough."

"You're not convinced?"

"We don't know much about their capabilities, sir. What if they can read our positron trail for hours after we've gone to lightspeed? I'm sure Lieutenants Pointer and Cruz took note of those huge sensor arrays on the Vraxar spaceship."

"We saw them," said Cruz. "I must admit they looked quite advanced."

"In that case, we should assume the worst and hope for the best. We'll need to come up with a way to both find the Gate Maker and also maximise the amount of time we have to attack it without molestation from a six-hundred kilometre, potentially unstoppable capital ship."

"I'll get to work on a solution," said Quinn.

"You've got Ensign Bailey to help out – does anyone else in the crew have experience you can call upon?"

"I'll look in if that's okay?" said Hawkins. "I did some time on engines."

"Good," said Blake. "See if you can come up with something before we leave lightspeed."

It was a big ask and everyone knew it. The Space Corps did its best to choose people who rose to the challenge rather than hiding from it and the crew got started.

Needing time to think, Blake dropped into his chair with its familiar smell and the supple creak of real leather. *Awful news*, Lieutenant Pointer had called it. It was worse than that. Since *Ix-Gorghal* had a method of following the *ES Abyss*, it would make completion of this mission to destroy the Gate Maker close to impossible. Looking further ahead, the crew of the *ES Abyss* were effectively cut off from home because there was no way Blake would be able to return to a Space Corps base with something as monstrously powerful as the Vraxar capital ship following behind.

The minutes went by while he racked his brains for a solution.

CHAPTER TWENTY-TWO

THE PLAN, when formulated, was simple enough and Lieutenant Quinn was the man to explain it.

"The primary aim is to earn us some time, both to locate the Gate Maker and, from there, to destroy it," he said.

"I'd like to think we might eventually escape ourselves," said Blake.

"One step at a time," admonished Hawkins.

"What do we have, then?"

"A computer-generated randomised path of varying-length lightspeed jumps," said Quinn.

For some reason, Blake felt disappointed at the straightforward nature. "That's it?"

"No, there's more. What we're going to do is aim on a slightly divergent course from where we expect to discover the Gate Maker. That will make *Ix-Gorghal* believe we're going elsewhere. Each time we emerge from lightspeed, we will deposit a few hundred shock drones and then perform a new transit."

"The shock drones will work?"

"That's what we're hoping. They do all sorts of tricks – you see, they're not just designed to confuse *known* technologies, they were built to work on the unknowns as well."

"I see. What exactly will they do?"

"They will confuse the Vraxar sensors for a short period and at the same time they will hide our positron trail behind a confusion of signals and broadcasts."

"You aren't convincing me, Lieutenant."

"In truth, I'm not convinced myself, sir. However, I genuinely believe a shock drone deployment will buy us some time and we're in a position where something is better than nothing."

"I won't argue that. Have you been able to come up with any forecasts?"

Quinn was a man who liked his forecasts and he brandished a sheet of old-fashioned paper with some rough sums on it. "Absolutely," he said. "Based on how long it took *Ix-Gorghal* to find us the first time, I have made some projections. If we rely purely on random lightspeed transits, by the time our modelling software has pinpointed the Gate Maker in about five hours, I believe we will have a fifty-minute lead over *Ix-Gorghal*."

"Assuming they can follow our trail of positrons," said Hawkins.

"The early indications are that we will be about eight further hours from reaching the Gate Maker, and by the end of that transit, we'll be a little over one hour ahead of *Ix-Gorghal*."

"What if we deploy shock drones in our wake?"

"If we do that, I estimate we could have anything from a fifty minute to a three-hour lead."

"Potentially less time than if we didn't deploy the shock drones? How does that work?"

Quinn looked deflated. "I don't know, sir. If I was a betting man, I'd go with a two-hour lead when we reach the Gate Maker."

Blake's head swum – he understood what Quinn was saying

well enough, yet he couldn't shake a conviction that his lieutenant had constructed a progressively higher tower of conclusions upon a foundation of turds, these foundations being laid upon a tiny island surrounded by an ocean of shit. The higher the tower went, the less stable it became and the more prone it was to toppling over and landing in the murky brown effluent around it.

There were times you just had to go with it.

"It's an excellent plan," said Blake.

"Really?"

Blake laughed. "It's an awful plan, but it's the best we've got."

Quinn also laughed. "If it fails, I'll deny all knowledge, sir."

"Too late, Lieutenant. I'll have an entry put into my log describing our intention to enact *Quinn's Folly*. If we're exceptionally lucky, it won't be the last entry."

They put the plan in motion.

Upon Blake's command, the *ES Abyss* exited lightspeed and ejected several hundred shock drones from its armoury. These drones were last-ditch countermeasures, intended to confuse enemy missiles. In this new age where the Space Corps' opponents were relying progressively more on beam weapons, the drones were somewhat less useful, but every fleet warship still carried a substantial number of these reflective, metre-diameter spheres with their tiny propulsion systems and sophisticated guidance jammers.

"There they go," said Hawkins.

"We're back to lightspeed again," said Quinn. "This trip has a thirty-minute duration."

The crew sat back to wait. Blake noticed there was a peculiar atmosphere on the bridge, as though no-one quite believed the circumstances. It was like being in a simulator designed by a cabal of insane senior officers, designed to test Space Corps personnel under the most absurdly testing conditions.

The feeling this was some bizarre, unwinnable trial was exacerbated when Lieutenant Quinn brought Blake's attention to a slight degradation he'd noticed in the output of the warship's engines.

"There's a fall-off in the region of one tenth of one percent," he said.

"Is that a confirmed average and not a fluctuation?" asked Blake.

"It's confirmed, sir. Early signs are the rate of drop is increasing."

"We're not going to lose the engines, are we?"

Quinn didn't answer directly. "If it happens, we're screwed without the Obsidiar backup."

"Does that mean we're going to lose the engines, Lieutenant?" Blake repeated.

"Probably not, though I can't tell you how far they'll degrade."

It wasn't good and Blake grimaced. The heavy cruiser had taken a thunderous blow from the Vraxar capital ship and he'd started to think they'd got away with manageable damage, like a soldier shot in such a way that the bullet missed every major artery and every vital organ on the way through.

"Keep me informed, Lieutenant."

After thirty minutes, the *Abyss* exited lightspeed, Hawkins released more shock drones and the heavy cruiser departed once more. All the while, the eight processing cores on the warship churned away at maximum utilisation as they worked on locating the exact destination of the Gate Maker spaceship.

"We've narrowed it down to this collection of solar systems here," said Quinn, several hours after the initial encounter with Ix-Gorghal.

"Anything significant amongst them?"

"Nothing jumps out."

"There's got to be something, otherwise why not simply stay within an hour of Dranmir instead of heading all this way?"

"There are a few hundred planets and a few dozen stars amongst all this lot if you want us to get hunting for a likely place," said Pointer.

"Do we genuinely want to find this Gate Maker earlier than planned?" asked Hawkins. "Won't that cut down our anticipated lead over *Ix-Gorghal*?"

"Potentially," said Quinn.

"I like the challenge and I like to know what's coming," said Blake. "At the very least we should try. This isn't a mission where we can hang around and await the optimum time to strike – the time to attack is *as soon as possible*."

"Do we even know for certain they are heading towards a planet or a star?" said Cruz. "Maybe they can make this gate out in the middle of nowhere."

"There's plenty of emptiness to choose from," Blake replied. "Which again begs the question why they didn't simply do what they're intending to do a few million klicks off the edge of Dranmir. They're certainly not scared of us and have no intention of running."

"I suppose."

"What exactly are we looking for?" said Hawkins.

"I expect most of these planets will be mapped and in the Space Corps database. We're looking for something unusual – a feature which makes a place different to every other."

The crew fell silent while they combed through the Space Corps' records of planets in the area they believed the Gate Maker had journeyed towards.

"Big planets, little planets, big suns, small suns," said Hawkins. "There's a bit of everything."

"Hot ones and cold ones," said Pointer.

"I've identified a couple of super-hot planets," said Quinn.

Blake looked up from his own screen. "Think about it – that one spaceship is going to attempt what a dozen Neutralisers failed to do. It's going to try and open what we assume will be a permanent gate for Vraxar ships to come through. It won't have escaped your notice that the Gate Maker was less voluminous than a single Neutraliser, therefore it makes sense they will need a way to either directly produce or extract energy."

"I agree," said Hawkins.

"If we approach the problem from that angle, does it provide any insights?"

"Nothing immediate," said Pointer.

The hunt resumed. Meanwhile, the *ES Abyss*'s engine output gradually fell, reducing their lightspeed multiple at the same time. The drop of two percent wouldn't be especially noticeable when the engines switched to gravity drive, but it was the potential end result which was concerning.

"We are re-entering local space," said Quinn, breaking the collective reverie.

They completed the routine of launching shock drones and vanishing once more to lightspeed, leaving behind a glittering array of robots to confuse the immense enemy they assumed was still in pursuit.

"We'll run out of drones eventually," said Hawkins.

"How long?"

"We've got enough for another five releases if we continue ejecting the same number of drones each time."

Blake checked the schedule of randomised jumps. "There's enough, as long as we don't need to repeat this tactic more times than we're expecting."

"Should I cut back the quantity of drones, sir?"

"No, don't make changes."

With two hours remaining of the predicted fission modelling time, Hawkins ventured a thought.

"Do we have any idea why the Gate Maker was so highly-polished?" she asked. "It seemed like a lot of effort if there wasn't a reason for it."

"Yeah – it would need to be specially buffed up after nearly every trip," said Pointer.

"Maybe it's meant to deflect sensors from a longer distance," said Cruz doubtfully. "Not that it would work very well."

"What if the Vraxar captain of that ship likes it to be shiny?" said Blake in exasperation. "What if there's no rhyme or reason for their destination other than they fancied a little bit of sightseeing?"

"Or what if they intend opening this gate at the place which will bring their fleet in at the closest point to these Antaron they plan to attack?" asked Pointer.

Blake threw his hands up. "I only like guessing games when I hit on the answer quickly."

"I never liked guessing games, even when I won," said Hawkins. "Where's the pleasure in relying on luck?"

In the end, it was Lieutenant Cruz who came up with the only idea which fit. At least it fit in a kind of so-unbelievable-there-must-be-something-in-it kind of way.

"If we look an hour or two outside of the projected destination area, there's the location of the old Helius Blackstar."

Everyone in the Space Corps was taught about the Helius Blackstar – the wormhole through which the Estral had once sought entry into Confederation Space until the rift was closed by the titanic blast of an Obsidiar bomb.

"The wormhole is gone," said Pointer. "There's just empty space there now."

At that exact moment, the modelling software updated its projection. The circle demarking the likely destination of the Gate Maker moved slightly across the star chart, until the furthest extent of the zone touched upon the location of the Helius Blackstar. The crew looked at each other.

"Why might they want to go to the location of an old wormhole?" asked Blake.

"An old wormhole which once connected to the middle of Estral territory, where the Vraxar fought their most extensive conflict," said Hawkins.

"A place they might still have a sizeable quantity of ships stationed," added Quinn.

"The Space Corps estimates the result of the Estral-Vraxar war become inevitable thirty-five years ago," said Blake.

"The mopping up exercise for an empire spanning thousands of worlds might take decades," said Hawkins.

"Or more," noted Quinn.

"I can see where you're going with this," said Blake. "You think there's a Vraxar warfleet parked up at the far end of the Helius Blackstar."

"It's a possibility," said Hawkins. "It strikes me that the Vraxar can never stop moving, sir. Even while they're fighting, they must have scouts spreading outwards, searching for the next target. They aren't like any other species – the Vraxar don't need a period of recovery after a war. In fact, an extended break in hostilities is unthinkable for them, since it might result in billions of their troops decaying and becoming useless."

"That fleet at Cheops-A...you think it was a *scouting* party?" Blake tried to inject a note of scepticism into his tones. He wasn't a good actor and he failed, not least of which because he was starting to believe Hawkins was onto something.

"It seemed like a lot of spaceships to us," said Hawkins. "To the Vraxar?" She shrugged.

Blake chewed his lower lip. "If we run with your idea for a moment, the only possible way for the Vraxar to make this work is for them to reopen the Helius Blackstar. Which is impossible, because it got torn apart by the largest bomb ever made. There's nothing there to open."

"That may not be quite true," said Quinn. "A wormhole forms because there's a weakness in the *fabric,* for want of a better word. That's the same fabric we go through in order to pretend physics don't exist when we travel at lightspeed."

"A spaceship only makes a little hole," said Hawkins. "It soon closes up."

"We *think* it closes up," corrected Quinn. "It makes it easier to believe we aren't damaging anything underlying the makeup of the universe. There are many schools of thought on the subject."

"None of which are relevant to this current discussion," said Blake sternly.

"Not necessarily," Quinn continued. "A wormhole is a larger hole than anything made by a spaceship. A much, much larger hole, which current thinking believes is a result of an inherent weakness in the fabric. So, the wormhole is like a big tear in the universe that a few brave souls have exploited to travel incredible distances in precisely zero amount of time."

"I should know this stuff," said Blake, cursing himself for letting his interests tail off once he'd been promoted to captain a few years ago.

"Yes, you should," said Pointer.

"Let's not all wade in," Blake replied. "I've just owned up to a weakness."

Quinn was impatient to give his conclusion. "It seems to me that the Helius Blackstar is gone, but the weakness which allowed it to appear in the first place still remains. Tassin-Dak specifically called the spaceship a *Gate Maker*. He didn't call it a Summoner, or a Mega Neutraliser or anything else that might define its purpose. The name gives it away. It's going to do something at the Helius Blackstar and allow a load of Vraxar to come pouring through."

Such was Quinn's certainty, Blake felt the man's conviction tugging at the threads of his disbelief. As if to drive it home, the next recalculation from the fission modelling software brought the site of the Helius Blackstar inside the possibility sphere.

"There you are," said Quinn. "That's where they're going."

Blake thought out loud. "The Vraxar can't rely on there being a wormhole everywhere they go, surely?"

"That's why they bring so many Neutralisers," said Hawkins. "To shut down resistance and to make a temporary wormhole for others to come, once they've found their prey."

It sounded logical. "The Vraxar must have learned about the Blackstar from Estral records," Blake mused.

"And bully for them, it leads straight to a primitive little backwater of space occupied by the Confederation," said Hawkins. "What's even more fortuitous for our Vraxar friends is the fact that this Confederation is only a short hop away from the next species on their hitlist. There's only one fly in the ointment for the poor, rotting Vraxar - we closed the door forty years ago."

"Now they have the means to open it," said Blake.

A soft beeping brought their attention to an alert from Quinn's console.

"The fission modelling has finished early," he said. "Come and look."

"I don't think I need to," Blake replied. "It's gone to the Helius Blackstar."

"Exactly right, sir."

"I'd like to get a message to Fleet Admiral Duggan. Do we have any Space Corps assets in the vicinity which can act as a relay?"

"No, sir," said Pointer. "I can send a message if you like and he'll get it in a few days."

"Let's not bother for the moment. How far away from the Helius Blackstar are we?"

"Nine hours, sir, assuming the failure rate of our engines stays as it is."

"We'll make one last entry into local space, dump all bar two hundred of our shock drones and then we'll head straight for the wormhole."

It took less than five minutes to accomplish this final attempt to confuse the pursuit of *Ix-Gorghal*. Then, the *ES Abyss* hurtled off on a new course, this one taking it directly towards a place where Blake was increasingly sure the Vraxar intended to reopen the Helius Blackstar wormhole. *A damned wormhole!* he thought, without even a grudging admiration for the remorseless, single-minded nature of the Vraxar.

The moment they'd started pursuit of the Gate Maker he'd known the mission was critical. Now it seemed somehow even more vital for them to reach the destination point and put a stop to the Vraxar's plans. The thought of witnessing thousands of their spacecraft spilling into Confederation Space wasn't a pleasant one and he mentally urged the damaged heavy cruiser to find an extra surge of power that would shave minutes or hours from the journey time.

The clock counted down slowly, taunting him for his fanciful thoughts.

CHAPTER TWENTY-THREE

IT WAS one of the worst journeys Blake could remember. He prided himself on his ability to let time glide around him while he remained staunch and unaffected by its passage. On this occasion, he felt as though he was caught in the turbulence of a great storm and it pushed him this way and that, scornful of his efforts to remain calm in the middle of it. Both he and the crew knew that the ES *Abyss* was far more vulnerable to attack with its energy shield gone. *They built them tough,* thought Blake, reflecting upon Fleet Admiral Duggan's earlier words.

"Probably not tough enough for what lies ahead," he muttered under his breath.

Blake spent a few minutes re-reading the databank records of the Helius Blackstar. The original location of the wormhole was an empty area of space approximately five days high lightspeed from New Earth. There were solar systems a few hours journey away, though nothing which could be described as being in the vicinity.

The Space Corps database contained a visual recording of the wormhole – it appeared as an area of utter darkness set against a sea of background stars. Blake found he could overlay a speckling of dots onto the image and these dots drifted slowly, inexorably towards the centre. Watching it was both frightening and thrilling.

Other than trawl through records from the past, there was little to fill the time. The crew were lost in their own thoughts and they hardly spoke; even the usually irreverent Lieutenant Hawkins remained quiet. Occasionally, someone got up for a scheduled break and disappeared from the bridge for a short time, often returning with trays from one of the replicators. The odours of food would have been appetising at any other time. At this moment they didn't appeal to Blake, even though his stomach occasionally rumbled angrily to remind him of his hunger.

"Maybe you should get some rest, sir," said Lieutenant Quinn. "We're due to arrive in three hours."

Blake looked up in surprise and realised it was his turn for a break. "There's no chance I'll sleep," he said.

"Want me to get the medic up here to give you something? We'll need to be on top form."

"Thank you for the concern, Lieutenant. I think I'll go for a walk.

The bridge door opened silently and Blake strode through. He didn't have a destination in mind and was only planning to stretch his legs for a few minutes. The passages of the ship were bathed in red instead of their usual blue-white, to signify the existence of a breach. Luckily, the Vraxar projectile hadn't penetrated as far as the living quarters and the heavy cruiser's interior remained sealed against the vacuum outside.

He walked, breathing in the cool air and flexing the knots from his muscles. It didn't take long for him to realise he didn't want to be anywhere apart from the bridge and he spun about halfway along a corridor and traced his route back. He stopped at a replicator from which he obtained an average coffee and several remarkably good doughnuts. He tried to eat a balanced diet in general and asked himself if placing a doughnut on each side of the scales would result in equilibrium.

Upon his return to the bridge, the sight of his plate drew forth several critical observations, which he gleefully ignored. For some reason he felt considerably more cheerful after his walk, as though he'd broken free from a thick covering of cobwebs which made everything appear grey. The crew caught this sudden optimism and the chatter started again. The bridge immediately felt alive, instead of being an enclosed room filled with people who expected to end up as Vraxar in the coming days.

Much of the remaining time before arrival was spent in discussion of what they were going to do about the Gate Maker.

"We don't want to arrive too close," said Hawkins. "Without our shield, we're a much easier target and we might get picked off before we've recovered from the transition to local space."

"I agree," said Quinn. "The trouble is, we need to destroy the enemy ship before it can open a portal to Estral Space."

"And before *Ix-Gorghal* gets there," said Cruz.

"We'll do a softly-softly approach and drop into local space at a million and a half klicks out," said Blake. "Once we've got the lay of the land, we'll perform an SRT to bring us where we need to be."

"Back in the days of the Estral wars, the Space Corps positioned a number of monitoring devices in the vicinity of the wormhole," said Pointer. "They were never decommissioned."

"Does that mean we can get a comms channel to Fleet Admiral Duggan?" asked Blake.

"Maybe. These monitoring drones weren't shut down, but I can't find out if they're still working and attached to the Space Corps comms network. If they're operational, we should be able to speak to New Earth."

"This is the type of situation where I'd value a second opinion," said Blake.

"I can tell you exactly what the Fleet Admiral's opinion will be, sir," said Hawkins. *"Blow the crap out of the Gate Maker and get yourselves home."*

"An accurate assessment, I'm sure," Blake agreed. "I don't suppose the Space Corps left any offensive hardware near the site of the wormhole?" he asked. "Such as Obsidiar bombs?"

"No. Monitoring gear only."

"Shame."

The conversation continued and the crew did their best to come up with a workable plan. There were times when information was so scant it was impossible to do anything other than guess and then assign a label of *plan* to the end product. This was one of those occasions. They had a good idea where they were going and a good idea of what was likely to be there. After that, the important details such as what were the capabilities of the Gate Maker, and how they would defeat it, were completely unknown.

"It seems reasonable to assume it can defend itself and that it possesses huge reserves of power," said Blake, speaking the obvious.

"And here we are without backup Obsidiar power," said Hawkins.

"The sensor scan we took when it came out of *Ix-Gorghal*'s hold doesn't show any visible seam on its surface," said Pointer. "That means no missiles, right?"

"But with the possibility of beam weapons," said Hawkins.

"It's a got a lot more volume than we have – there's plenty of room for all sorts of unpleasant technology inside," added Quinn.

Blake called a halt to proceedings. "I don't think we're going to conjure up anything of value by continuing with this. We'll need to think on our feet and take whatever opportunities arise."

"Ten minutes!" yelled Lieutenant Quinn suddenly.

The warning came as a shock. The first part of the journey had felt to Blake like he was wading in treacle, whilst the latter third had flown by so fast he felt cheated out of this tiny portion of his life. The others looked similarly dazed, though it didn't stop them reacting properly and getting on with their final pre-arrival checks.

"Two minutes!"

With the screens of his console wrapped comfortably around his seat, Blake got himself ready. A light appeared on his navigational screen and an alert bleeped. A few seconds later, the *ES Abyss* grumbled and shook as it emerged from lightspeed.

A well-oiled routine commenced.

"Activating stealth modules," said Quinn.

"Commencing scans," said Pointer. "Nears are clear."

Blake used the control bars to get the heavy cruiser moving. The stealth modules sapped the already depleted engines and the warship responded sluggishly. After a few seconds it topped out at sixteen hundred kilometres per second – a relative crawl in comparison to its usual maximum.

"Lieutenant Cruz, how are you getting on with those monitoring drones?"

"I'm hunting for them, sir. They're not on our network and I believe they may have been left on an old-generation network the Space Corps no longer uses."

"Can you access it?"

"Yes. I need to dig through the archives for some access codes."

"Keep on it. I want command and control to know where we are and why."

"I've already sent a low-speed signal as agreed," said Cruz.

"Good."

It usually took Blake a few seconds to orient himself with the surrounding area when he arrived somewhere new. His head darted left and right across the navigational console and sensor feeds until he felt everything click into place. He changed course slightly, aiming the *ES Abyss* directly for the database coordinates which identified the former position of the Helius Blackstar.

"I need some updates," he said.

"I've switched directly to the super-fars," said Pointer. "I'm trying to get a focus on the target area."

"Bring it up on the screen when you find it."

"I'm still attempting to link to our monitoring drones," said Cruz. "There were twenty in all and they're definitely on an old version of our comms network. V99.12xw according to the records – that's dated twenty years ago."

"You can still reach them, can't you?"

"Yes, it won't be a problem."

"Got it!" shouted Pointer.

Every pair of eyes on the bridge turned towards the main viewscreen. The distance was extreme and the image wobbled with the infinitesimal movements of the sensor modules. Blake found himself squinting to try and make out extra details.

In the middle of the screen, the spherical shape of the Gate Maker sat motionless – indicators on the feed showed it was positioned exactly in the centre of the old wormhole, down to the millimetre. Great sparks of energy flashed out from the edges of the spaceship, jagging away in colours of green and blue. These bolts extended for thousands of kilometres in all directions and came with such frequency they made it difficult to see the Vraxar craft in the centre.

"I don't think they're finished," said Blake.

Quinn had his mouth open in wonder. "They've definitely started."

"Will any of that sensor data tell us how long until they're done?"

"I wouldn't like to guess, sir," said Pointer. "There's so much energy concentrated about the Gate Maker it's difficult to understand what the hell is going on."

"It's strange...it feels like our sensor arrays are being pinned onto that spaceship," said Cruz. "I've never seen this happen before."

"We're going to make a short-range transit – aim for a hundred thousand klicks from the Gate Maker. Then, we're going to fire missiles at it until it blows up."

"Ready when you are, sir," said Quinn.

"Activate."

The *ES Abyss* shot forwards, the double transition sending a much stronger vibration through the hull. The heavy cruiser emerged into local space at precisely the intended spot. Blake got his bearings and set them on a circular course which would take them around the Gate Maker whilst maintaining a constant distance.

"Get that sensor lock back up."

"On it."

"And reactivate the stealth modules."

"They're coming online right now, sir."

"There's our target," said Pointer.

The *ES Abyss* was much closer than before, though the only sign of this was the added stability on the sensor feed. Where before the image had wavered, now it was rock-steady. The Gate Maker continued pouring energy into space, a huge dark spot in the centre of incredible chaos.

"Fire," said Blake. "Lambdas only."

Hawkins acknowledged and sent the launch command. Lambda missiles burst from their tubes and sped towards their target. Blake's tactical screen filled with tiny dots.

"Fire again as soon as reload is complete."

"Yes, sir."

The second salvo followed the first, and another four hundred advanced missiles twisted and turned through space towards their target.

Blake intended this as a probing attack, to see if he could prompt a response from the enemy ship. The response came quickly. A wave of invisible force rippled outwards from the Gate Maker, expanding in all directions. The first salvo of missiles met this wave and a moment later the second wave did the same.

"Those missiles are dead," said Hawkins. "Guidance and detonation systems gone."

The wave enveloped the *ES Abyss*, sending needles bouncing from one side of their gauges to the other and back again. Three of the eight processing cores went straight to one hundred percent utilisation and remained there for a second before slowly dropping.

"What the hell?" asked Quinn. "That was like the anti-missile system we've seen Neutralisers and the Vraxar battleships use. Except that one was far more powerful."

"I want another launch – stagger it this time. Lambdas, Shimmers, Nukes, Lambdas, Shatterers. Then try and hit them with a particle beam."

It took a few seconds for Hawkins to set up the firing pattern. Once done, she triggered a sequence which would launch the missiles in a set pattern. The crew watched anxiously as the warheads headed through space.

"They've used that energy wave again," said Quinn.

"Let's hope they can't use it too regularly," Blake replied.

The energy wave trashed six hundred inbound missiles and sent the warship's instrumentation into a temporary frenzy of misreads. The *ES Abyss* was equipped with a rapid-reload mechanism for the Lambdas and it spat them out in a near-continuous stream. It was the Shimmers and nuclear missiles which Blake was most keen to hit the target and he clenched his fists, willing them onwards.

"There's another energy burst from the Gate Maker," said Quinn. "And a fourth."

"Shimmers and nukes have been disabled."

"Damnit!" snarled Blake, thumping his fist down.

"If you want my opinion, they aren't even trying, sir," said Quinn. "There was only a two-second interval between those last two energy bursts."

"I'm going to use the particle beam," said Hawkins. "There's no overcharge without the Obsidiar core."

"Give them the front and rear, Lieutenant."

The ES *Abyss*'s front and rear beam domes hummed and thumped. Invisible lines of energy connected the warship and the Gate Maker for a split second before the discharge was complete.

"That's done...absolutely nothing?" said Pointer.

"Looks like," replied Hawkins.

"There's a slight increase in their hull temperature where we hit them," said Quinn. "They're either dispersing the energy internally or our particle beam is being broken up when it travels through those energy bolts its giving off."

"At least it's defensive only," said Blake. "I'm sure it would have fired at us if it was capable. Turn the Bulwarks on it."

"The Bulwarks are set to automatic," said Hawkins.

The ES *Abyss* was fitted with eighty-four of the large-bore, high velocity cannons. It could only bring fifty of them to bear on the Gate Maker at the same time. The rapid-fire thrum echoed through the walls and hundreds of thousands of projectiles streaked towards the enemy ship.

"They've got an energy shield," said Quinn. "We might knock it out eventually."

"Not before the Bulwarks burn out and shut down," said Hawkins.

"Maintain fire at thirty percent of maximum, Lieutenant."

"Roger."

Lieutenant Cruz cleared her throat. "I've joined the monitoring drones' local comms network."

"Patch us through to New Earth Central Command Station," said Blake.

"The drones are waking up from ultra-low power sleep. It's going to take a minute before they're warmed up."

"Tell me when you can make the patch."

"The output from the Gate Maker has just made a big jump, sir," said Quinn.

The intensity of greens and blues climbed noticeably on the viewscreen. Not only that, but the lines of energy leapt progressively further and further away from the centre. The colours dimmed and Blake thought for a moment it was the sensors adjusting the brightness for comfort. It wasn't.

"The blues are fading out," said Pointer.

"And the greens are darkening."

"I get the feeling we're too late, sir."

"There are only nineteen drones on the network, not twenty," said Cruz, more to herself than anyone.

"We're going to have to do something," said Blake.

"No, there are twenty drones, one of them is still offline for some reason."

"Forget about the drones, Lieutenant."

Blake knew there was only one course of action open to them. Their weapons were ineffective against the endless reserves of the Gate Maker. Time was running out and he was certain the Vraxar were close to forcing open the wormhole. The only hope was a high-speed collision into the Gate Maker's shield in the hope they could overload it and make the enormous spaceship vulnerable to missile fire.

"It's not offline, it's being *held* offline," said Cruz.

With his hands tightly on the control bars, Blake prepared to turn them in towards the enemy spaceship.

"Oh crap!" said Cruz.

She was another of the crew who rarely swore and her exclamation was enough to jar Blake to attention, though not enough to stop him beginning his manoeuvre.

"We need an SRT! Now!" Cruz shouted.

"What?" said Quinn. Too late, he saw the fleeting fission cloud of a spaceship arriving from a short-range jump of its own.

Blake pulled the control bars hard left, his new course fixed in his head. Nothing happened. The lights on the bridge flickered, went out and returned. One-by-one, the crew's consoles shut down. The distant pounding of the Bulwark cannons stopped, leaving the bridge utterly quiet.

"Neutraliser," said Blake. "How?"

CHAPTER TWENTY-FOUR

"IT WAS out near one of the monitoring drones. I didn't catch it straight away," said Cruz glumly.

"Not your fault, Lieutenant. We were acting under pressure and it was my choice for us to make the quick lightspeed jump towards the Gate Maker."

"I'm tapping into the residual power," said Quinn. "We're not going to have many options."

"I know," said Blake. "I'd like to see what we're facing."

The consoles came online, though most of the screens showed only partial information and many of the warship's facilities were offline, inactive or just plain inaccessible.

Pointer was able to get something from the front sensor array. "Check this out," she said. "It won't look great."

The warship's sensors couldn't focus over long distances when they were running off the residual power which remained in the Gallenium engines. On this occasion, the enemy spaceship was close enough to make out the details.

"Look at the state of it," said Hawkins.

The Neutraliser was badly damaged. Much of its front nullification sphere had deformed from the effects of heat, whilst its main connecting struts were bent as if they'd been subjected to intense flames which had warped the metal. Blake guessed what this spaceship was.

"It's the *Ir-Klion-6*," he said. "It's the one Fleet Admiral Duggan told us about."

"The final vessel of the twelve which brought *Ix-Gorghal* through," said Hawkins.

"That may be the last Vraxar Neutraliser in Confederation Space, and here it is, right where we didn't want it."

"Tough luck for us."

"Are any weapons available?"

"I might be able to get a few Lambdas chambered. It'll take out the final residual power."

"Best hold off. Can we get a message out through those monitoring drones?"

"I think so. We won't be able to hold a channel open, so it's outbound only."

"Fine – make command and control aware of what we've found."

"Do you want me to pass on any recommendations, sir?"

"I don't think so. They've got people who'll know what to do."

"I've sent the signal and received an acknowledgement from the drone telling me it has been successfully relayed."

"What do we do now?" asked Hawkins. "And why haven't they killed us?"

"I don't know, Lieutenant."

"I've got a good idea why that is, sir," said Pointer. "They're waiting for *Ix-Gorghal*. Tassin-Dak wanted information from us, but he had no way of getting us away from the *Abyss*. This

Neutraliser just needs to hold us here until *Ix-Gorghal* arrives. The Vraxar said he was carrying a billion soldiers and we can't hold off that many."

"*Ir-Klion-32* had a good few million as well," said Blake. "When it comes to numbers, we've got one hundred and twenty soldiers onboard, plus crew."

"How long until *Ix-Gorghal* gets here?" asked Hawkins.

"Anything from thirty minutes to two hours," said Quinn, not making an effort to sound convinced at his own estimation.

"We can't just give up!" protested Cruz.

"Who is giving up?" asked Blake. "Get through to the troop's quarters and tell everyone to get suited up, if they aren't already dressed."

The internal comms system used hardly any power and Cruz had no problems sending the command. While she was busy, Blake walked to the bridge locker and began dragging suits off the rack and dropping them onto the floor. There were also gauss rifles and pistols, as well as a couple of grenade belts. He picked out a rifle and tested its weight.

"Our turn," he said, pulling a suit up over his uniform. "Leave your consoles and come over here."

The others joined him in a group, fighting to get into the spacesuits as quickly as possible so they could return to their stations.

The lights on the bridge brightened slightly and Blake saw lists of numbers scroll across several screens. He dashed to his console and attempted to access a few of the spaceship's critical systems.

"Are we back online?" he asked.

"I don't think so," said Quinn, scratching his head.

"What's happening?"

"There's inbound comms," said Pointer. "The source identifies itself as *Ir-Klion-6*."

Blake was rapidly becoming accustomed to surprises and this one was no more a shock than several others he'd experienced recently.

"What do they want?"

"To speak to you."

"Of course."

The connection was made and a Vraxar from the Neutraliser spoke through the bridge speakers. The tones were unmistakeably similar to those of Tassin-Dak and a picture was starting to build in Blake's mind about the aliens' command structure.

"I am known as Renklan Vir," said the Vraxar. "I command the *Ir-Klion-6*."

"I am Charlie Blake and I command the *ES Abyss*."

"*Ix-Gorghal* comes and Tassin-Dak is not happy at what you have done."

"Aren't we all children of the Vraxar? Or is that just the kind of crap you inject into the minds of conquered species?"

"Your words mean nothing. We have come and we will subject your race to conversion. Insolence is of no consequence."

"I assume you desire more from this conversation than a casual exchange of minor insults?"

"I have been instructed to bring you to the *Ir-Klion-6*. This time you have no choice in the matter, since we have disabled your Gallenium engines and therefore your ability to launch your weapons."

"We have an Obsidiar bomb," said Blake, testing his luck again.

The Vraxar laughed. "There is no Obsidiar bomb, else you would have used it on *Ix-Gorghal*."

"Why would we allow you to bring us to your ship?" asked Blake. "Are you suggesting we voluntarily permit ourselves to be subjected to your truth drugs, followed by a conversion into one of your rotting soldiers?"

"Not everyone, Captain Charlie Blake – we only need you. The rest we will allow to leave on one of your shuttles."

"In spite of your success when it comes to murdering other species, you don't have a very good grasp of persuasion, do you?" asked Blake. "Let me enlighten you - in order to be successful at persuasion, it is vital that you make the other party believe what you say."

The Vraxar laughed again. It was the all-knowing sound of someone who had the upper hand. "What do you have to lose? Either we kill you or we let you go."

"I don't intend being the one to tell you where to locate the rest of the Confederation's worlds. You won't find anyone here willing to betray our entire species."

"Your denials are only delaying the inevitable. *Ix-Gorghal* is in your territory and soon our Gate Maker will create an opening for thousands more of our fleet. We have the databanks from your warship Determinant and eventually we will unravel the secrets they contain."

"If everything is going so smoothly you won't be too disappointed when I tell you to piss off, will you?"

The connection went dead.

"I think you annoyed him, sir," said Pointer.

"We've taken a particle beam hit aft," said Quinn. "And now a second one."

Hawkins laughed. "It doesn't look like they're going to wait around for *Ix-Gorghal* to get here, does it?"

"Their commanders are easily angered," said Blake. "It's something to bear in mind for the future."

The damage reports appeared on Blake's screen. The *Abyss*'s armour plating had dissipated most of the heat, leaving the spaceship with only minor additional damage. As he watched, further reports were generated.

"They've turned their dark energy beam on us as well," said

Quinn. "Two hits and they've put a big crater in our starboard side."

"The bastards are leaving us with just enough power to see what they're doing to us and not enough to do anything about it," said Pointer.

"There was no choice," said Blake simply.

"You don't need to say anything else, sir," said Hawkins. "No one deals with the devil and comes out a winner. The only thing Renklan Vir had to offer was death and there was nothing you could do to change it."

"Definitely," said Quinn. "I don't even think he expected to get anything out of this. All he did was show there's cruelty underlying the Vraxar. There's a race amongst them who controls the others and they aren't in it just for survival – this is something they enjoy."

"That's what I thought as well," said Cruz. "That conversation was part of a stupid game and we'd lost before it started."

Another particle beam hit the *ES Abyss* and another. The Neutralisers differed in how many beam domes they had fitted and the *Ir-Klion-6* had twelve visible. They fired sporadically.

"Renklan Vir is stretching this out on purpose," said Blake.

"Yep."

The Galactics were excellent damage soaks and the *ES Abyss* absorbed many direct hits. The warnings on Blake's console turned to red alerts, which then became critical alerts. Several of their sensor arrays were disabled, followed by the navigational system. Finally, the life support system shut down entirely. Meanwhile, an alarm pealed incessantly on the bridge, accompanied by a strobing red light. The alarm was just loud enough to make conversation uncomfortable and Blake shut it off.

"Keep me updated on our status," he said. *For all the good it'll do us.*

Pointer was able to bring up a feed showing the upper section of the heavy cruiser's hull. It was an unrecognizable mess of burning metal and rivers of molten alloy.

"Here's the rear view."

The *Abyss* was leaving a trail of orange sparks and a streak of flame across the blackness of space.

"It would be beautiful if I didn't know what it was," said Hawkins.

"They've more or less burned out the engines," said Quinn. "Even if they stopped firing now, the Space Corps shipyards won't be able to repair us."

Blake felt something catch in his throat. The ES *Abyss* was a proud warship and it was terrible to see it being hacked slowly to pieces and unable to respond.

"We've had a breach into the lower maintenance decks," said Quinn.

"Do we have enough power to seal the area?"

"Yes, sir, it's closing off."

"Any casualties?"

"None reported."

"Tell the troops what's coming," said Blake. "Wait. It needs to come from me."

"I'll get you through."

"Lieutenant Holloway?"

"Hello, sir. It's getting hot down here. We've been looking at the sensor feeds."

"This is the end, Lieutenant."

"Is there anything we can do, sir?"

"I'm afraid not. We've got no power for weapons or escape and the enemy captain is determined to fire upon us until we are destroyed."

"I would have liked a chance to fight."

"I'm truly sorry, Lieutenant. It's a soldier's lot."

"Maybe in the next life, huh?"

"At least the next life isn't going to be as a Vraxar."

Holloway gave a laugh free of bitterness. "That's something to celebrate."

"There're a few of the guys who've had a good run. Tell them I'm sad it had to come to an end."

"I know the ones you mean, sir."

"I'm sad for everyone, not just those."

He cut the channel, unable to speak longer. The Neutraliser continued firing its particle beams and one-by-one the *Abyss*'s remaining sensor arrays shut down.

"We'll be blind before we're dead," said Pointer.

"We've got heat penetration just beyond the starboard bridge wall," said Quinn. "I'm not sure I want to die this way."

Blake had no words to offer. He'd failed and it was a hard thing for him to face up to. He kept his eyes fixed on *Ir-Klion-6* and felt his futile hatred seething within. The feeling was so strong it squeezed his chest and throat, making it hard for him to swallow.

"One more chance," he said. "One more chance to kill these bastards."

The image feed had fallen to an extremely low resolution. However, it wasn't quite so grainy that it hid the beam of thick blue light which struck the *Ir-Klion-6*, nor did it disguise the magnificence of the plasma flames which roared wildly from the point of impact, until they surrounded the Neutraliser and hid it within their deadly grasp.

Blake found himself standing, his eyes wide. His mouth struggled to form the words his brain was trying to feed it with. In the end he could only lift one arm and point at the screen. The others had seen it too and their expressions told a story encompassing every single emotion across the entire spectrum of emotions.

The flames hadn't even started to recede when large-yield plasma explosions appeared amongst them, bursting with violent energy. Blake lost count of how many blasts detonated off the Neutraliser's shields. He recognized the type and the word jumped from his mouth.

"Shatterers."

All at once, the *Ir-Klion-6* was engulfed in an explosion of such monumental proportions, the entire vessel was lost amongst a white-hot sea which dwarfed even the mighty Vraxar Neutraliser.

A corner of Blake's mind shouted at him to get moving – it ordered him to break the shackles which kept him frozen in front of the unfolding spectacle. The rest of his mind responded, bringing action to his limbs and his voice.

"Move!" he bellowed. "Take a visor and get to the shuttle bay!" He sprang across the bridge, dragging Hawkins and Ensign Park to their feet. He waved his arms forward, urging the others to follow.

The loudness of his words and the suddenness of his actions spurred them on. With hardly a pause in his stride, Blake stooped to gather up a visor for his spacesuit and dropped it over his head. He turned to make sure the others were with him and then he raced towards the bridge exit. The heavy door shuddered slowly upwards, as though it was drawing on the last vestiges of power available within the *ES Abyss*. Blake didn't wait and he ducked beneath it, half-rolling through the gap and coming to his feet already running.

His visor established an interface with the internal comms and he patched through to Lieutenant Holloway.

"Lieutenant Holloway, get your troops to the rear shuttle bay. We're leaving on Shuttle One."

"I thought we were dead, sir?"

"No one's dying, Lieutenant. Did you get bored watching the sensor feed?"

"It lost power a couple of minutes ago. What did we miss?"

"The *Sciontrar* has come – it's kicking the crap out of the Neutraliser."

"Does that mean the shuttle's engines will fire up?"

"They have to."

"I've always liked the Ghasts, sir."

Holloway spoke in such a deadpan fashion that Blake felt laughter rise up inside. There was an edge of madness to it and he refused to succumb, especially since death still held them all within its cold embrace.

"You might get a chance to thank them later. Get moving."

It was a long enough journey to the rear shuttle bay when you were simply disembarking for shore leave. When the entire ship was in danger of breaking up and the metal walls smoked from the heat of particle beam strikes it felt much longer. Blake sprinted at the head of the group, occasionally slowing to allow the stragglers to catch up. His visor HUD informed him the temperature inside this section of the spaceship was well in excess of three hundred degrees, which was close to exceeding the suit's insulating capabilities. He increased his pace, not wanting to suffer the agonising death of burning.

Just when Blake truly began to believe that a miraculous escape was within reach, he discovered it wasn't to be so easy. The crew were within two hundred metres of the rear shuttle bay entry area and running along a wide, straight corridor, when a blast door rumbled jerkily shut ahead of them. Blake didn't slow and ran straight up to its access panel and planted his open hand onto the surface. The door didn't open.

"My suit is picking up a draught," said Cruz.

Everyone understood immediately.

"There's been a breach through the hull," said Pointer. "We need to get this door open."

"It's locked precisely because there's a breach," said Blake angrily. He slammed his palm onto the access panel for a second time. "It won't open."

"You'll need to override it, sir. If the vacuum doesn't pull us out, we'll burn alive."

The corridor was hot and getting hotter by the moment. The walls heated the air and created shimmering patterns which were drawn away towards the source of the hull breach. The crew began hopping from foot to foot, trying to delay the inevitable blistering of their spacesuits.

Blake looked back the way they'd come. There was another route to the shuttle bay, but it was an additional two hundred metres, with no real possibility the other blast doors were open.

"Lieutenant Holloway, where are you?" Blake spoke quickly, eager to get this conversation finished.

"We're entering the shuttle boarding zone, sir."

"All of you?"

"Yes, sir."

The troops were quartered a lot closer to the shuttle bay than the bridge and they'd acted quickly enough to avoid falling victim to the internal vacuum seals.

"We're stuck behind a door here."

"I can send Clifton that way if you want, sir? He might be able to make an opening for you."

It wasn't really an option – the internal blast doors were thick and strong. It would take a huge quantity of explosives to break through, which would leave the surrounding walls so hot it would prevent passage.

"Don't send Clifton. Get on the shuttle – if you need to leave, get out of here at once. No heroics."

"I'll tell the others to board, no guarantees on the heroics."

It wasn't something Blake wished to argue over. He dropped out of the comms channel and used his suit to connect to the *ES Abyss*'s internal security systems. These security systems were a set of control modules which were closely tied to the warship's life support. Since the life support was disabled, everything attached ran at a crawl. After a few seconds, he tied in successfully and sent a command code for the blast door to open.

>OVERRIDE CODE ERROR: NOT RECOGNIZED

He swore inside his visor. The escaping air plucked at his legs and he worried it would become strong enough to drag the crew outside. He had no intention of sticking around and he tried his codes again.

"What's up?" asked Hawkins.

"Something must be scrambled. It's not taking my codes."

Hawkins kicked at the door in an unexpected display of frustration. "Damnit!"

The crew searched for something to hold onto. Once the air was sucked clear, they'd be able to survive the vacuum in their suits. Unfortunately, the corridors of a fleet warship were kept clear of intrusion. Even the wall-mounted maintenance consoles were flush to the metal.

"Dragged into space or burned alive. That's not how I planned to go," said Pointer.

"I think I've found what's wrong," muttered Blake. "The command codes aren't reaching their destination."

"Can I help?" asked Hawkins.

"Wait - I'm trying something."

He tried again and his heart jumped.

>PRIORITY OVERRIDE REQUEST ACKNOWLEDGED. HULL BREACH IN SECTOR 9F-3. PLEASE CONFIRM.

>OVERRIDE CODE: BLAKE. CONFIRMED.

The door clunked once, rose a few inches from the floor and then stopped. Lights on the access panel dimmed and failed.

Quinn shuffled from foot to foot. "That's the residual power gone."

The internal doors had no other method of opening and they were too heavy to be cranked open by a mechanical jack. In desperation, Blake dropped to his knees and looked through the gap – it was much too small for a child, let alone an adult. Hot air whistled through the opening, washing over his face.

It wasn't the captain's place to say what everyone was thinking. *We're screwed*. He didn't speak the words but couldn't bring himself to give a motivational speech. An undulating movement on his forearm caught his eye and he watched with fascination as the surface of his spacesuit started to blister. The temperature had risen beyond four hundred degrees in the few seconds he'd been checking beneath the door and it was more than the suits could withstand.

Something else caught Blake's eye. The lights on the access panel reappeared and the green light for *open* glowed strongly. The blast door made a groaning scrape and then it rose smoothly into its recess in the ceiling.

"Go!"

The crew didn't need to hear the words in order to act. As a group, they piled through the opening, with Blake coming last. The access panel on the far side of the door also glowed green and he pressed it with his fingers. The door descended at once, closing off the passageway behind them.

"Move!" shouted Blake.

They moved. The shuttle access area wasn't far ahead and they sprinted towards it, their eagerness to live giving strength to their legs.

"What the...?" asked Cruz.

"The Ghasts must have finished off the *Ir-Klion-6*," panted

Blake. "Our engines have started generating power again. Enough to get that door open, anyway."

"Let's hope the troops haven't left us."

"They won't have had time. The shuttle's engines will have only just come online."

"Still..."

Blake got the message and he connected to Lieutenant Holloway. "Where are you?"

"In the docking bay. The shuttle is warming up."

"Don't go without us. We'll be there in a few seconds."

"And we'll be waiting."

They reached the shuttle access room. The airlock door was sealed but opened readily enough to Blake's command. The crew dashed into the airlock tunnel, closing the first door behind. The second iris twisted open, allowing them access to Shuttle One. There was standing room only in the passenger bay but in the circumstances, it was unimportant.

"Close the door and let's get the hell out of here!"

Blake pushed his way through the groups of soldiers until he reached the cockpit door. He opened it and found all the seats inside were taken.

Lieutenant Holloway greeted him warmly. "Captain Blake - you're just in time. Want a seat?"

"No – as you are. I'll stand."

With its engines straining, Shuttle One sped over the ES *Abyss*'s hangar bay floor. The heavy cruiser was burning hot and the shuttle started smoking at once. Lieutenant Holloway kept a tight hand on the controls and piloted the tiny vessel out into space. Once clear, she accelerated hard in order to put as much distance as possible between the two.

"Show me the *Abyss*," said Blake.

One of the co-pilots – a man whose name Blake didn't recognize – focused the rear sensors on the dwindling shape of the heavy cruiser. The *Abyss* was gone, of that there was no doubt. Its front section glowed white like a star and there was a huge split across the mid-section. The gap widened and before Blake's eyes, the heavy cruiser broke into separate pieces. He hunkered down on the floor, bereft.

CHAPTER TWENTY-FIVE

BLAKE WASN'T permitted time for misery or reflection. Only seconds after Shuttle One's escape from the wreckage of the *ES Abyss*, a comms request came through.

"You'll need to take this one, sir. It's someone calling himself Tarjos Nil-Tras from that there Ghast battleship."

Blake clambered to his feet. "Patch it into my visor."

"Yes, sir."

The familiar voice of the Ghast thundered into Blake's earpiece. The translation modules on the spacesuits were less sophisticated than those fitted to a fleet warship and the alien sounded like he was chewing on a mouthful of gravel.

"Captain Charlie Blake," he said. "We arrived in time."

There was no pride in Nil-Tras's voice – the words were a simple observation of events.

Blake felt humbled. "Thank you, Tarjos."

"I am bringing the *Sciontrar* closer to your shuttle. We have a central bay you can use. It will be easier if you hand over control of your vessel to us."

"Agreed." Blake muted the comms channel and spoke briefly

to Lieutenant Holloway, advising her to accept the incoming pairing request from the *Sciontrar*.

"There is no time for manual docking – you need to get onboard quickly," Nil-Tras explained. "We cannot afford to divert from combat for long."

"The Gate Maker?"

"Is that what you call it? It is dismissive of our missile bombardments."

"You need to destroy it. The Vraxar are attempting to open the Helius Blackstar and we believe they have the bulk of their fleet waiting on the other side."

"You are better informed than we are," rumbled the Ghast. He laughed in sudden good humour. "We simply saw an enemy ship and thought we'd better destroy it. Now we know the reasons."

In the front seat, Lieutenant Holloway lifted a clenched fist in Blake's direction and raised the thumb. *Pairing complete* the gesture said. Blake noticed a sudden lateral force which told him the shuttle was banking sharply to the left.

"Have you used your anti-shield weapon on the Gate Maker?" asked Blake.

"We used it on the Neutraliser. The weapon takes some minutes to prepare for another discharge. Every new weapon our labs produce comes with this limitation or that. I complain, though in truth I am grateful." He laughed again.

The words reminded Blake of the many stories he'd heard about the humanness of the Ghasts. Nil-Tras talked an old hand from the Space Corps.

"We think *Ix-Gorghal* is coming," Blake said.

"We were unable to determine if it followed us or followed you and we didn't wish to test it by waiting in one place."

"My engine man produced an estimate of its anticipated time

of arrival at the Helius Blackstar. I'm afraid I have completely lost track of time."

"We know it is coming and we can only act as fast as we are able. We will either destroy this Gate Maker and escape, or we will not. What use is it forever checking the seconds which pass?"

"I like your outlook, though I don't think I'll be able to change."

"We are initiating the docking routine. My technicians advise there will be no problem with the coupling in our bay."

"I'll speak to you shortly, Tarjos."

"Come directly to the bridge and you may be in time to witness the destruction of the Vraxar vessel."

The Ghost had an unshakeable confidence in his own ability and the strength of his battleship. Blake was beginning to understand why they made such formidable opponents – they just never gave up.

"There's the *Sciontrar*," said Holloway. "It looks neat."

Neat wasn't exactly the word Blake would have chosen to describe a vessel with such a titanic amount of firepower. It was fixed on the centre of the shuttle's viewscreen, only the background movement of stars indicating how rapidly the battleship was travelling. The *Sciontrar* looked relatively undamaged – there was a pattern of heat damage which covered a circular area a few hundred metres in diameter. Other than that, it looked like it was ready for anything. *It may have to be,* thought Blake.

It took less than two minutes to complete the docking routine. Either the Ghosts lacked the Space Corps' concern with safety, or they'd initiated an emergency procedure designed to bring home damaged shuttles as quickly as possible. Blake didn't care which – he was simply glad there was no delay.

The shuttle's viewscreen filled up with the slab-sided flank of the Ghost battleship. The hangar bay doors slid aside at the last possible moment and even then, they only opened partway.

"Still on full throttle," gulped Lieutenant Holloway, pressing back into her seat. They rocketed through the doors, with the *Sciontrar*'s docking computers applying the brakes at precisely the right moment to bring them to a timely stop. "Whoa shit!"

"I thought you'd always liked the Ghasts, Lieutenant?"

"I have, sir. It's their docking computers that piss me off."

Blake smiled, feeling part of his burden fall away. The shuttle came to a standstill, hitting the airlock with a solid thump. Blake stumbled, righted himself and then dashed for the exit. He pushed his way through the passenger bay until he reached the shuttle's external door. The light on the panel was red and he stared, daring it to remain so. He was on the verge of punching it when the red light changed to green and a cheery alert went *ding!*

"Lieutenant Hawkins, look after everyone. I'm off to the bridge."

"I can't even look after myself, sir."

He ignored the response – Hawkins knew her stuff and she'd do what was required. The outer door opened, revealing a Ghast-sized passage, lit in cold blue. There was a secondary airlock door twenty metres along, which was already open, providing reinforcement to the notion that safety was a secondary concern to the Ghasts.

The airlock passage led directly into the central section of the *Sciontrar*. Blake paused at the end, looking left and right. He'd seen file pictures of the Cadaveron class Ransor-D which the Space Corps had captured many years ago. The *Sciontrar* appeared similar, yet newer. In the past, the Ghasts were known to fill their ships with personnel to oversee many of the tasks which were automated on a Space Corps warship. Blake saw no sign of technicians, though there was a huge bank of screens embedded in the wall to his left. Further along, he could see a room which was filled with shapes he couldn't make out.

The interior of the *Sciontrar* was not silent. Blake was

attuned to spaceships, wherever and by whomever they were built. He sensed the underlying thrum of the battleship's immense gravity drive and when he touched the walls, he could feel the vibration and imagine the desire of the engines to be unleashed, to test themselves against the *Sciontrar*'s extraordinary inertia.

It wasn't only the engines Blake heard. There were other sounds – he noticed a series of booming thumps, coming from above and below. It was the sound of heavy-duty mechanical reloading arms pushing missiles into their launch tubes in preparation for firing. The Ghasts had diverted to pick up the people from the stricken *ES Abyss*, but it hadn't stopped them keeping up their bombardment of the Gate Maker.

Blake was on the verge of guessing at a direction, when he heard heavy footsteps coming from the right. He headed towards the sound and stopped short when an armed patrol of Ghasts emerged from a side passage. In the flesh, they were bigger and broader than he imagined they'd be. Blake wasn't a short man, but against the Ghasts he felt distinctly under-sized. The aliens wore uniforms of pale blue, which covered their grey skin everywhere apart from their heads. Each member of the patrol had thick, black hair and their faces, while human in many respects, were an equal part alien.

"Captain Blake?" asked the lead Ghast, his voice scratching out through an interpretation module fixed to his shoulder. This one was pushing eight feet tall and held a mean-looking repeater in one hand. There was no threat in his manner, only curiosity. Out of politeness, Blake lifted his visor and positioned it on top of his head.

"Yes. Your Tarjos invited me to the bridge."

The Ghast grinned, revealing a row of perfect white teeth. "We will take you there."

Blake's escort took him through the *Sciontrar* at a fast walk.

The journey wasn't far and Blake guessed that the central docking bay was intentionally placed to allow easier access for the crew. On the way, they passed a number of other Ghasts wearing uniforms of different colours. Some carried devices which may have been analytical tools. Not one of them talked or offered a greeting.

The group of seven went upwards in an airlift. The Ghasts remained silent, though there was no attempt to intimidate their guest. Afterwards, they passed through a small room and entered a short corridor which ended at a wide flight of steps. These steps were difficult for Blake to ascend - the height of the risers didn't help, but in reality, he knew his reserves of strength were failing. There was a door at the top, made of a featureless grey alloy which gave every impression it was five metres thick. With barely a pause, it whisked open, revealing that it was, in fact, closer to nine metres thick. The Ghasts evidently didn't like the idea of having anyone break in, and, given the capabilities of the Oblivion class battleships, it seemed wise that they didn't take any chances.

Blake took in the sights – the *Sciontrar*'s bridge was relatively compact when taken against the overall size of the vessel. It was a rectangular room, twenty metres along its longest wall and fifteen along the other two. The blue light was more subdued here and it blended with the pastel colours of text and images upon the many operator consoles arranged evenly around the plain metal floor. Blake estimated there to be twenty-five Ghasts in here, each of them staring intently at a screen or panel. They spoke little and the loudest sound was a humming which had no visible source and which reminded Blake of air conditioning or cooling fans.

Only one of the Ghasts was standing. This one had a uniform of a deeper blue with no other adornment and had his back to the door. The alien turned at the sound of arrival and strode amongst the banks of consoles towards Blake.

"Captain Charles Blake. I am Tarjos Nil-Tras of the *Sciontrar*."

The Ghost was seven-and-a-half feet tall and broader than most of his fellows. Like the others, his musculature was natural, rather than honed in the gym. He waited for a response.

Blake didn't know if he was expected to say something in particular or make a specific gesture of greeting.

"An impressive spaceship," he said, trying out the compliments route.

"It is," said Nil-Tras.

"What of the *Kalon-T7*?"

"It did not survive the encounter with *Ix-Gorghal*."

"I am sorry."

"They did what was necessary."

"How did you get here?"

Nil-Tras's eyes glittered with internal conflict. "The same way you managed. Our projection was less accurate than yours and we have been on a fruitless hunt through a series of nearby solar systems."

"How did you know to come to the Helius Blackstar?"

"A signal from one of your old monitoring drones reached your Fleet Admiral and from there to my Subjos. I was glad to hear you made it so far."

"I hope the Vraxar despise our persistence."

Nil-Tras gave a short bow of his head to signify agreement. "Come."

With that, the Ghost returned to the front of the bridge and stood directly before a bank of many screens. Blake caught up and his eyes jumped from screen to screen. Each display showed a feed from one of the battleship's sensor arrays, most of which were capturing the bleak emptiness of space. The largest screen showed something else.

The Gate Maker was visible in the centre of the display. The discharges of blue had vanished entirely, and the greens had become so dark it was difficult to distinguish them from the background. Still they fired, their span and frequency noticeably stronger than the last time he'd seen them. Blake felt as if he was watching a million different limbs pushing and tearing at the fabric of space and in a way, he knew that was what the Vraxar were doing.

"The Gate Maker vessel appears to have bottomless wells of power with which to repel our attacks," said Nil-Tras. "We are running low on ammunition and not one of our missile waves has penetrated its countermeasures. Our Vule cannons are not affected, but they cannot fire for extended periods."

"How long until you can fire the anti-shield incendiaries?"

"We call it the Particle Disruptor," laughed Nil-Tras. "A dramatic name for a weapon which requires in excess of thirty minutes to recharge."

"How long until it's ready?"

"You were just in time. Look over there."

Nil-Tras raised an arm and pointed at a console to one side, which had three Ghosts seated in front of it. Blake wasn't practised in the alien language and he was unable to decipher the symbols covering most of the screens. The most important part didn't require an understanding of the speech. He saw a graph with a long Y-axis, against which a thick green bar was making steady upwards progress.

One of the Ghost crew spoke urgently and Nil-Tras responded in the alien speech. Blake detached the earpiece from his visor and pushed it into his ear in time for it to interpret the rest of the conversation.

"As I told you, the enemy vessel's power discharge has stopped its rate of increase, Tarjos," said the Ghast.

"How long until it is finished?" Nil-Tras responded.

"I think it is already finished."

"Then we are too late?"

"Fifteen seconds until we can fire the Particle Disruptor," said another Ghast.

Blake found he couldn't take his eyes away from the gauge. At the same time, he detected a high-pitched whine which passed the threshold into audibility and rose in time with the power meter of the disruptor weapon.

Another of the Ghasts joined the conversation, his voice emotionless in spite of the significance in his words. "There is a new area of ultra-high gravity, centred upon the Vraxar spaceship. It is increasing exponentially."

"[Translation uncertainty: *Shit* or *Crap*] we can't allow them to complete their mission," said Nil-Tras. "Disengage our energy shield and activate lightspeed transit towards the enemy. We will ram their shields at our highest speed."

"It is too late, Tarjos," said another of the Ghast crew. "The new gravity will crush us immediately."

"If that's what it takes," snarled Nil-Tras.

"The Particle Disruptor represents our greatest hope, Tarjos. We cannot fire it if we are crushed."

"Five seconds remaining."

"In that case, we wait."

In those last few seconds, the whining abruptly turned into a howl of incredible anger. The bridge of the *Sciontrar* shuddered and Blake fought for balance. He wasn't sure if any of the crew announced the weapon's discharge. They didn't need to – the Particle Disruptor emitted a low bass thump which ground remorselessly through his body. Everything went quiet, leaving Blake's head pounding.

The main screen showed the result. The Particle Disruptor's beam lanced through the green-black sparks and struck the Gate Maker's energy shield. Moments later, the Vraxar ship was held within the ferocious plasma fires which spread rapidly from the centre. Blake found himself willing the Ghasts on, hoping their weapon would be as effective as it was before.

"I had concerns," said Nil-Tras, sounding anything but worried.

"About what?" asked Blake.

"I wondered if those emissions of energy jumping from the enemy ship would interfere with our Particle Disruptor."

"No sign it happened."

"Their shields have yet to fall." Nil-Tras switched to giving orders. "Resume missile bombardment."

"The gravity is too much – they will be disabled before impact."

"Resume."

"Acknowledged."

"What are the readings from the enemy vessel?"

"There are no fluctuations, Tarjos."

"We may lack the required capability to complete this task."

"The Vraxar spaceship has destroyed our missile wave before the gravity could do so. The *Sciontrar*'s ammunition stocks are below twenty percent."

"Keep firing."

The plasma surrounding the Gate Maker began to dwindle, its brightness reducing and becoming patchy in places. Blake ground his teeth together, producing a scraping sound he could hear clearly in his head.

"The new wormhole is stabilising with a diameter of twelve hundred kilometres," said one of the Ghasts.

"First power fluctuations detected in the enemy vessel," said another, with no more emotion than if he'd been reading from a shopping list.

Blake was unable to keep quiet. "It's working!"

"What about their energy shield?" asked Nil-Tras.

"It is failing."

"The enemy countermeasures have destroyed our second and third missile waves."

"They're not helpless yet," growled Nil-Tras.

"The wormhole is no longer stable. It is fraying at the outer edges and its diameter is reducing. Now eleven hundred kilometres across."

The fourth wave of Ghost missiles crashed into the Gate Maker's shield. Many of the warheads were destroyed by the gravity so close to the centre, but more than two hundred warheads detonated against the Vraxar shield, creating a subdued cloud of heat and energy. Blake had seen the explosive force of the latest Ghost Shatterers and he could only imagine the reserves of the Gate Maker if it was able to maintain its shield through everything being thrown against it.

"The enemy shield is gone."

"Excellent," said Nil-Tras.

"The wormhole is collapsing, Tarjos. Our missiles should be more effective."

It was the beginning of the end for the Gate Maker. The bolts it spat out with such raw energy seemed to shrink inwards, becoming brighter and greener as they did so. Without an energy shield to stop them, the fifth wave of Ghost missiles plunged into the armour plating of the Vraxar ship. Even lacking an energy shield, the Gate Maker was enormous and the detonations only extended over a fraction of its surface.

The *Sciontrar* may have been low on ammunition, but it still carried thousands of warheads. Nil-Tras ordered them launched in tight waves of three hundred, with the high-yield Shatterers in between. Waves six and seven caused extensive damage and the Ghost sensors were able to filter out the plasma light in order to show the patchwork of deep craters beneath.

"They don't seem interested in escape," said Blake.

Nil-Tras's expression gave the first discernible indication of concern. "No, they don't. They are doing everything they can to maintain the new wormhole, even though it means the destruction of their spaceship."

The eighth wave of missiles reached its target. Blake already knew the Gate Maker was designed with defence in mind and he saw how tough it was with or without its shield. The vessel's hull was a pocked mess of burning metal and some of the craters were hundreds of metres deep. It seemed impossible it would hold out for much longer.

Blake guessed the reason behind their stubbornness and he didn't like it. "They want to hold the wormhole open long enough for their fleet to come through."

"It's crumbling," said one of the Ghost crew. "They don't have time to bring many others."

The words triggered something in Blake and he felt his body pump a vast quantity of adrenaline into his veins. "Maybe they only want one ship to get through."

"One ship?" said Nil-Tras. "That is an outcome I will settle for."

"Not if it's what I'm thinking it is," said Blake, with growing alarm.

"The Vraxar ship is on the verge of destruction. Soon the wormhole will collapse entirely."

"A fission cloud has appeared at the wormhole and there is a trail of positrons, Tarjos. Something came through."

"Where is it?"

"First estimations suggest it was ejected many millions of kilometres beyond."

Blake was aware of the principles – to get through a wormhole, you got as close as you dared, launched into a lightspeed jump aimed directly at the centre and then, when you'd come out the other end, activated a second lightspeed transit to escape the gravity of the wormhole. The Vraxar had got something through and it would likely emerge from lightspeed somewhere in the vicinity.

"The Gate Maker is shutting down, Tarjos. I suggest we cease fire and conserve our ammunition."

"Not until that wormhole is gone."

Blake took little satisfaction watching the final throes of the Vraxar spaceship. It remained in the same spot, no longer a perfect sphere, with chunks of it beginning to separate. With its structural integrity gone and its power source depleted, the weight of the still-collapsing wormhole pressed down upon it. The Gate Maker was enormously dense and it resisted the tremendous forces.

It ended with little drama – the wormhole collapsed into nothingness, leaving the ruined Gate Maker behind as a record of events.

"Is it a threat?" asked Nil-Tras.

"I do not believe it is, Tarjos. Its power source has failed and there are many breaches through its external plating."

"Leave it, then. We will give our scientists the opportunity to study what remains."

"What came through?" asked Blake.

"We do not know. We captured details of its fission cloud, though its proximity to the wormhole will make it difficult to interpret the data."

"There is an approaching vessel, Tarjos. It is attempting to suppress its inbound signature."

Blake knew what was coming. "*Ix-Gorghal*! We need to get away from here."

The Ghasts were a practical race. They didn't waste time looking startled or blurting out useless questions. One of their navigational team, who was sitting within two metres of Blake, simply reached out and pressed an indentation on his console. The *Sciontrar* entered lightspeed, a fact Blake only recognized through years of experience.

"They will follow us, Tarjos Nil-Tras."

The Ghast seemed entirely unfazed by the notion. "We will deal with that when the necessity arises. Come with me, it is time to eat."

Nil-Tras's response was not quite what Blake was expecting. Nevertheless, he went along with it and followed the Ghast captain to an alien replicator. A minute later, he found himself holding a huge plate covered in several different-coloured pastes, all of which smelled like mushrooms. This abrupt change of pace couldn't dispel the unease he felt about what exactly it was the Vraxar sent through the wormhole.

With the encouragement of his host, Blake sampled the contents of his tray and discovered they tasted exactly like they smelled.

CHAPTER TWENTY-SIX

THE ROOM WAS dark enough to reflect the mood of its occupant. Fleet Admiral Duggan remained in contemplation for some considerable time – long enough for Cerys to surreptitiously scan his life signs for anything of concern.

Eventually, Duggan reached forward and pressed the switch on an old-fashioned lamp which his wife had given him years ago. He preferred modern furnishings yet didn't want to hurt her feelings by telling her he hated it, nor could he bring himself to drop it repeatedly onto the floor until it broke.

The lamp had a low-power bulb which failed to illuminate the entirety of his office and created deep pools of gloom in the corners. His eyes were as sharp as ever – a blessing he never overlooked – but he didn't wish to risk damaging them by working in such poorly-lit conditions.

"Cerys, turn on the overheads," he said.

The lights came on, filling the room with the Space Corps' not-quite-perfect copy of natural daylight. Duggan squinted until his eyes adjusted.

His desk was covered in folders, each containing a report

from one department or another. The news was a mixture of good and bad, and Duggan wished he could live to see just one day where the news was completely and utterly *neutral*.

He picked up his copy of Captain Blake's report on the recent mission. In spite of his slight over-exuberance when it came to captaincy, Blake was nothing if not thorough when it came to his documentation and the folder was thick.

Duggan skimmed over it for the third time, occasionally giving a half-smile at the details. Blake had acquitted himself well, even though he'd lost one of the Space Corp's most capable warships. Sometimes the result was worth the cost and there would be no punishment in this case.

Time and again, the report hinted, implied or just outright stated that the *ES Abyss* was a far less capable vessel than the *Sciontrar*. That was expected, since the *Sciontrar* was a battleship and one of the newest in the Ghost fleet. It was still troubling – it appeared the aliens had begun to open up another technological lead. There were gaps here and there in the Ghost capabilities and Duggan had a few new factories coming onstream soon that would push humanity once more to the fore. In theory it didn't matter, since they were allies. In reality, Duggan preferred to be ahead of the game rather than playing catch up.

There was another report on the table, this one being the cause of his disquiet, and also the reason he most worried there'd never be an opportunity for the Confederation to fully flex its military muscles.

The report was from his Critical Data Analysis team. They'd thrown every available processing resource at the fission data captured by the *Sciontrar* and had come up with a result. Their analysis confirmed the arrival of a single Vraxar ship, which had attempted to disguise its fission signature when it performed a lightspeed transit away from the wormhole created by the Gate Maker. Duggan had no idea why it needed to hide anything.

The analysis team had helpfully provided an estimate of the new ship's dimensions. It was bigger than *Ix-Gorghal*. Duggan cast his mind back to his conversation with the captured Vraxar. It had provided him with another name and said the Vraxar wanted to bring a second ship through at the same time as *Ix-Gorghal*. He knew the name of what had come – it was *Ix-Gastiol*. Now the Vraxar had their two most powerful spaceships in Confederation Space and they also had the *ES Determinant's* memory arrays.

The one ray of hope was that the enemy hadn't yet cracked the static data on the array. When they did, there would be no hope. Like all good leaders, he always had something in reserve. He picked up a third folder, entitled *Project: Last Stand* and opened the brown cover. Reading it brought tears to his eyes and he wondered what humanity had done to be brought to the brink in this way.

Follow Anthony James on Facebook at
facebook.com/AnthonyJamesAuthor

ALSO BY ANTHONY JAMES

The Survival Wars series

1. Crimson Tempest
2. Bane of Worlds
3. Chains of Duty
4. Fires of Oblivion
5. Terminus Gate
6. Guns of the Valpian
7. Mission: Nemesis

The Obsidiar Fleet series

1. Negation Force
2. Inferno Sphere
3. God Ship

Printed in Great Britain
by Amazon